She walked around us. I saw that she had a narrow nylon sack hanging down her back. In it, there were two store-bought arrows. She stopped about fifteen feet from Roland. "You're Redhawk?" she demanded.

"Who the hell are you?" he snarled.

"I have a message for you," she said. In one swift movement, she whipped an arrow out of her sack, set it to the bow, pulled back, and let the arrow fly. The next thing we saw was its shaft quivering in Roland's chest.

Roland let out a bellow of shock. Clutching the arrow, he scrambled to his feet. "Bitch!" he exclaimed in outrage.

In the next moment, she did it again.

★

"Mountain legends, Native American history, and lessons in wilderness survival add texture to the tale."

—Ft. Lauderdale *Sun-Sentinel*

"Andreae stocks her trailbags with interesting people..."

—*Kirkus Reviews*

"Suspenseful moments and well-drawn, complex relationships provide the high points."

—*Publishers Weekly*

Also available from Worldwide Mystery by
CHRISTINE ANDREAE

GRIZZLY
TRAIL OF MURDER

CHRISTINE ANDREAE

A SMALL TARGET

WORLDWIDE®

TORONTO • NEW YORK • LONDON
AMSTERDAM • PARIS • SYDNEY • HAMBURG
STOCKHOLM • ATHENS • TOKYO • MILAN
MADRID • WARSAW • BUDAPEST • AUCKLAND

For Morgan and Tim

A SMALL TARGET

A Worldwide Mystery/February 1998

First published by St. Martin's Press, Incorporated.

ISBN 0-373-26264-7

Printed in U.S.A.

ACKNOWLEDGMENTS

Warmest thanks to Steve and Sue Rolfing, to Ward McKay and to Maggie Plummer for their help with my research and for their attentive readings. I am also grateful to Anna Collins, Suzanne Kilgore, Harry Papagan, Robin and Denise Pfau, and Theresa Reynolds for their continuing support and encouragement. As always, thanks to the real Andy.

Heart shots are always fatal, but the heart is a small target for the archer unless the shot is taken at very close range.

—Fred Bear, *The Archer's Bible*

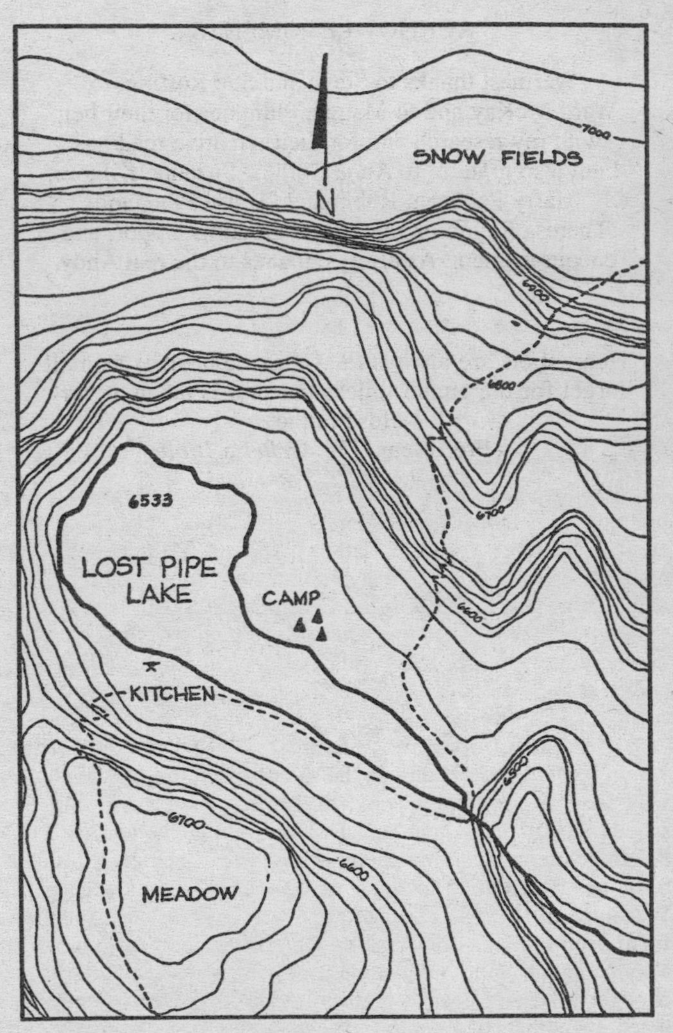
N
7000
SNOW FIELDS
6900
6800
6700
6533
LOST PIPE
LAKE
CAMP
6600
KITCHEN
6500
6700
6600
MEADOW

ONE

I HAD PACKED for Montana's high country, not for a funeral. I had extra wool socks in my duffel and extra AA batteries for my headlamp. I had polypro long johns thick enough for Everest, and khaki shorts that looked as if they'd survived Burma in World War II. But no skirt—never mind a black dress.

"Don't worry about it," Pete Bonsecours said when I called him from the motel. Big help. Pete was a friend. He was also an outfitter who ran llama pack treks into the Mission Mountains, a spectacular range on the west side of the Continental Divide. He had persuaded me to sign on as camp cook for a postseason excursion. Not, I admit, that it took a lot of persuading.

I should say that I would trust (and have trusted) Pete with my life. But I wasn't sure I trusted him on what to wear to a Catholic funeral on an Indian reservation. His genes were half-Indian, but he was a newcomer to the Flathead reservation. I knew he could read the subtleties of animal tracks in the wilderness, but how tuned in was he to the nuances of attire in church? I didn't think we could afford to be religiously incorrect. We had taken six paying clients on our trek, and two of them had ended up murdered. One of them, Roland Redhawk, was being buried today.

"Let me speak to Dolores," I said. Dolores was married to Pete. She came from a Salish family that had lived on the reservation for five generations. In the summer months, she went along with Pete as expedition cook, but this particular trip had been scheduled for September and Dolores, a reading teacher in the Salish-Kootenai school system, was back in her classroom. I'd been teaching three sections of English Composition 101 in Washington, D.C., all summer and, even before Pete's invitation, I had been thinking about taking the fall semester off. One of the advantages of being a part-time professor is that I don't get paid enough to be steadfast. Moreover, since I have two slender volumes of published verse on my *vita,* I qualify as a creative type in the eyes of college administrators. And creative types, as everyone knows, are *supposed* to do flaky things like take off to go cooking in the wilds of Montana.

It took Dolores a long time to get to the phone. Over a buzz of voices in the background, I could hear their three-year-old son crying. "Sorry to bother you," I apologized when she came on the line, "but I was wondering what to wear to the church. All I've got is jeans and a tweed jacket I wore on the plane. You think I should go and buy a skirt somewhere?"

"You're fine. We don't worry much about clothes here." There was a pause. "You want to go?"

"It's better than sitting around here in the motel watching flashbacks. Maybe it will help me end it. I think I'm having what my mother would call 'intrusive recall.'"

"Did Pete tell you that Charlene asked him to be one of the pallbearers?"

"Really?" Charlene Redhawk was our dead client's brand-new widow. I digested the news for a moment. "So it's okay, then?"

"I hope so." She sounded dubious.

I felt a rush of protective anger. "Dolores, I don't see how anyone could blame Pete."

"Anyone can sue."

"That's ridiculous! It's not like we were careless or anything. At least not in Roland's case. It was totally beyond our control—like getting hit by lightning. An act of God."

"If God had money, you think people wouldn't sue Him?"

"Her," I corrected automatically.

"Lee," she said, and there was a smile in her voice, "I hate to tell you this, but out here on the res, God's still He."

ACCORDING TO THE notice in the "Walking On" section of the *Char-Koosta News,* a Mass of the Resurrection would be celebrated on Saturday morning for Roland at the mission church in St. Ignatius. The mission had been founded by Jesuits back in 1854 and, I must confess, I was expecting something pioneerish—a log cabin with a stubby steeple, perhaps. Certainly, on that bright autumn morning, I was unprepared for the sight of a brick church with soaring Gothic windows and a hundred-foot-high bell tower. It stands against the blue wall of the Mission Mountains like a great cathedral of Europe, dominating the town's low rooftops.

Walking inside is another surprise. Like a Victorian Easter egg, the pale blue walls are trimmed with gold filigree. Rows of medallion-shaped frescoes float like bubbles on the high, curving ceiling. Pastel blue windowpanes diffuse the space with a watery light. For a peculiar moment, I felt weightless, as if I were swimming inside a heavenly aquarium.

Even more peculiarly, the cavernous interior was empty. No congregation waited in the pews. I checked my watch. It was eleven o'clock, time for the service to begin. There was a respectable-sized crowd milling around outside the church. Why was no one coming in? I picked up a tourist brochure from a rack and slipped into a back pew. In the brochure, I found a poignant old photo of the mission's Boys' School: close to a hundred native boys were buttoned snugly into jackets. Their round, dark heads were shaven, like new recruits in an army.

A movement in the aisle made me turn. A tall dark suit was standing beside the pew. I looked up, expecting an undertaker, and saw Luke. Agent Luke Donner, State of Montana's Criminal Investigation Bureau. He smiled. "Long time, no see," he said.

Stunned, I stared at him. Without his battered cowboy hat, his head looked smaller, less heroic than I remembered, but it was Luke all right. He wasn't wearing a suit. He was wearing a charcoal grey sports jacket, a white shirt, and new, dark jeans. His jacket had a relaxed Italian look and his designer tie, a print of large lavender squiggles, was daring—at least by my ex-husband's standards.

Suddenly I felt shabby in my battered tweed jacket. Worse, I felt a hot red flush rising into my face. I ducked my head and slid over, making room for him. "What are you doing here?" I demanded.

"Minding my business." His rugged face was deadpan, but his eyes teased boyishly.

It took a minute to sink in. "You're on the case? I thought the FBI was handling it."

"They were." Then he added with disgust, "Like a goat rope."

"A what?"

"They messed up. The lab people in Missoula complained to the attorney general."

"Wait a sec. What's a goat rope?"

"Oh, a bunch of women with ropes try to catch a goat. Ends up in a god-awful mess."

"This is some kind of rodeo event?"

Luke waved it away.

"Sounds hilarious," I said drily.

He grinned. "They also screwed up on jurisdiction. A couple of the members of the tribal council complained to the governor. Turns out this is the only reservation in the country where the state has jurisdiction over felonies. The legislature passed some act back in 1960."

"I see," I said. But I didn't see at all. "So who's in charge?"

"Me." The corner of his mouth twitched like a cat that had just swallowed a big fat federal canary.

Behind us, the heavy church door opened. Luke swiveled. A rectangle of white light spilled up the aisle. Two women, one fat, one thin, stood silhouetted in the doorway. Luke watched them walk up the aisle, his eyes intent on their faces.

I felt a stab of alarm. "You don't think she's going to show up?"

"It's a possibility," he said casually.

"I thought that only happened in the movies the killer shows up at the funeral."

He didn't answer.

THE GIRL had come out of the woods above us on the field of boulders. She was pale and slight and carried a primitive bow. Under her matted hair, her eyes had been calm. Her expression hadn't changed when she shot off her arrows. But it wasn't her face that kept looping through my mind. It was the image of her torn sneaker: not a high-performance shoe, foam padded and reinforced with leather, but a plain canvas sneaker, like the ones I used to wear as a child in the fifties. A red sneaker faded to pink, mud-caked and tied with brown shoelaces. On the right one, there had been a drop of blood astonishingly red on the faded canvas. I would know the girl in those sneakers. But would I know her with clean hair and in heels?

ABRUPTLY, LUKE STOOD UP and left the church. His boot steps echoed behind me. I sat there gazing stupidly at the sea of empty pews ahead of me. Up front, at a side altar, a fresco depicted Saint Joseph standing ankle-deep in fluffy clouds, holding the baby Jesus like a modern-day dad. I thought about Luke and *his* son. He'd gone back to his wife on the boy's account. "Barb," he called her. He and Barb had been separated when we met, and on-again, off-again after that.

Like a transcontinental yo-yo, I'd been there during a couple of the off-agains. Two winters ago, we'd spend an extremely promising week together, back-country skiing. Last winter, during Christmas break, Luke invited me out for more winter wonderland fun. We had a great time together, but I wasn't all that surprised when, at the end of the trip, he put me back on my plane with an "It's a far, far better thing I do" speech and went back to his son's mother. He might have been Bogie putting me on the last plane out of Casablanca.

He never called or wrote. The larger part of me (i.e. my ego) was wounded, but a smaller, less-accessible part was relieved. What would I have said if he'd asked me to move to Montana? Would I have risked changing my life? "Barb" had spared us both the next step. That was over a year ago. I hadn't heard from him since. If it hadn't been for the killings, I might never have seen him again.

I looked at my watch again. Half an hour past show time, and no sign of a priest or a coffin. I stood up and, turning to go out, I noticed a pair of large, contemporary oil paintings hanging in the shadows under the choir loft. One portrayed the Virgin in fringed white buckskin, carrying the baby Jesus in a cradle board on her back. The other showed a mature, solidly built Jesus in a chief's bonnet. The portraits were the church's only visual concession to an Indian aesthetic. The artist had painted Jesus standing over a campfire. Under a red Hudson Bay blanket, he revealed a red, thorn-encircled heart. He looked far more masculine than the Italianate Jesus in older frescoes. In fact, the more I looked at him, the more he looked like my friend Pete: both had the same square face and torso, the same high cheekbones, the same thin bow-shaped mouth. But the face of this Jesus had the serenity and compassion of a wise old man. For a fleeting moment, I felt the urge to cry on his shoulder.

Instead, I stepped out of the dimness of the vestibule and stood blinking in the noonday sun at the top of the brick steps. Knots of people stood waiting on the dry grass below. A TV van was parked on the other side of the chain-link fence. I spotted Luke beside another van, talking to a young Indian woman behind the wheel. Near a side gate in the fence, a young white man stood idly tapping a skinny reporter's notebook against the leg of his jeans. His egg-shaped body had a soft-boiled look. He sported a black turtleneck a la Jack Kerouac and a stressed-leather bomber jacket à la Banana Republic.

I trotted down the church steps and walked over to him. "Hi," I said. "Where is everyone?"

"At the longhouse."

"What's the longhouse?"

"That's where they hold the wake. They carry the coffin over here when they're done."

"Thanks," I said. "Who are you with?"

"The *Missoulian.* Crime beat." He didn't exactly swagger, but the words came out of the side of his mouth, tough-guy style.

A NEW GATHERING of cars and pickups turned into the parking lot. Photographers and newspeople moved into place. By the time the cortege came into view, clusters of spectators lined the wide street at the side of the church. A priest in white vestments led the procession. A line of children carrying flowers made a horseshoe around the coffin, which was carried on the shoulders of six men. I spotted Pete, his face unreadable. Only one of the pallbearers wore a sport coat. The rest wore work jackets. I need not have worried about not having a black dress. Charlene Redhawk, a blunt-faced woman with a skinny greying braid, walked behind her husband's coffin in an emerald green polyester pants suit and a magnificent antique squash-blossom necklace that looked too heavy for her drooping neck and shoulders. Sunlight glinted on heads of blue black hair, on red gladioli, on yellow and orange mums, on beaded belt buckles and silver cuffs. I wondered whether the vibrant splashes of color would turn tawdry once inside the church's watery blue sanctuary.

The pallbearers carried Roland Redhawk's coffin up the steps. The polished cherry-wood casket glinted richly in the sunlight. Its silver fittings looked fancy enough for a pope. Either Roland's trading-post business was more lucrative than one might suppose, or his widow, Charlene, had gone into hock for his send-off. The crowd surged up the steps after the coffin.

Luke found me. "You going in?"

"I don't know," I said.

The *Missoulian* reporter approached us with his pad. "Luke Donner?" he asked.

"Not now," Luke said firmly.

"Who's she?" he demanded rudely.

"*Newsweek.*"

The reporter looked as if he couldn't decide whether to suck up or sneer. Luke took my elbow and steered me over to the privacy of a blue spruce planted along the fence line. Suddenly I felt like an invalid. Against the jagged blue backdrop of the Missions, a stand of yellow aspens looked translucent. "Tell me what happened," he said gently.

TWO

THE MISSION MOUNTAINS are a young range whose high, jagged peaks look newly broken. Massive and uncomfortably sharp, they loom out of dark pine forests. In the upper reaches of the forests, hidden between the peaks, lie scatterings of lakes and tarns. The smallest ones, bright blue specks on the map, are still unnamed, but the one where the killings took place is called Lost Pipe Lake. It sits some six thousand feet above sea level on the Indian side of mountains.

"Indian side" because the Missions are split down their long backbone into two jurisdictions. The western flank belongs to the Flathead Indians a confederation of the Salish, Kootenai, and Pend d'Oreille tribes. The east side belongs to our government and is managed as a wilderness by the United States Forest Service. In the late 1970s, the Bureau of Indian Affairs, another arm of our government, had plans to log the slopes on the Indian side of the mountains, but a trio of Salish grandmothers organized a Save-Our-Heritage movement which stopped all timber sales and eventually persuaded the tribal council to protect their side of Missions as wilderness area the first tribally managed wilderness in the country.

Our trek to Lost Pipe Lake had been sparked by a tribal-sponsored conference on "Low-impact Tourism" held on the reservation below the mountains. Workshops run by directors of agencies with names like "Touch the Earth" and "Lac du Flambeau Heritage Project" addressed the problems of tourist impact on natural resources and native cultures. After the last session on Friday afternoon, a variety of optional activities had been arranged for the weekend. The menu included a tour of the National Bison Range at the southern end of the reservation; a cruise on Flathead Lake at the northern end; an evening of traditional Indian dances at the Salish-Kootenai Community College in Pablo; an early-morning bird walk at Safe Harbor Marsh, recently purchased by the Nature Conservancy.

By way of promoting their new llama-trekking business, Pete and Dolores Bonsecours were offering conference-goers a llama-packed picnic lunch on Saturday. Their flier for the outing was a Xeroxed sheet with a sketch of a string of llamas across the top. The drawing was amateurish, but caught the elegance of the creatures' carriage. They looked like a line of humpless camels in an Egyptian frieze. In the accompanying brochure, Pete billed his llamas as "the wave of the future in back-country recreation."

"Llama's," his text explained, "are browsers, rather than grazers. They consume less grass than horses and can subsist on low-protein foods like pine needles and sedges nibbled along the trail. Their feet are padded and do not erode the soil like horses' hooves. A llama has as little impact on the wilderness as a white-tailed deer." (Padded feet may not seem like a big deal unless you've seen the way hoof traffic, after a spell of rain, can churn footpaths into canals of shin-high mud.)

A week after Pete's material was mailed out with the conference registration packets, the Bonsecours had two calls, both from conference-goers with special requests. The first came from a filmmaker named Gwen Mears, who said she was working on a documentary for PBS about "the greening" of Indian Country. Dolores, who took the call, thought she sounded a bit misty about Indians. Nonetheless, when Mears said she and her partner wanted to include footage of the Bonsecours and their llamas in the back country, Dolores couldn't suppress her excitement. She explained to the filmmakers that getting them and their gear up into the mountains would entail two overnights. No problem, Gwen Mears said. Dolores happily penciled them in for the week after the conference.

Pete took the second call. A secretary had him hold five minutes for a "Mr. Herron." Herron didn't introduce himself when he came on the line. He announced that he was flying out from L.A. for the conference and wanted to take his "boy" up to Lost Pipe Lake afterward. Pete was surprised that he knew the lake—even for locals, it was off the beaten track.

Herron went on to complain that he'd been trying to arrange a horse-packing trip for his son, but the outfitters he'd talked to claimed that the Mission Wilderness was closed to commercial horse packers.

"That's right," Pete said. "The traffic was destroying the trails."

Herron snorted at the regulation. "Yeah, but private parties can go in with their own horses. I'll make it worth your while to take us in as your guests," he offered.

"Sorry," Pete said. "I traded in my mules a couple of years back."

Herron laughed humorlessly. "A friend of mine on the tribal council told me you still had horses."

"A couple. But not for pack trips."

"So I'm stuck with llamas?"

"There's still horse packers in the Bob Marshall Wilderness," Pete suggested. "Big Salmon Lake makes a nice trip."

But Herron was set on Lost Pipe Lake. Pete booked him without asking why. When Dolores asked her husband why he hadn't asked, he shrugged.

Annoyed, she said, "Ours is not to reason why."

Whereupon Pete went stony and didn't tell her that Herron had sounded like an ass on the phone. Not that it would have made any difference, as Dolores said later. Herron wasn't the first turkey they'd catered to and certainly wouldn't be the last.

In any case, after going round and round on the logistics, they agreed that in fact, Lost Pipe Lake would make a breathtaking backdrop for the filmmakers. The trail up to Lost Pipe Lake was steeper than Pete would have chosen; but after a summer of trekking, his llamas were in peak condition.

When he called me in Washington and invited me to come along, I asked, "Why me? Doesn't your brother-in-law still sub for Dolores?"

"You're more photogenic."

"Uh-huh."

"And a better cook."

"Thanks. But I'm not Salish. I thought you said it was a film about Indians."

"And tourists."

I groaned. "Did I ever mention I was camera shy?"

Pete pondered this. "You don't want to come?"

"Of course I want to come. It sounds neat. I'm just not feeling very rich at the moment."

"We'll pay your way."

"You will?"

"Plus wages."

"Damn!" I laughed. "You sound too fat! I'm coming!"

Pete said earnestly, "We owe you a lot more than airfare."

Three years before, on a horse pack trip with Pete in the Bob Marshall Wilderness, fate dealt me a trump card and I'd used it to save Pete's business. Since then, there had been times I wished I'd finessed something for myself as well. Now, however, with Pete on the other end of the line, I found his gratitude embarrassing.

"I mean it, Lee," he insisted.

"Can I fly first-class?"

"What?" He sounded shocked.

"I'm *kidding,* Pete. Now, should I buy a Hawaiian shirt for my cinematic debut?"

"We're talking eco-tourists, not *Gilligan's Island,*" he rebuked. "Think recycled fleece."

WHEN I TOLD my mother that I was "taking the fall semester off," as the kids say, she objected, "But Lee, you are forty now."

"Forty-one, Mom."

"It is not an age to keep running away." Her slight-but-charming Viennese accent surfaces when she is distressed. My mother, Dr. Marcella Romann-Squires, is a clinical psychologist who believes in stages of growth. She worries that I'm not on track. At the same time, she is a devout Jungian.

"I need to feed my soul," I told her. I felt a bit fraudulent saying this. It sounded so extravagant. Nonetheless, it was true.

My mother acknowledged the appetite of my soul with a nod. It was August in Washington and we were sitting in her air-conditioned office drinking iced Earl Grey out of handblown Irish glass tumblers. Around the neck of her linen blouse, she had draped a filmy cotton scarf. On my neck, scarves usually end up looking like bibs, but my mother has a gypsy's knack for them. Above the folds of bright cotton, her cap of cropped hair looked as glossy as a blackbird's. At sixty-nine, she has no more than three grey hairs. She let out a resigned sigh. "I hope you'll be careful," she said.

"I'll be careful."

"I do worry. For a poet, you seem so unaware of your process."

"It's like sex, Mom. Get too analytical, and it evaporates."

When embarrassed, my mother's voice becomes vague. "Ah, yes," she drifted off. "Like Eurydice."

WHEN I'D COOKED for Pete in the Bob Marshall, his mules had carried a metal wood-burning stove, complete with collapsible chimney pipe, and pantry panniers heavy with sacks of potatoes and generic cans of peaches-in-syrup and peas-and-carrots. Llamas, however, carry less weight than mules, so Pete had switched to a two-burner propane stove and Ziploc bags of home-dried apples and zucchinis. His postconference picnic on Saturday was my shakedown cruise: a chance to learn the stove's quirks under Dolores's supervision. The new stove wasn't the only change. The old-time Montana meat-and-potato menus, standard among outfitters, had shifted toward New Age Third World beans and grains. I was looking forward to the challenge: our promotional picnic offered lima bean and dill soup, rye bread with Gouda, crudités and crackers with hummus. Peppery slices of buffalo salami saved the meal from vegetarianism. For dessert there were carob brownies and mint tea.

"You too pure for caffeine these days?" I asked Dolores. I tried to sound casual. Virtual brownies were one thing, but the prospect of camping without morning coffee worried me.

"You think Pete's gonna roll out of the sack for mint tea?" she said.

TEN PEOPLE signed up for the picnic, including the two filmmakers, but not "Mr." Herron and his son. In terms of packing the food, only one llama was necessary. But Pete said llamas do better in groups, so he brought eight, the maximum number of livestock allowed into the tribal wilderness. At the trailhead, as Dolores unloaded them from the trailer, Pete gathered us into a group around a large chocolate-colored llama named Jake.

I had to smile seeing Pete—a hard-bitten horse-and-mule man—holding his exotic beast by a shiny blue nylon halter line. The picture was incongruous, like one of those trick photographs with a famous head on the wrong body. Then it dawned on me that llamas, in fact, were as indigenous to the Americas as Indians. Suddenly Pete, broad as a barrel, his bandanna tied around his jet black hair (he was letting it grow) began to look properly authentic beside his large, elegant llama. The alpine peaks behind them helped. We might have been setting out to explore the lost Inca city of Machu Picchu.

Pete's voice brought me back to Montana. "What do you know about llamas?" Pete asked us.

"They spit!" exclaimed a freckled woman in a salmon pink wind suit. The other guests laughed nervously.

Pete nodded. "Yep. But they've got a bum rap for it. Dogs bite, too. But neither act up very often. With llamas, spitting's a defensive weapon. Something like tossing a stink bomb. The smell's real foul, but it's as bad for the spitter as it is for the target, so they only use it as a last resort. Mostly, they spit to warn each other off, to establish rank. If a llama habitually spits at humans, it usually means he's been mistreated—same with a dog that bites. So relax. We've raised these llamas to be comfortable with two-leggeds. This big fella here's called Jake. He's going to carry our kitchen."

Jake's long, rabbitty ears swiveled like antennae. Beneath luxuriant lashes, his large black eyes took us in. Pete went on jovially, "Llamas are pack animals, but they aren't like horses or mules. If anything, they're like cats. They tend to be reserved. They've got lots of nice fluffy fur, but they really don't like to be cuddled by humans. You know what it's like when you're standing in line and someone crowds you? Makes you kinda edgy, don't it? We all need our own space. Respect your llama's space, and he'll work more happily for you.

"Okay, Lee, he's all yours. This is our cook, Lee Squires."

I stepped forward, took Jake's halter, and looked up at his proud head. Delicately, the llama lowered his nose down to mine. I suppressed a giggle. Jake's black nostrils felt velvet-soft and dry. His breath came in strong, warm puffs that had a faint straw-like odor. I breathed my own air into his nostrils and felt a strange, primitive kind of intimacy with the beast. Then my giggle broke loose, and Jake pulled back disdainfully.

Pete looked surprised. "He's taken a likin' to you, Lee," he said with amusement.

Gwen Mears, who had been filming on her knees with an industrial-size videocam, stood up. "Excellent," she said happily. She and her partner, Mary Ann Dellarobbia, were both somewhere in their twenties and both recent graduates from NYU's prestigious Tisch School of the Arts. Gwen was the more striking: tall—about five eleven—with perfect milky skin and dark copper-colored hair, which she wore in one long, thick braid. In a former life, she could have modeled for a Pre-Raphaelite painter, but the pearl in her left nostril was brutally contemporary: it shone like a major new pimple. Mary Ann was smaller and dark, with the sad eyes and big breasts of an Italian Renaissance madonna—a madonna with a Brooklyn accent. She sounded like a character in a blue-collar sitcom.

The two of them conferred, then turned their Betacam on a plump, middle-aged white woman decked out in the most extraordinary costume. While the rest of us wore jeans and sweatshirts, bandannas and baseball caps, this woman sported a Tyrolean hat, complete with jaunty little feather, a fitted tweed jacket, corduroy knickers, kneesocks, and hiking boots. She could have passed for a British country squire, circa 1920. All she needed was a shotgun in the crook of her arm. Her name was Felicity and, like the filmmakers, she lived in New York City.

Pete assigned Felicity a small cream-colored llama named Fluffy. As a pair, they definitely had visual impact and I wasn't surprised to see the filmmakers singling them out for their film. At first I suspected the younger women of a satiric impulse—Felicity's outfit might not have turned heads on Madison Avenue, but out in the woods, the effect was bizarre. Felicity herself, however, turned out to be engagingly genuine. She had a pointy nose and bright hazel eyes under the felt brim of her hat. There was nothing pompous about her. Like a child playing dress-up, she relished the effect of her costume. "I'm not sure knickers aren't too *boyish* for me," she confided to Gwen and Mary Ann.

"No, no!" they laughed. "You're perfect!"

The destination of the day was a glacier-carved lake at the base of the Missions. The lake was a solid eight on the scenic scale, but the trail that led to it was an easy three-mile stroll. To rate a ten, I think some huffing and puffing is required; perhaps this is the puritan in me. Nonetheless, in my experience, the greatest vistas, the ones that clear the mind and remain in the heart, need to be *achieved.*

However, I was not complaining. I had flown in late the night before, and my brain felt as if it were still over Kansas. If I didn't move too hard or fast, it might catch up to me. Our parade reached the lake before noon. It was a cool, overcast day—more November than September. Gusts of wind rippled the black mirror of the lake, shattering reflections of yellow aspen at its edges. Dolores and I set up the stove in the lee of a pile of grey boulders and got the lima-bean soup going. It needed a kick, I thought. I found a small plastic bottle of rice vinegar and added a couple of squirts. We tasted. "Not bad," Dolores conceded.

The guests scraped the pot, then wandered off to explore while we cleaned up.

The filmmakers brought the woman in the Tyrolean hat over to Pete. "We're trying to persuade Felicity to come up to Lost Pipe Lake with us," Mary Ann said.

"Can you take another?" Gwen asked.

"Sure," Pete said.

Felicity, her face flushed with pleasure at the invitation, protested weakly, "I don't know."

"You've *got* to be in the film, Felicity," Gwen said firmly.

"But I'm an asthmatic," she said worriedly.

They all looked at Pete. "The air's real clear up there," he said reassuringly. "Makes breathing easy."

"You have medicine, don't you?" Mary Ann demanded in Brooklynese.

"Yes, but—"

"Well, then," Mary Ann said, as if it were settled. "You can deduct it as a business trip." She turned to Pete. "Felicity has her own travel agency—specializing in adventures—float trips down the Amazon, South African safaris, you name it."

"Thrills for the carriage trade," Felicity said wistfully. "I'm afraid I'm mostly a desk-chair adventurer myself."

"We can take it as easy as we need to," Pete encouraged.

Felicity thought a moment. "Could I have Fluffy again?"

"No problem."

"I've gotten rather attached to her," Felicity mused.

"Him," Pete corrected. "They're all gelded males. Females are too expensive to use as packers. A good breeder will set you back three, four thousand dollars."

Felicity drew a breath and straightened her tweed shoulders. "Well," she said determinedly, "I'll do it. I think I need more risk in my life."

Pete gave her a bemused smile. "Back in the days of the Incas, whenever the ruler traveled some place, a white llama wearing gold earrings and a red shirt walked before the ruler."

Felicity perked up. "I don't suppose you'd let me pierce his ears?" she flirted.

"Why not? You provide the gold, I'll poke the hole for you."

"Forget that," Mary Ann said.

SO WE HAD a party of seven for Lost Pipe Lake: Pete and I, the two filmmakers and Felicity, their adopted tourist, and the two Herrons, *père et fils*. At the last minute, Pete added two more customers. On Sunday afternoon (we were to depart for Lost Pipe Lake early Monday morning), a battered pickup pulled into the Bonsecours drive and a tall old man slid out of the cab. Under his billed cap, his beaky yellow face had a sunken look, as if imploded by disease, but his black eyes were sharp and his step was strong. His name was Edmund McNab a Salish descendant of a Scottish fur trader named Angus McNab who followed Lewis and Clark's route into the valley. Pete called him "Eddie." He was a friend and neighbor, a retired mechanic who still "kept a hand in" the car-repair business. Without his help, Pete declared,

Mission Mountain Outfitters would have floundered for want of operational wheels.

Eddie's face remained impassive at this praise. We sat in the kitchen, drinking coffee. Dolores's mother, Rose, put a box of powdered doughnuts on the table. Three-year-old Paul Bonsecours played with a pair of ice trays on the kitchen floor. Eddie and Pete talked about a cracked universal. Dolores made a second pot of coffee. "Hear you're headed up to Lost Pipe Lake," Eddie said at last.

Pete nodded gravely.

"Never been up there, myself."

Rose, a squat woman with a round face and a frizzy home permanent, looked up at him in surprise, then looked away quickly.

Pete kept his gaze on the remaining doughnuts. "We've got room for one more. You want to come along?" he invited.

"I reckon," Eddie said.

THAT NIGHT, while Pete was washing up the dinner dishes and Dolores and I were organizing the trip's groceries, the phone rang. Pete dried his hands on a towel decked with bleached holly boughs and answered it. He listened for a long time.

I picked up a Ziploc packet of featherweight shriveled disks. The blue felt-tipped label said; "Egp, 2# fresh. 8 serv. Squeeze after rehyd." "What's this?" I asked Dolores.

She glanced at it. "Eggplant. For eggplant parmesan." She consulted the master menu sheet. "It's a backup," she said.

"You mean in case we get stuck up there?"

She shrugged off my worry. "In case you need extra."

Pete said into the phone, "Look, I'd like to help you out, but the regulations don't allow groups larger than eight. You'd make it nine."

"Have you got stuff for a cake?" I asked Dolores.

She frowned. "What kind of cake?"

"Any kind. Something to stick candles in. The girls said Felicity's going to turn fifty on our first day out. Guess what her last name is?"

"Whose?"

"Felicity's."

"What is it?"

"Parsley."

Dolores crinkled up her face. "Felicity *Parsley?*"

"Forsooth."

Pete held up a hand for quiet. "Roland, I can't do that," he said into the phone. "He's the one who set it up." Something in Pete's voice alerted us. "Look," he argued, "I can keep an eye on him as well as you."

Dolores and I listened to Pete listening.

Then he said dubiously, "Yeah, if you can get it in writing from the tribes, it's okay with me."

"What?" Dolores asked after he hung up.

"That was Roland Redhawk." He turned to me. "He's real active in PERTEC that's Protectors of Earth's Rights Tribal Environmental Council. He also runs a trading post up near Polson. Part museum, part convenience store. Sells beads to the tourists." Pete permitted himself a small smile.

"He's Salish?"

Pete scratched the back of his neck. "I don't think so. Maybe part Lakota? I think that's what I heard."

"Mostly Wannabe, if you ask me," Dolores said crisply. "So he wants to go along with you?"

"He says Bernadette Walker asked him to keep an eye on Herron. Turns out he's a big-shot developer from L.A."

Dolores looked thoughtful.

"Who's Bernadette Walker?" I asked.

"She's on the tribal council," Pete said. "One of the first women ever elected—and when it comes to environmental issues, let me tell you, she makes Greenpeace look tame. She'd outlaw all recreational use of the wilderness, if she could get away with it. She fought our llama business tooth and nail."

"What's she up to now?" Dolores demanded irritably.

"I don't know. But she's willing to pay Roland's way."

It took Dolores and me a good hour to measure out and add three days of extra portions to all the food bags. We resealed and relabeled; then I poured myself a healthy shot of bourbon from the canteen I'd brought along. I didn't offer Pete any. He didn't drink. But Dolores took a splash in her diet cola and we toasted the expedition to Lost Pipe Lake. We were feeling happily silly—even Pete was grinning away—when the phone rang again.

Dolores didn't move. Pete leaned back in his chair and plucked the receiver off the wall phone. "Hey," he said.

Then he said, "Huh." He tipped his chair forward. There was an animal tension in his wide body, as if he might suddenly spring out of his chair. I remembered that he'd gone through college on a football scholarship. But he remained motionless. "You've got it in writing?" he asked. Then he said, "No, that'll be fine." He sounded surprised. "Right. See you in the morning."

In one motion, he hung up and stood up. "Roland's gotten a tribal dispensation. We can take nine llamas up to the lake. With Bernadette Walker's stamp of approval."

"I don't get it," said Dolores.

"Roland says our client from California wants to build a ski resort below Lost Pipe Lake. Herron gave a presentation at the conference. He's proposing a state-of-the-eco ski resort—complete with casino."

Dolores groaned. "Another casino scheme?"

Pete's mouth tightened. "Apparently, Herron's been dangling big fat golden carrots under the tribal council's various noses."

We sat still for a moment, digesting the news.

"Will the council bite?" I wondered.

"Not if Bernadette has anything to say about it," Pete answered.

"She's actually sending a *spy* along with us?"

"I guess you could look at it that way," Pete said.

I felt annoyed. I resented the intrusion of local politics into our wilderness trek. "Don't you think your friend Bernadette's overreacting?" I complained.

Pete's face closed. "Maybe," he said coldly.

Shit, I thought. I'd offended him.

THREE

PETE BONSECOURS was born thirty-something years ago to a French-Canadian father and an alcoholic Salish mother. When I first met him, he had no interest in his Salish heritage—in fact, it was something he preferred to ignore. Now that he had embraced his Indian side, however, our common ground appeared to have turned fragile. I felt as if I had waltzed blindly out onto thin ice. Pete's stony face was a loud warning crack.

"So educate me," I said, dismayed and exasperated. We sat up talking past midnight, long after Dolores went to bed. Pete's dark eyes didn't have the convert's fanatic gleam, and his voice never got out of low-key. Nonetheless, beneath his exposition of history and semantics, there was a deep reservoir of passion.

I learned that the term "Flathead" (as in "Flathead Lake," "Flathead River," and "Flathead National Forest") is a white man's misnomer for a Rocky Mountain tribe that spoke Salish. Although their Salish-speaking cousins on the Pacific Northwest coast flattened their heads through ritual binding, the inland Salish kept their heads au naturel.

I also learned that "Flathead Reservation" is a double misnomer: the valley is not the sole province of "Flathead" Indians. Although two of the three tribes on the reservation are Salish-speaking, the third tribe, the Kootenai, is a linguistic isolate.

Lesson number three: the word "reservation," which denotes a place set aside for Indians, is—to put it mildly—incorrect. Back in 1855, by the terms of an agreement called the Hellgate Treaty (Pete pulled out a Xeroxed copy), the Indians ceded some 12 million acres of what is now western Montana and Idaho in exchange for a broad valley protected by the wall of the Missions and watered by winding rivers. (According to a wistful historical marker on present-day Route 93, which bisects the valley floor, the original reservation was "almost entirely virgin prairie, unplowed, unfenced, and beautiful to see. You rode a saddle horse to get places. Some people wish it were still like that.") Despite the treaty, at the beginning of this century, our government opened the reservation to white settlers. Over 90 percent of the productive farm land was allotted to non-Indian homesteaders and merchants. The Indians became a minority on their own "reserved" turf.

They still are. Pete gave me a tribal brochure that lists the reservation population at 19,628—3,771 Indians and the rest "non-Indian." With carefully modulated pride, he pointed out that, over the last sixty years, the Indians have managed to buy back over half of their reservation from white landowners. So if the word "developer" is enough to make any greenie wince, the specter of a white developer packs a double wallop for "red" greenies.

THE FOLLOWING MORNING, I drove Pete's van north on 93 toward Flathead Lake. Compared to the jewellike lakes high up in the mountain's pockets, Flathead Lake, with its mists and white gulls and pine-covered islands, is like the arm of some northern sea—an arm about thirty miles long. The lower half of it is part of the reservation and at the town of Polson, the tribes have built a lakeside motel complex called the KwaTaqNuk Resort, where the conference was held. I met our guests by the registration desk in its split-level, earth-toned lobby.

Charlie Herron was less arrogant in person than I expected from Pete's account. He stood an inch or so taller than me—about six feet in well-worn hiking boots—and his hair was thick and yellow. He was in his late forties, handsome in a country-club sort of way, and determinedly fit: his arms and legs were as tan and muscular as a tennis star's and there was no hint of softness at the waist of his cargo shorts. He radiated enough physical energy to move and shake a bus full of politicians. Felicity, still in her country-squire knickers, was definitely charmed. Under the jaunty brim of her hat, she batted her high-fashion navy blue lashes at him. The filmmakers, Gwen Mears and Mary Ann Dellarobbia, were cool, bordering on chilly. They were suited up in matching khaki vests, the multipocketed kind favored by newsanchors in war zones.

As we loaded the van, Herron was savvy enough to help Felicity with her bag and to let the younger women cope with their own gear. In the bustle of leaving, Herron's eight-year-old son was scarcely noticeable. His name was Kevin. He was a skinny kid with mouse-colored hair in a salon cut. In an orange XL T-shirt and shorts large enough for a circus fat man, he flapped nervously around the parking lot.

By nine o'clock we were under way. Sunlight glinted off the soft blue surface of Flathead Lake. In a shoreline park, the lawn was emerald under yellowing maples. We turned off the highway onto a gravel road that ran, straight as a grid line, into the high dark blue wall of the Missions. Behind me, in the back of the van, conversation turned to the conference and Charlie Herron's proposed ski resort. Lost Pipe Lake, he'd been told, might serve as one of the reservoirs he could tap for water to make snow. He talked excitedly about solar-powered lifts and compost toilets and an underground lodge where elk could graze on its sod roof. I glanced in the rearview mirror at Gwen and Mary Ann. Their smooth young faces were skeptical and contemptuous. Clearly they were disgusted by Charlie's spiel. Felicity, on the other hand, smiled and nodded encouragingly, though I had the feeling she would have listened with equal attention to a blow-by-blow description of how he flossed his teeth. Not surprisingly—though I have to admit that people's self-images often do surprise me—Charlie Herron saw himself as ecologically enlightened. His dream of a downhill wilderness included "wildlife viewing stations" along the trails so skiers could "interface" with nature.

"Winter," he enthused, "is the best time to see animal tracks. I went snowshoeing last December with a Zen monk friend of mine. He's written this best-seller about tracking as a spiritual discipline—how it expands and intensifies perception."

"Really?" Felicity said.

"Yes, we spent two hours looking at mice tracks, and I swear, it was fabulous!" Herron laughed. His good spirits were infectious. His manner was a lot more appealing than his mission.

"You know," he said, lowering his voice as if speaking confidentially, "if we can get this thing off the ground, there are all sorts of possibilities—a mountaintop retreat center, for example, where skiers could meditate and tune into what nature has to teach. Maybe we could even have tracking classes."

"Taught by Zen monks?" Mary Ann asked from the backseat.

"Why not?" Charlie said brightly. "Think of it. The purity of those frozen peaks, sitting Zen in a place where grizzlies sleep beneath the earth, then a run through virgin powder—"

"Followed by a quick game of craps," Gwen intoned from the backseat.

"What about the indigenous trackers?" Mary Ann demanded.

Herron blinked. "Excuse me?"

"The Native Americans."

Charlie's handsome face was perplexed.

"She means you should use Indian trackers, Dad," Kevin piped up. It was the first time he'd spoken. In the rearview mirror, I could see everyone looking at him.

Charlie Herron laughed good-naturedly. "Point well taken," he said. He twisted back to Mary Ann and Gwen. "Sometimes I get lost in my own sales pitch," he admitted. "Kevin here keeps me on track." He gave his son's head an affectionate rub.

PETE, WHO HAD driven the llamas in his trailer, met us at the trailhead. He and his Salish friend Eddie McNab (I was relieved to see that his sickly color had improved overnight) were unloading the llamas, tying them to a nylon picket line strung between soaring Douglas firs. Roland Redhawk, the tribal spy, was unloading llama packsaddles, nylon panniers, and Jake's plywood kitchen boxes from the back of Eddie's elderly pickup. I was not prepared to like Roland. I suppose I pictured someone more secretive, a sneak keeping tabs on us from behind trees. But Roland was a good-humored, outgoing sort and when we shook hands, I felt a friendly little ding of generational kinship. He was wiry, five seven or eight, with faded brown hair pulled back off his high forehead into a ponytail. Under his plaid flannel shirt, he wore a blue tie-dyed T-shirt. On his wrist, he wore a heavy silver cuff set with a massive hunk of pale, veined turquoise. The bracelet looked old. (Felicity admired it extravagantly.) I was too busy loading up to say anything more than hello, but my first impression was that Roland was a benign, aging Deadhead.

Pete did his briefing on the nature of llamas and assigned them to the guests. When Felicity was reunited with Fluffy, she tied a large red silk scarf printed with black flowers around his long neck. "There you go, darling!" she exclaimed. "It's the best my suitcase could do for a red shirt. Doesn't he look royal?" she demanded. Then, despite Pete's suggestion about not getting too cozy with the animals, she flung an arm around Fluffy's neck and buried her face in his shaggy cream-colored fur. Fluffy's ears flattened, but he bore the embrace without flinching. "Listen!" Felicity exclaimed. "He's singing to me!"

We stopped. In fact, the llama was humming. It was a soft minor-key hum that sounded remarkably human. Gwen clapped on her earphones and rushed over with her sound boom. Fluffy's hum rose in pitch. Kevin's llama, a tall rusty-colored animal with white markings, joined in. Its name was Ringo.

"Are they really singing?" I asked Pete.

"More like whining. It's their way of complaining."

"Oh," I said, disappointed.

Pete gave me a wry smile. "People tend to get romantic about llamas. This summer I took out a journalist who wrote about how their humming was like the sound of a ship creaking at sea." He shook his head in disbelief.

I thought about it. "Have you ever been on a sailboat?"

"Nope," Pete said.

"Sometimes, when you're going along at a good clip, the stays—the wires that hold up the mast—make a humming sound. Maybe that's what he meant."

"She," Pete corrected.

"E-flat! He's singing E-flat!" Felicity called out excitedly. She hummed the note back to Fluffy.

"Shouldn't you say something to her," I wondered.

"Why?"

"Sort of like teasing a whiny kid, isn't it?"

He was not concerned. "They're animals, not kids. They can put up with it."

CHARLIE HERRON strode over to us with the hard-shelled black briefcase he'd loaded into the van.

"You bringing your office along?" Pete joked.

"A piece of it," Charlie answered. "It's a satellite phone. Which animal is safest?"

"Safest is locking it in the van."

Charlie Herron shook his head. "It's coming along. I've got some bids coming in."

Pete didn't look happy, but he took the case and weighed it in two hands. "About twenty pounds?"

"Eighteen-and-a-half."

"Why don't you take Carbon—the black one over there. He'll take the extra weight. You can strap it on top of his panniers. He's pretty reliable."

"'Pretty reliable' isn't going to cut it." Herron's voice was snappish. He caught himself. "Sorry, Pete," he apologized smoothly, "but that little miracle of modern communication you're holding cost me twenty thousand."

By this time, the whole group had tuned in. Pete raised an appreciative eyebrow. "In that case," he said mildly, "you might want to do what the girls are doing with their camera."

"What's that?"

"Carry it yourself."

Charlie's jaw dropped half an inch; then he clamped it shut. An angry flush rose from the neck of his polo shirt, but before it could erupt, Roland stepped forward. "Hey, Pete," he suggested, "I threw a light pack in Eddie's truck, just in case. I'll be glad to carry it. I'd like to see one of those things in operation." He turned to Charlie. "Roland Redhawk," he introduced himself. "I caught your presentation at the conference. Impressive, man. Like, we could use more people with your kind of vision around here!"

Uriah Heep in tie-dye. Charlie Herron stared, as if Roland had just crawled out of a psychedelic VW, then turned back to Pete. Without a word, he took the black case from Pete's wide, callused hands and strode off.

"Charming," Gwen muttered.

Felicity gave her a stern look, then glanced pointedly at Kevin. He appeared to be absorbed in Ringo. "Hi, sweetheart," Felicity cooed to Fluffy.

THANKS TO THE MAGIC of Velcro straps and thumb-press buckles on Pete's spiffy new tack, loading his llamas was much faster and easier than loading his mules—a procedure that took at least an hour and required wrapping up all the gear in canvas tarps, roping up the bundles, then tying them onto the mules' backs with a series of packer's hitches and knots. Mules may have a high nostalgia quotient, but I have to say I didn't miss them. I managed to load my entire kitchen on the llamas' backs inside of ten minutes.

Gwen and Mary Ann, who wanted their hands free for their equipment, declined to lead llamas, so Pete led the way with their llamas tied one behind the other in a short string. Mary Ann carried the camera in an aluminum case on a backpack frame. Gwen had the sound equipment in her day pack. Pete's llamas carried their tripod and some forty pounds of battery packs and tapes—enough for six hours of filming which, Mary Ann said, they'd probably edit down to four minutes or less.

Felicity fell in with Fluffy behind the younger women. Charlie Herron went next, Carbon's lead in one hand and his black case in the other, like a commuter striding importantly toward his train. Kevin, who had been tugging on Ringo's lead, and had finally gotten him started, was about to step in after his dad, but Roland ditched in front of them, leaving Kevin at the rear of the line with Eddie and me.

Roland's rudeness annoyed me. "You want to be up with your dad?" I asked Kevin, ready to intervene.

"That's okay," he said simply. "I think Ringo's the sort of person who likes the end of a line."

The trail, which was scarcely wider than a deer track, paralleled Angus Creek, a drainage named after Eddie's forebear, Angus McNab. I was struck by how quiet the llamas were. They moved almost silently. As we climbed up through the forest, Jake's breathing behind me was louder than his footsteps. The track steepened. No one complained at the frequent stops to oblige the filmmakers. We would catch our breath while Gwen and Mary Ann hiked up ahead to set up; then we would parade past them. Mostly they shot from the ground, lying like snipers on their bellies at the side of the trail, sound boom and camera aimed no higher than our boots and the llama's dainty feet.

After an hour of shifting his telephone from one hand to the other, Herron decided that Carbon was trustworthy. With Roland's help, he secured the machine onto the llama's back.

Once a deadfall blocked our way, and we stopped while Pete lit into it with his ax. Mary Ann knelt to film Pete's massive back, the white chips flying, the arc of flashing steel. Gwen caught the *thunck, thunck* with her mike. Between her earphones, her face was spacey, as if she were listening to three sound tracks at once.

Charlie Herron and Roland stood by like supervisors on a construction site. When the log finally cracked and buckled, they manfully pushed and dragged it off the path. Charlie, who had removed his windbreaker, looked particularly manful. He was packing what looked like a 9mm automatic in a black Cordura nylon shoulder holster.

Felicity exclaimed with awe, "You're carrying a gun!"

Slowly, Gwen swung the sound boom in their direction. Underneath his lavender polo shirt, Charlie Herron's firm chest expanded several notches. *Bite your tongue, Squires,* I told myself.

"We're in bear country," he told Felicity.

"Is it loaded?" she asked.

He raised a sun-bleached eyebrow. "Not much good unloaded."

Roland put in, "This time of year, the grizzlies are active in the woods. They like to chow down on pine nuts before their long winter's nap."

"Oh?" Felicity said nervously.

"Pine nuts have a high fat content," he explained as Mary Ann panned them with her camera. Charlie Herron and Felicity waved and smiled, but Roland turned his back abruptly and walked off into the trees.

"Oh, come on," Gwen muttered, annoyed. The filmmakers moved over to Kevin, who had been given the office of llama holder. He sat on a log, holding the leads of Ringo, Carbon, and Jake, engaged in a one-sided conversation with them. Sunlight slanted through the pines above him, giving the scene a holy look.

Gwen adjusted dials on her mixer. "Tell me about your llamas, Kevin," she said.

PETE SHEATHED his ax and walked over to Herron. "Thanks for your help, Charlie," he said.

"No problem," Charlie said.

"I'd be obliged if you'd stow your weapon in your pack. The tribes don't allow firearms in a wilderness area."

Charlie nodded pleasantly, but made no move to undo his holster.

"What about the bears?" Felicity asked.

"Well," Pete said slowly, as if considering bears for the first time. "We're probably making enough noise to warn them off. More likely to meet one of the tribal rangers than a bear." He turned to Charlie. "And if we do, you're likely to lose your gun, and I'm likely to lose my license."

Charlie unarmed himself, wrapped the shoulder straps around the holster, and buried the packet in a pannier.

EDDIE ASKED ME TO take his llama. "I might take a detour on the way up," he said. I tied the animal's lead onto the back of Jake's saddle.

"No problem," I told him. He was sweating heavily, but I pretended not to notice. Whatever was the matter with him, he obviously didn't want it made an issue.

We moved on. Ahead of me, I could hear Charlie sounding off to Roland on the subject of tribal red tape. By the time we found a clearing to stop for lunch, the two men were discussing the concept of "mining trash" on the reservation for postconsumer building products. Score one for Roland's suck-up skills.

While our clients broke out water bottles and sandwiches (an inch of smoked turkey dressed with pesto between thick slabs of Dolores's wheat bread) from their day packs, Pete and I tied the llamas to trees and relieved them of their packs. Calmly they sank down in to the "kush" position, legs folding underneath them camel-fashion. There was no sign of Eddie. "You think he's okay?" Felicity worried.

"Sure," Pete said. "He grew up in this country."

"He doesn't look very well," I noted.

Pete gave a fatalistic shrug. "I told him if he didn't make it, I'd plant him on the way down." The corner of his mouth twitched.

"This is a joke?" I said.

"Hey," Charlie Herron said sincerely, "Not a bad way to go. Hell of a lot better than being hooked up to a bunch of machines."

Felicity smiled uncertainly. She had removed her hat and her hair, dyed a cherry-brunette, was plastered in damp sections to her head. Underneath her sunglasses, she looked pale.

"How are you holding up?" I asked her.

"Well," she said cheerfully, "I'm here. You don't have to break out the shovels on my account."

"I think you're great," Mary Ann encouraged her. "I can't see my mom doing something like this." She hefted her camera up onto her shoulder.

Felicity held up a warning hand. "Oh no, you don't! Not without my hat!"

Gwen laughed. "Hey, hat-hair's part of the wilderness experience!"

As Mary Ann panned the group, Roland, who was stretched out on his back with his eyes closed, rolled over onto his stomach. "We're gonna get you, Roland," Gwen teased. "Sooner or later."

Pete grinned at me. "Talk about camera shy."

THE TRAIL DETERIORATED as we climbed. Conversation stopped. We crossed the creek. One of my boots slipped off a rock and filled with icy water. The llamas stopped midstream to cool their feet, but showed no interest in drinking. Like camels, Pete explained, they had little need for water.

Concentration became key: *Watch your step*, I chanted to myself. My view went no farther than Ringo's rump in front of me. Below his bustlelike tail, the insides of his long hind legs were hairless, nature's way of preventing overheating. They looked as smooth and shapely as a showgirl's. The outsides of his legs, however, were shaggy, and the contrast was bizarre: Ringo looked as if he were wearing dark, furry chaps over white spandex dance tights.

Somewhere around six thousand feet up, my own huffing and puffing became louder than Jake's heavy breathing behind me. Thirst tickled my dry throat; in my wet boot, a heel blister announced itself. It was almost four when we finally climbed out of the woods onto a high meadow strewn with purple asters. I felt as if I had scaled the seven-story mountain of Purgatory and reached the outer circle of Paradise. Even in late afternoon, the alpine brightness was dazzling—"like day added to day," *giorn a giorno,* as Dante put it.

"Here we are," Pete announced. We led the llamas across the meadow and looked down on Lost Pipe Lake. It was obvious how it came by its name: a high cirquelike wall of grey rock at the north end made the pipe's "bowl." At the southern end, the blue green water narrowed into a roughly carved "stem." Here the terrain was flatter, the shore rimmed by dark pines.

"I feel like I'm dreaming," Felicity sighed.

The two filmmakers stood still, appraising the scene with professional eyes. At the bowl end of the lake, the rock wall rose about seventy-five feet above the water. Large maps of snow on its lower slopes were perfectly reflected on the lake's glassy surface. "The light is incredible," Gwen said. "It's so *clear!*"

"No pollution up here," Pete said cheerfully.

"Will you look at that!" Felicity marveled. On the opposite shore, the low sun hit a tall evergreen tree leaning out over the water. Its feathery needles were golden and in the evening light, the tree glowed like a treasure of Byzantium.

"Why is it yellow? Is it diseased?" Gwen asked.

Pete shook his head. "It's a larch. A deciduous type of fir. They lose their needles in the fall."

Mary Ann slipped out of her pack and took a light meter out of her pocket. "The magic hour," she said happily.

Pete looked as pleased as a successful host. He pointed across the "stem" of the lake to a clearing among the pines on the far shore. "We'll pitch the tents over there. We'll set up the kitchen on this side, just in case our food draws a bear."

"Wait a sec," Gwen ordered. "Can we go through that again?" She dove into her pack for her headphones and mike.

Mary Ann held a light meter up to Pete's face. Then, like a dowser sweeping for a well, she took a second reading off Charlie Herron's face.

"Hey," he objected. "We've done the supernumerary bit to death. Time for a swim."

"Go ahead," Pete said. "Leave your llamas up here with us. We'll give them a chance to graze a bit, then bring them on down."

"You're going to swim?" Gwen asked. She looked torn between photo ops. But Charlie and Roland didn't wait for her to make up her mind. They took off down the trail at a jog. Felicity and I followed more sedately. By the time we were halfway down the path to the lake, Roland and Charlie had scrambled up onto a slablike boulder and out of their clothes. We stopped to watch them dive into the turquoise water. Charlie Herron executed a respectable swan dive and was followed more awkwardly by Roland. Seconds later, they surfaced, gasping with the shock of the cold, and swam frantically to shore. They might have had sharks on their heels.

Felicity and I laughed. The men staggered out of the water. Despite the cold, Charlie wore his nakedness aggressively. His tan lines at biceps and thigh emphasized his muscular white-ness. Dripping wet, his torso shone like marble hoisted from a Homeric sea. He hopped up onto the boulder where he'd left his clothes, but ignored them, and instead surveyed the shimmering lake.

"Buns of steel," Felicity muttered wistfully.

"Very scenic," I allowed.

Roland was more modest. Hunched over and shivering, he picked his way around the rocks toward his clothes.

"I thought Native Americans weren't supposed to be hairy," Felicity whispered.

Front and back, Roland's beige body was thickly thatched with dark hair.

We turned our eyes back to the lake. "I'm going to give it a try!" she exclaimed happily. She started on down the path.

"You going in?" I asked, surprised.

"I'm just going to stick my feet in," she called back.

THE EVENING FELT like a festival. I set up a red-and-white striped kitchen fly on the west side of the lake and picked a bouquet of asters from the high meadow. On the opposite shore, Pete and Eddie—who, despite our concerns, had ambled casually into camp—picketed the llamas and set up the tents: a green pyramid, a pair of blue domes, a red lozenge. The bright nylon shone like party balloons. For supper, I grilled our defrosted salmon steaks over a pine wood fire. On the propane stove, I managed not to curdle the béarnaise. While I whisked away with a pair of forks, Felicity, who had chilled her silver flask in the lake, doled out tots of Stoli, and we toasted her fiftieth birthday. (Pete and Eddie raised melamine cups of coffee, Kevin, a cup of Kool-Aid.) Over the salmon, we toasted her again with a Pinot Grigio. Gwen and Mary Ann had packed in a couple bottles for the occasion and they had climbed halfway up the rock wall to chill them in old snow. By the time we had blown out the candles on a carrot cake from Dolores's freezer, I was grateful that I hadn't had to cook it up from scratch. It felt much later than seven o'clock. Felicity made a pretty speech about new friends. Across the lake, distant snowy peaks were bathed in a rosy alpenglow. Above them, the deep blue sky was pricked with early stars.

Charlie Herron sent Kevin around the lake to fetch his satellite phone from their tent and Kevin trotted back with it, begging, "Let me do it, Dad! Can I do it? Please!"

"Hang on there, Bud," Charlie said. "We've got to check the map. The mountains may screw up transmission."

While the rest of us watched, Kevin set the briefcase on the ground, snapped it open and, as his father directed, rotated the lid around the evening sky. Beside the phone's keypad, lights began to blink.

"Getting warm," Kevin said. "Contact!" He pushed a switch. "You're locked on." Charlie picked up the handset and punched a number into the keypad. He listened for several moments, then hung up. "Would you believe, busy?" he announced. He sounded more pleased with his toy's performance than frustrated by the busy signal.

We settled in around the fire with coffee. Charlie doctored his and Roland's coffee with a flask of Scotch. By unspoken but common consent, we had avoided the subject of Charlie Herron's plans for the lake. But when Gwen and Mary Ann began talking about a Native American sweat ceremony they had attended in Taos, the developer was inspired. "Hey," he exclaimed, "we could have après-ski sweats! How's that for a tie-in?" he demanded.

"Pitiful, man," Roland said. The disgust in his voice surprised us all. "Sweat lodges are part of our religion. You know the problem with white people?" he demanded. "You want to skim native spirituality off the surface. You don't understand that our religion's inseparable from our economic life."

"Exactly," Charlie agreed, his voice slurred but jovial. "Exactly my point."

I glanced over at Pete. In the firelight, his face was expressionless.

"Are you Salish?" Felicity asked Roland.

"No Salish blood in me." He didn't elaborate.

Charlie looked at Roland. "I wish I could think where I met you," he mused. "I *know* we've met before."

"In a previous life," Roland joked.

Charlie poured another drink into his cup. "No." He shook his head deliberately. "It'll come to me. I never forget a face."

Bored with the conversation, Kevin pestered his dad to try the phone again. His voice was whiny, on the edge of exhaustion.

"Time for bed, pal," Charlie ordered.

"I'm not tired," Kevin countered.

"Go on, I'll be along in a few minutes."

Kevin didn't move.

"Look, son, I said, Go to bed."

Pete stood up. "I'm going over to check on the llamas," he announced. He turned to Kevin. "I'll walk over with you, if you like. We can stake Ringo right outside your tent. He'll take good care of you. Llamas are great watchdogs."

"Do they bark?" Kevin asked.

"No, but they'll give an alarm. Some people say it sounds like a turkey gobbling, but I think it's more like an old Chevy turning over on a cold morning.'' He made a grinding, mechanical sound at the back of his throat.

Eddie raised an eyebrow. "That's a Chevy?'' He stood up. "About my bedtime, too,'' he said.

Kevin wasn't persuaded. He tugged at his dad's arm.

"I told you, I'll be right there,'' Charlie said.

"But it's dark,'' Kevin complained.

"Oh, for Crisake!'' Charlie said angrily.

"Hey, Kevin,'' I intervened. "Take the kitchen lantern with you. You can leave it on outside your tent.'' I turned to Pete. "We have extra batteries, haven't we?''

"Sure do,'' he said.

IT WAS DARK by the time Pete got Kevin settled in his tent and strolled back around the lake to our campfire. A three-quarter moon had risen over the top of the rock wall and cast a wide yellow path across the black water. Farther down the shoreline, the lantern glowed like a mooring light. Charlie tried his satellite phone again, made contact with an answering machine in L.A., then went to pour another drink and dropped his flask. The liquor chugged out as he fumbled around in the dark for it. I caught the civilized scent of malt whiskey on the cool night air.

"Do bears go for Scotch?'' Gwen quipped.

"Scotch and girly meat.'' Roland said solemnly. He made a smacking sound with his lips. He wasn't much better off than Charlie.

Pete scooped up the flask and handed it to Charlie, who shook it, then turned it upside down. It was empty. "Fuck,'' he said crossly.

"Hey, man,'' Roland said, "I've got some more in my bedroll.''

I waited for Pete to object, but he said nothing. Charlie picked up his satellite phone, and the two of them staggered off. We followed the progress of their voices around the dark perimeter of the lake.

"Maybe they'll fall in and drown,'' Mary Ann said. She sounded hopeful.

"They're going to wake Kevin up.'' Felicity disapproved.

"I doubt it," Pete said. "He was pretty bushed."

By the light of the campfire, I finished up the dishes, then tossed a couple of ropes up into the upper branches of a sizable fir and hoisted the food panniers out of harm's way. This, of course, unleashed Pete's collection of bear stories. He had a new one I hadn't heard before about a grizzly killing a llama. I threw another log on the fire. We forgot about Charlie Herron and Roland Redhawk.

Afterward, we figured it must have been close to nine when we heard the first shots. They sounded muffled, like a double backfire down a city street.

"What was *that?*" Gwen demanded.

I felt a sinking sensation. "Pete?"

But he was already on his feet. There was another retort—this one sharper—then two more. "Stay where you are," Pete ordered. He took off into the dark at a run.

"What's the matter?" Felicity cried in alarm.

No one answered.

Then Gwen said, "That was a gun, wasn't it?"

"They're probably just fooling around," I said.

"Creeps," Mary Ann said disgustedly.

"Do you think it could have been a bear?" Gwen wondered.

"Maybe," I said, though we had not heard any noise from the llamas. I would have thought a bear would have set them off.

"I hope no one's hurt," Felicity worried.

We waited and listened and stared into the dark across the lake. Moonlight washed the upper slopes of rocky cirque and silvered the sides of the nylon tents, but the rest was inky blackness. Then we saw small figures moving across the spot of lantern light. "Pete," I yelled. He didn't answer. Led by Felicity's flashlight, we followed the path around the stem of the lake to our tent site. As we came out of the woods, I saw Pete's broad shape and Eddie McNab's thin one silhouetted by the lantern. They were standing over a form sitting with his back to us, head down. I couldn't see who it was—Roland or Charlie—but whoever it was, he looked sick. I felt a small flash of serves-you-right superiority—odious, given my own penchant for booze but, I have to say, satisfying nonetheless. Pete's and Eddie's postures were casual. Whatever had prompted the gunshots, everything looked normal. "Hello!" Felicity called out, gaily waving her light at the group.

Eddie detached himself and walked purposefully toward us across the moonlit clearing. Felicity lowered her light as he approached. Shadowed by the bill of his baseball cap, his face was invisible, but his voice was substantial enough. "Herron's dead." Eddie announced flatly. "Redhawk shot him."

FOUR

ROLAND REDHAWK sat on the ground. He didn't look up as we approached.

Pete held the gun nonchalantly at his side. It might have been a stone picked up to pound a tent peg.

Charlie Herron lay face up at the edge of the circle of lantern light, about twenty feet from his tent. His eyes were open. Already death had begun to draw his lips back into a rictus that showed the edges of his teeth. They had a Hollywood regularity I hadn't noticed before. His fleece jacket was open and the entire front of his shirt was wetly dark. We stared, disbelieving.

"What happened?" I said.

"They had a fight," Pete answered.

"It was an accident," Roland said. His voice was slow and dull. "He was pissed. He got his gun and started waving it around. I tried to take it away."

"He had no pulse when I got here," Pete said. He looked at his free hand, then wiped it on his jeans. "Didn't think about rubber gloves."

"You don't think he's got AIDS?" Mary Anne said, her nasal voice shrill with horror.

"Oh my God," Felicity said.

"Did you *pack* rubber gloves?" I asked.

"No." He held up the gun. "Can you find something to wrap this in?"

"Sure," I said. I didn't move. Neither did anyone else.

"Jesus," I said. "I don't believe this." I felt a surge of anger at Pete: *He should have taken Herron's gun.*

Mary Ann burst into tears. Felicity put an arm around her and ushered her away from Herron's body.

"What are we going to do?" Gwen asked.

Pete shifted from one foot to the other, as if his boots hurt.

"I'll go out," I said firmly. "If I leave now, I can get to the van before morning." While I didn't relish the idea of negotiating the trail at night, the notion of taking charge while Pete hiked out was even less appealing. "Who should I call—the sheriff?"

Pete thought about it. "Call Fish and Game. Tell them what happened and where we are. Then call the tribal police. They'll notify BIA and the sheriff. The nearest phone's back on 93. There's a convenience store on the left—just after the big sign for jerky. You'll find quarters in the glove compartment."

Roland mumbled something.

"What?" Pete said.

"Let your fingers do the walking." The words came out sloppily.

We stared at him. He let out a sigh I could smell. "Use the phone." He nodded toward Herron's black case. It lay by a clump of bear grass, a dark rectangle in the dim outer circle of lantern light.

"Can you work it?" Pete asked.

"The boy can."

Kevin. Stunned, we all turned and stared at his tent. Moonlight bleached the side nearest us. No sound or movement came through the taut nylon.

In an appalled whisper, Gwen protested, "He *couldn't* have slept through it."

Pete and Eddie were looking at me.

"What? You want me to..."

"You'd be better at it," Pete said.

I felt another flare of anger. "Why?" I demanded.

"Because of your"—he hesitated, then finished awkwardly—"your experience."

"You mean because eleven, twelve years ago I had a daughter go and die of leukemia? I fail to see how that qualifies me to break the facts of death to a kid I met this morning."

He looked stricken.

"Pete, I never talked to Rachel about her dying. I—" I stopped. I looked down at my boots, then up at their anxious faces. It wasn't the time for true confessions. I took a breath. "Okay," I agreed. "I'll do it. But before I get him out of his tent, get Pops covered up, will you?"

EIGHT YEARS OLD. I tried to remember eight. Rachel hadn't made it that far. She had died three days after her fourth birthday. Outside Herron's tent, I called out, "Kevin? Kevin, it's me, Lee." I knelt down and found the tent's zipper. "Kevin, I need to talk to you. I'm going to come in. Okay?" He made no sound, but I could hear him listening. The plastic zipper made a leisurely ripping sound. I stuck my head into cold darkness. "Where are you? I can't see." I heard a small nylon rustle from the bag on my right. I crawled in. "Kevin, give me your hand."

I patted the bag. Kevin wriggled inside it. I caught the smell of urine. His hand found mine. His was icy. I held on tight. "Have you been awake the whole time?" I asked.

He didn't answer.

"Kevin, your dad's been shot."

"Is he dead?"

"Yes," I said.

For several giant-size seconds neither of us said anything. Then I couldn't stand it any longer. "Come on," I told him. "We need to get you into dry clothes before you freeze." *Freeze to death,* I almost said.

He gave me his flashlight. I fished through their leather-trimmed duffel and found a pair of Kevin-sized jeans and a sweater.

"That's Dad's," Kevin said.

"Well, where's yours?"

"I don't know."

"Put it on for now," I ordered. "Your dad won't mind."

He didn't move. Across the moonlit wall of the tent, Pete's and Eddie's shadows slid back and forth. A plastic tarp scraped and crackled. I could feel Kevin shivering. "Come on," I said. "Get dressed. Do you want some help?"

"No."

"Do you want me to leave?"

"No," he said, his voice rising in panic.

"Hey, I'm right here. See?" I turned the light on myself. I made a face at him.

He giggled. Then he worried, "Dad's going to be mad."

Shit, I thought. "About what?" I tried.

"My mom said he'd get mad if I wet my new sleeping bag." His voice was tearful.

"Dead people can't get mad, Kevin. They don't feel anything. Your dad's dead." *The feminine touch: gentle as a bulldozer.*

Kevin was quiet a moment. Then he asked, "Can I see him?"

"Not right now," I said briskly. "We need your help. Do you think you can show Pete how to work your dad's phone?"

"Oh, sure," he said cheerfully.

WE CRAWLED OUT of the tent and joined the group. They had moved the lantern away from the body and stood huddled around it as if it could warm them up. Everyone looked guilty—everyone except Roland. He sat hunched over on the ground, his head resting on his knees, snoring soddenly.

Moonlight bounced off the blue plastic tarp that covered Charlie Herron's body. The tarp, anchored around the edges with rocks and logs, gave death a familiar, homemade look: it might have been covering the last of someone's winter woodpile, or protecting spring seedlings from frost. "Is he under there?" Kevin asked.

"Yes," I said.

"Let me see."

I looked at Pete and Eddie. *Your turn, laddies.*

"The police need to look him over first," Pete told Kevin. "You'll see him later, with your mom."

"Where did he get shot?"

"In the chest."

"Was there lots of blood?" Kevin wondered.

"Oh, dear," Felicity interrupted, her voice anxious and breathy. "How about a nice cup of cocoa? I'm sure we all could use something hot. Do you have any cocoa?" she asked me.

"Yep," I said, back on firm ground. "Cocoa we got. And chamomile tea, too. That's what Mrs. Rabbit gave Peter after his escapade in Mr. McGregor's garden," I blathered idiotically.

"Do you remember Peter Rabbit, Kevin?" Felicity wheezed sweetly.

Kevin ignored her. Maybe *Jurassic Park* would have worked better. "Did the bullets go through his heart?" he asked Pete.

"Looks that way."

"My mom says he hasn't got one," he cracked.

Felicity broke the shocked silence. "Children don't understand," she murmured to Gwen and Mary Ann.

Surprisingly, Eddie spoke up. "Looks to me like that's exactly what he's trying to do."

KEVIN HAD no problem with the satellite phone. Pete sat on it for over an hour answering questions and when he finally signed off, he was still uncertain exactly who was in charge of the investigation—the sheriff's office or some arm of the federal government. A pair of tribal rangers from Fish and Game would hike in at first light, and a Bureau of Indian Affairs investigator would accompany them; but after that, no one was sure.

I steered Pete out of earshot of the others. "Does Eddie know what happened?" I asked.

Pete shook his head. "He was asleep at the far end of the clearing. The shots woke him up."

I looked up at the lopsided moon. "And he didn't see anything?"

"He got there the same time I did. We tried CPR, but—" Pete stopped. When he started again, his voice was harder. "Roland wouldn't shut up. Eddie and I were trying to do something for Herron, and there was Roland breathing down our backs, going on and on about self-defense. He claims Herron came at him with the gun."

We stood still, trying to read each other's faces in the dark. "You think it was an accident?" I asked.

"I don't know." He paused. "Did you ask Kevin what he heard?"

"No." I took a breath. "I had the feeling he knew his dad was dead—even before I said anything. But I didn't want to quiz him."

"They were both pretty drunk," Pete said.

"Drunk doesn't rule out murder," I said. "What's your sheriff like?"

"Doesn't much like getting out of his chair, from what I hear."

We stood there a moment longer, postponing reentry into the

group, into decision making. The night seemed very quiet. "It'll be all right," I said lamely.

"Yeah," Pete said.

EDDIE TOOK KEVIN and four of the llamas up to the high meadow. "No point in having him hang around here," Eddie observed laconically. Pete gave Kevin his own sleeping bag and the lantern and told him that he and Eddie were assigned to the "meadow watch." Kevin seemed content.

We repicketed the rest of the llamas closer to the tents. ("They'll help keep unwanted visitors away," Pete said with a practical nod at the body under the tarp.) Then we gathered wood and rocks for a campfire. There was little comfort in it. Roland lay passed out on the ground beside it, and his comatose breathing was scarcely conducive to conversation. Felicity and the two girls withdrew to their tents. I brought my sleeping bag over to the fire and sat up with Pete listening to Roland's wet snorts and a distant chorus of coyotes.

It was a long night. I slept a couple of hours, curled up in my bag with my back to the fire. I woke up shivering in the dark. The bag was damp and I had a sore shoulder, a stiff neck, and a dry fuzz on my tongue. Herron's body was still there under its tarp: I hadn't been dreaming. Pete and Roland were flat on their backs, apparently impervious to the cold. Irritating little pops came out of Roland's open mouth. Pete was making a chesty rumble. I threw more wood on the fire and gave Roland's boot a kick. He kept on popping.

The sky turned grey about seven. There was a heavy layer of frost on the tarp over Herron's body. I could hear the girls stirring in their red dome. One of them groaned. I walked around the shore back to our kitchen. The lake breathed a grey mist. A woodpecker's sharp staccato broke the stillness. I made coffee on the stove. Mary Ann and Gwen showed up with all their equipment. They wanted sunrise on the lake. I poured them cups of coffee, then carried the pot back to the tent area.

Pete and Roland were now both vertical. Pete had thrown a new log on the fire, and it was smoldering damply. Roland Redhawk stood hunched over it. The collar of his army fatigue jacket was turned up, and his head poked out from it tentatively, like a nervous turtle's. Although the sun wouldn't rise for another hour—one of the disadvantages of fall camping—Roland was wearing aviator shades. He accepted my coffee wordlessly, holding the cup in both hands while I poured from the pot. The steam made half-moons on his dark glasses. Below them, his skin had a grey cast and there was grey in the stubble on his chin. He did not look well.

Pete on the other hand, looked rested and capable. He had tied a clean bandanna around his head and his black hair was glossy as a crow's wing. Under his red-and-black wool shirt, thick as a horse blanket, he was wearing Herron's black nylon holster. Herron's gun, wrapped in a plastic food bag, was in the holster.

Pete escorted Roland over to the kitchen, but Roland declined food and settled under a tree away from the group eating breakfast around the fire. I had decided that we deserved double rations. I cooked pancakes and elk-meat sausage, plus a two-dozen-egg frittata with potatoes, onions, and basil. There was no point in saving provisions. The trek was over. Pete planned to hike out as soon as the rangers arrived and took charge. The filmmakers had no objection. The day promised to be clear, and they figured they could shoot enough footage of the lake and the llamas before we left.

"We'd like you in it," Gwen said to Pete. Her milky skin looked bruised under her eyes, and her heavy braid had frayed all along its length.

He brightened. "No problem."

She lowered her voice. "What about Kevin? Can we use him?"

Pete rubbed the back of his neck. "I guess that'd be up to him."

Kevin was sitting beside Eddie under a crooked pine, cross-legged, breakfast plates in their laps. Eddie's was empty—he had taken only one pancake. Kevin was operating on the frittata, removing each speck of basil from the eggs like a surgeon picking out shrapnel.

"Hey Kevin," Mary Ann said, "will you help us out with our movie today?"

"Okay." He flicked away another speck of basil.

"Great!" Gwen and Mary Ann chimed simultaneously.

Their enthusiasm gave Kevin second thoughts. He looked at Eddie. "Are you going to do it?"

"Nah."

"Oh, come on, Eddie," Gwen protested. "You've got to be in it, too."

Eddie looked bemused.

"Please?" She pressed. "Pretty please?"

"Hey," Mary Ann coaxed, "all you gotta do is sign right here on the dotted line, and you, too, can be a big movie star."

"Me and those old AIM Indians," Eddie said sardonically.

Mary Ann perked up. "You were AIM?"

Eddie shook his head. "Not much of that around here. Those guys were city Indians, mostly."

"What's AIM?" Felicity asked.

"American Indian Movement," Mary Ann explained. "It was big out here in the seventies, but back east, the media was pretty focused on Vietnam and Watergate. I mean, scarcely anybody's heard of Wounded Knee."

"Wounded Knee?" Felicity said. "I thought that was a battle back in the last century."

Mary Ann looked pleased, as if Felicity had proved her point. "It wasn't a battle. It was a massacre. The Seventh Cavalry slaughtered a band of Sioux women, and children. The few men with them had already been disarmed. That was back in 1890. I'm talking about a protest in 1973. Wounded Knee II, they called it. Hundreds of Native Americans from tribes all over the country drove into the village of Wounded Knee, South Dakota, and took it over. The Justice Department sent in armored personnel carriers with .30-caliber machine guns. They sent in FBI, police, U.S. marshals with M-16s—and gave them enough ammo to wipe out every Indian in the Dakotas. They even had Phantom jets doing fly-overs. I talked to one guy who'd flown missions in them over in Vietnam. He comes to Wounded Knee, and now *he's* the 'gook' his own bombers are hunting *him*. Weird."

"So what happened?" Felicity wondered.

"AIM held the village for over two months. There was some

shooting. A couple of people were killed. Then the leaders gave themselves up. Several of them went to prison."

Eddie stood up and put his empty plate in the washbasin. "A bunch of troublemakers dressed up in feathers and red windbands," he said bluntly. "Violent men who were drunk half the time. They weren't no warriors. They were cop killers. Now Hollywood's gone and turned them into heroes."

Mary Ann bristled. "If you're talking about Leonard Peltier, you're misinformed," she declared hotly. "He was set up by the FBI."

Gwen jumped in. "Let's not get political," she said firmly. "We're working on a documentary about Native American attitudes toward land use."

A smile worked its way across Eddie's rumpled face. "That's not political?"

Gwen winced, then gave Eddie a little nod of concession. "We'd really like to try some shots of you and Kevin with the llamas," she persisted.

He shrugged. Then, solemnly, he held up his hand as if he were about to be sworn in. "Me Tonto," he announced.

Mary Ann rolled her eyes. "Tonto we can do without."

"Who's Tonto?" Kevin asked.

"The Uncle Tom of the Woolly West," Mary Ann cracked.

Felicity turned to Kevin. "Tonto," she said with dignity, "was the faithful companion of The Lone Ranger. Do you know who The Lone Ranger was?"

"No," Kevin said.

She explained. We sipped coffee and listened attentively. For a moment, I was no longer perched on a log in the wilderness. I was tucked into my father's worn leather armchair watching The Masked Stranger right wrongs on black-and-white TV. The screen had rounded corners.

"He'd always leave a silver bullet before he rode off into the sunset," Felicity said. "It was his trademark." She paused, then allowed herself a nostalgic smile. "I used to listen to it on the radio. Mondays, Wednesdays, and Fridays at seven-thirty." She turned to Kevin. "When I was your age, TV hadn't been invented yet."

Kevin wasn't impressed. "Why did he wear a mask?"

Felicity thought about it. "I guess he was like Batman, in that regard. He preferred to keep his identity a secret."

"Did Tonto wear a mask, too?"

"No."

"How come?"

"His identity didn't count," Mary Ann said gloomily.

FELICITY VOLUNTEERED to help with the breakfast dishes and Gwen and Mary Ann, who were waiting for the sun to appear over the top of the peaks, joined in.

"Kevin seems like he's doing okay," Mary Ann observed. She sounded surprised.

"Poor kid," Gwen said.

"You think he'd like to talk to his mother on that machine?" Felicity wondered.

"You could ask him," I said.

"Do you think they're together?" Felicity persisted. "I mean Charlie and Kevin's mother. I had the feeling maybe they were divorced."

"I don't know, Felicity," Mary Ann said dubiously. "You want to call her up, break the news to her, then say, 'Here's Kevin'?"

"Why do you think they're divorced?" Gwen wondered.

Felicity flushed. "I just felt he was available," she finished delicately.

"I'm sure he was," Mary Ann said ironically.

"Felicity," Gwen declared, "the guy was bogus. He didn't give a shit about Indians all he wanted was their land." She glanced in Roland's direction and lowered her voice. "Let's face it. Roland did the world a big favor."

"*Gwen,*" Felicity protested, her voice genuinely shocked.

THE SUN APPEARED through the dark pines across the lake, turning the flat grey water to green and striping its surface with long, skinny shadows like the grain in a piece of polished malachite. Watching a movie in the making proved as exciting as watching a writer at work. At various spots around the lake, a tangle of llamas, people, and movie equipment would unfold, parade a couple yards, then stall out. I packed up the kitchen and took down the fly. "You want me to strike the tents?" I asked Pete the next time he passed through.

"No, leave them up till the authorities get here. They'll want to see the setup. If all our other gear is ready to go, it won't take long to pack up the tents. You could clean up both fire rings, though. And Lee?"

"What?"

"Keep an eye on Roland, will you?"

"What about you?" It came out more sharply than intended.

Pete's lifted his straight eyebrows in surprise and pointed out the obvious: "I'm busy with the girls."

"Pete, I'm sorry. I won't be responsible for Roland."

His dark eyes searched my face as if he couldn't believe I was serious.

"I mean it."

"You want the gun?"

I glanced over at Roland stretched out under a scraggly pine on the far side of the kitchen. Judging from his appearance, his hangover was genuine. If my own morning-after experiences were any indication, Roland wasn't going anywhere. And even if he was, I wasn't going to shoot him. "No. I don't want the gun."

He walked off. His face said: *What's your problem?*

I FINISHED CLEANING UP the campsite, then went over to Roland. "Hey," I said. In the purplish mirror of his shades, a dead overhead branch was twice reflected, once across each eye. It looked creepy, like the artwork for a Stephen King best-seller.

"What?" His mouth scarcely moved.

"Time to move."

He didn't budge.

Thanks Pete. Thanks a lot. "You okay?" I asked Roland.

"I feel great."

"Come on, we're going over to the tents."

He sat up slowly. He waited a moment, then stood up. There were pine needles in his ponytail.

Over at the tents, he found another tree. Felicity crawled out of her tent, wearing fresh makeup and a shirt that looked freshly ironed. In her hand, she had a yellow cardboard panoramic camera. "I thought I'd get some pictures of the girls filming," she explained. But she made no move to join them. "Do you think it'd be all right if I, uh—" With her camera, she made a vague gesture that encompassed the entire campsite. Our eyes, however, landed on the blue tarp. "I hope you don't think I'm being ghoulish," she said apologetically. "It's just that no one at home is going to believe this."

THE SUN WAS heating things up. I fished Kevin's sleeping bag out of his tent. It was hot inside and the sodden polyester bag stank. The ecologically pure thing to do would have been to haul water from the lake into the woods behind the tents and wash it out there with our biodegradable soap. But to get enough water to do the job was going to take a bucket brigade. The lake could handle one little boy's pee. I walked over to Roland.

"I'm going down to the lake, around by those the rocks."

He grunted.

"You're coming with me. Sorry, but I'm supposed to keep you in sight."

"Christ Almighty," he muttered. But to my surprise, he got to his feet. At the tents, I gathered up Kevin's bag. Roland caught the stink of it and grimaced. "What the fuck is that?"

"Piss," I said. "Funny thing, Roland. Kevin happened to wet his bag last night."

"Hey," he said weakly. "I feel bad about the kid, okay? But these things happen. Like, it was an accident. What was I supposed to do—like, let the jerk Glock me?"

I said nothing.

"I swear to God, it was an accident. I was trying to get the gun away from him—"

I held up a hand. "Roland, I really don't want to hear it." Which wasn't entirely true. As much as anyone, I wanted to know what had happened around the campfire. On the other hand, the cloying note of self-pity in Roland voice disgusted me. There was no way I was going to play mother confessor to the man. Let him unload on the cops.

WE DIDN'T speak to each other again. At the bowl end of the lake, Roland eased himself out of his fatigue jacket, carefully folded it into a pillow, and lay himself down in the shade of a smooth grey boulder. I unzipped Kevin's bag and, at the edge of the lake, threw it out over the water, as if I were fluffing a down quilt over a bed. I watched the pale blue nylon slowly sink under the surface. The mud at the water's edge sucked at my boots and the moss-covered rocks were slippery. I picked my way through them to a boulder of my own. For maybe fifteen, twenty minutes, I dozed in the sun.

Gwen's and Mary Ann's voices woke me. They were scouting out another camera angle. Mary Ann carried the camera with her. Gwen had the tripod and a battery pack. The llamas and the rest of the party had parked themselves across the lake. "Let's try them against that wall, with the lake in the foreground," Gwen said. She looked up at the sky. "Another half an hour, the sun will be on it."

Mary Ann hoisted the camera to her shoulder and peered through the lens at the slope of dark rock that curved around the north end of the lake. Patches of old snow filled its crevices. Above the snow, the bare rock had the drama of a ruined battlement. "A bit closer, I think," said Mary Ann.

"You want us to move?" I asked them.

"I don't think so," Gwen said. "At least not yet."

They carried their gear twenty yards farther up the rocky shoreline and set up the tripod on a slab of granite.

Ten minutes later, Gwen came back. "Can we get that bag out of the way?" she asked. "I'll give you a hand with it."

We took off our boots and hobbled across sharp rocks into the water's edge. Cool black mud squished between my toes. I waded in and swirled the bag around, stirring up liquid clouds of mud. The cold made my feet ache. We lifted the wet bag out of the water. It felt as if someone had filled it with stones. We let it drip a minute, then staggered out of the water with it. "My feet are numb!" Gwen declared. Then something caught her eye. "Who's that talking to Mary Ann?"

I turned and looked. Mary Ann's back blocked our view of someone in baggy camouflage pants. Then Mary Ann turned and the stranger—a young woman—started walking toward us. Her step was brisk and confident, but she walked with a limp.

"Is that one of the rangers?" Gwen wondered.

"I don't know," I said. If it was, she looked like she'd had a rough time on the way up. Her tan T-shirt was torn and caked with dirt, and her hair, a thick rug of snarls, had twigs in it. Across her cheeks, there were smudged black lines. They looked purposeful, as if she had drawn them with charcoal. In her left hand she carried a simple wooden bow about five feet long. The wood was caramel-colored and smooth, but unvarnished. It had the handmade look of the Boy Scout projects my brother used to bring home.

She stopped about five feet away. She considered us and the muddy mass of blue nylon at our feet. She frowned, as if trying to decide which rule we had broken. "Hi," I said.

She didn't answer.

Gwen and I glanced at each other. I asked the girl, "Are you all right?"

She focused. "What?"

"You okay?" I repeated.

"Oh." The question seemed to surprise her. "Yeah, sure." Her voice sounded younger than she looked, though it was hard to say what age she was.

"Are you with the tribal rangers?" Gwen asked.

"No," she said. "I'm on my own." *Oh-own,* she said. There was a lag in her long "o's." "I'm looking for Roland Redhawk."

"Over there," I told her. Alerted by the new voice, Roland was sitting up. He leaned back against his boulder, arms folded across his chest, legs crossed casually, in a posture of studied nonchalance. Beneath his mirrored glasses, his mouth was a taut line.

She walked around us. I saw that she had a narrow nylon sack hanging down her back. In it, there were two store-bought arrows. She stopped about fifteen feet from Roland. "You're Redhawk?" she demanded.

"Who the hell are you?" he snarled.

"I have a message for you," she said. In one swift movement she whipped an arrow out of her sack, set it to the bow, pulled back, and let the arrow fly. The next thing we saw was its shaft quivering in Roland's chest. Roland let out a bellow of shock. Clutching the arrow, he scrambled to his feet. "Bitch!" he exclaimed in outrage.

In the next moment, she did it again. Her second arrow went cracking through the left lens of his shades into his left eye. Roland fell back. His head made a sickening thump against a rock.

"Oh, my God!" Gwen said.

The woman bent over Roland, put a foot on his chest and, straining, yanked the arrow out of his heart. Without stopping to look at it, she bounded past us in the direction from which she'd come. Barefoot, I lurched toward Roland. Gwen was clutching my arm. "Let go!" I yelled.

"Mary Ann!" Gwen screamed. "Get her!"

FIVE

MUFFLED BY the church's heavy doors, prayers chanted for Roland Redhawk drifted over my head, up toward the Missions' dark peaks.

"So she got away," Luke said.

"I could have stopped her," I told him. "If I hadn't been barefoot, I could have saved whatever monumental amount of dollars this womanhunt of yours is costing."

Luke frowned. "The girl was armed, Lee. Don't beat yourself up about it."

"I'm not."

"Hmm."

"Well, maybe a kick or two in the rear," I allowed. "Talk about Three Stooges. Gwen and I were slipping around like a pair of mud wrestlers, and Mary Ann was zoned out filming the scenery. She was almost at the end of a cartridge, and was using it up so she could reload for the next take. She thought Gwen was yelling at her to get the girl on film. She swung the camera around and zoomed in on the girl running toward her. Then she ran out of film."

"It's an incredible shot," Luke said.

"You've seen the video, then."

"Yep." He let out a wistful sigh. "Pretty spot, up there." We looked out at the ranks of the Missions looming above the valley floor, their flanks dark as cobalt under snowy peaks. Lost Pipe Lake lay to the north—another country, another dimension.

"How long did you stick around after the troops arrived?" he asked.

I shrugged. "Pretty much all afternoon. We went through the whole name, rank, and shoe size bit. At one point it looked as if they were going to confiscate our boots. Finally Pete got permission to leave, so we took down the tents, loaded up the llamas, and started back down around five o'clock. Everyone was ready to get out of there, even if it meant walking all night, but Eddie found us an old campsite about a mile down the trail, and we spent the night there. Two of the tribal police came with us. I gathered the FBI told them to get lost. They were not what you'd call happy campers. Maybe they said three words."

"Every cop wants to work a homicide. That's where the glamour is," Luke stated with a resigned shrug. "Then pretty soon they realize they don't know what they're doing. By the time we get there, the scene's been trampled in a turf war, and everyone's ego is out of joint."

"It wasn't simply jurisdictional jealousy," I told him. "There was Roland, dead on the rocks with an arrow sticking out of his eyeball, and this white guy—a real cutie—made a crack about open season on prairie niggers. A couple of his chums started snickering. The cops from the tribe were standing right there."

Luke's jaw tightened. I waited for him to say something. He didn't.

"It's just hard to believe all this shit is still going on out here," I insisted. "Back east, everyone thinks Native Americans are a superior form of human being."

"That's because they don't live with them," he said flatly.

I looked at him.

"Were you born with a bleeding heart?" he asked.

But I wasn't ready to drop it. "Look, first we beat the Indians into the ground, then we hate them some more. It's depressing."

"That it is. Do you remember who did the interviews at the scene?" Like a doctor with a good bedside manner, it was hard to tell whether he was probing or making small talk.

"It wasn't that organized. Everyone was asking us what happened. Mostly they were interested in the video. I don't remember anyone taking notes. From what we saw of it, the whole thing looked pretty zooey. The FBI agents and the deputies were running around waving their walkie-talkies and calling for helicopters and dogs while the tribal police were trying to measure rocks."

"Did anyone talk to the boy about what he'd seen?"

"Kevin? Not that I know of. With a killer on the loose, Herron's death took a backseat. It's not like there was any question about who did it."

A warm breeze from the parking lot blew the smell of dust and axle grease across the churchyard. I felt a loosening sensation, as if a large knot had been eased inside me. I remembered one of the things I'd liked about Luke: he was a talented listener. He stood beside me, his stance relaxed, hands in pockets, eyes scanning the media people in the yard, the pickups in the parking lot, the road along a line of dust-whitened willows that led out to 93. In the sharp noonday sun, the collar of his dress shirt was immaculate against the tanned skin of his neck; but in the shadow under his jaw, he had missed a little patch of stubble. I felt an urge to reach out and touch it, to feel the prickle of it under the tip of my forefinger. *License my roving hands.*

From the swarm of questions in my mind, I picked a businesslike one. "Have they located Kevin's mom yet?"

"Nope," Luke answered. "Herron's office has no idea where she went. They've been separated for the last year."

"That's what Felicity thought."

"What?"

"That they were separated."

The word hung heavily between us. He didn't pick it up.

"When did you get here?" I asked.

"Drove up from Helena last night."

"So how's Helena?"

"Good."

"Great." I sounded as bright as a new penny. "You and Barb still together?"

His mouth tightened for a second. "Yeah." He looked into the distance, then met my gaze. His eyes were light brown flecked with green. Like a trout stream, it was hard to read the shadows.

"It's working out, then?" I fished.

"Sure," he said uncomfortably.

Sure.

Behind us, the doors of the church opened. Suddenly Luke was energized and focused. "Okay, keep your eyes open. If you think you see her, don't get near her. She might be armed, and we don't want anyone to get hurt. Just let me know if you can. Or give a nod to the driver of that van." He indicated the young Salish woman in the battered van parked by the chain-link fence. "That's our surveillance van. We'll get the crowd on video here and at the graveside. If she shows up, we'll see who she talks to, who she's with." He paused. "I don't want you near her," he repeated. "It's not your job. It's mine."

"Okay," I agreed.

He looked surprised.

"Look. I blew it up at the lake. But that doesn't mean I feel the need to redeem myself with a flying tackle right here in front of everyone on the grass."

"Okay," he said cheerfully. "Catch you later."

"Yeah."

He stopped. "What's the matter?"

I took a breath and grabbed one at random. "I'm not sure I'll recognize her."

"Don't fix on faces. You saw the way she moved, her body language. Keep your focus soft. Pay attention to shape and movement."

"Like looking for wildlife?"

"There you go."

THE PALLBEARERS carried Roland's coffin down the steps. Their faces were grimly concentrated. TV cameras trailing technicians on the ends of black umbilical cords followed the procession to the hearse. I found Dolores with her mother Rose. Dolores was wearing stonewashed jeans and a cream-colored wool jacket. After Paul's birth, she had cut off her waist-length brown hair to her shoulders and although she usually pulled it back into a beaded clip, in honor of the funeral she was wearing it in a soft pageboy that made her look like a suburban teenager. She was, in fact, a year or two over thirty. Rose, her mother, was the same height, but rounder and less upscale-looking in a frizzy home permanent, brown slacks, and a windbreaker. Standing with them was an older woman smoking a cigarette. She had wispy white hair and a round golden-colored face that reminded me of a sagging jack-o'-lantern. Rose introduced us. Her name was Louisa.

"Lee was up at Lost Pipe Lake," Dolores told her.

Louisa's hazel eyes sharpened with interest. "Oh, you're the cook." Her voice was much younger than her face.

"Yes," I said.

She turned to Dolores. "Paper said Eddie McNab was there, too."

"Yes," Dolores said. There was a final note in her voice, as if she'd just closed a door.

Rose didn't notice. "Eddie asked Pete if he could go along with them," she informed Louisa.

Louisa's eyebrows shot up. "Is that a fact?"

Rose confirmed it with a nod, then pulled a pack of Kools from her windbreaker and lit up. "Can't think why he'd take the trouble. Seems downright gruesome to me," she observed.

"You can say that again," Louisa said.

"Gruesome? Why's that?" I asked them.

Louisa took a drag on her cigarette. "Considering what happened up there—"

Dolores cut her off firmly. "That's ancient history, Louisa."

Rose studied her cigarette. I was surprised to find that I wanted one. It had been almost ten years since I had quit. Now the reek of them repelled me. I found it hard to believe that once upon a time cigarettes were an après-sex pleasure. I'd learned how to write without them and how to drink without them. But evidently I hadn't learned how to get through a funeral without them.

"Pleased to meet you," Louisa said to me. She moved off.

"What's ancient history?"

Dolores dismissed my question with a shake of her head. "Louisa should mind her own business."

"You should mind your manners," Rose rebuked her daughter.

Pete joined us. "You coming with us to the interment?" he asked me. "Charlene's giving a feast afterwards, real traditional."

I hesitated. "Felicity's leaving this afternoon. I told her I'd meet her at the motel for a late lunch."

The three of them stood together, solid as a bulwark. I wanted to be taken into their circle of safety, to hug them and be hugged back. But none of us made a move. I felt gangly and pale beside them, an outsider. "See you later," I said lamely.

ON THE WAY BACK to Polson, I gave myself another kick. If I was feeling excluded, I had only myself to blame. I had turned down the chance to break fry bread with them and try camus, an indigenous wild bulb more authentically Salish than southwestern fry bread. Moreover, after getting back from Lost Pipe Lake, I'd opted out of Pete's and Dolores's nest. A continuous stream of curious and sympathetic friends had flowed through their house. An anonymous motel room seemed preferable to the sofa bed in their very public living room. When I told Pete I needed some space, he had suggested the KwaTaqNuk and magnanimously insisted on putting the room on his Visacard. Moreover, he had given me use of the van I was now driving. What more did I want?

More, a little voice piped up.

I rolled the window down and drove with the wind thumping gently on my eardrums. On the west side of the valley, banks of grey clouds rolled in over the brown hills. At Ninepipe Wildlife Refuge, where the reservoir lay level with the road like a flooded field, the glassy surface of the water sharply mirrored the clouds moving overhead. I pulled off the highway into a parking area and got out of the van for a look. Billowing clouds above, billowing clouds below. It was unsettling. I might have been staring at a hole in the earth, a tear fringed by reeds and rushes. I half-expected a bird to swoop out of the sky and fly right through the watery opening, down into an undersky. I caught the stink of something dead. Rotting fish entrails spilled out of a garbage can by a gate posted "Off-Limits." I felt as if I had stumbled into a landscape of potent metaphors—metaphors whose meaning eluded me. I climbed back into the van and I spent the rest of the way back to Polson composing a sisterly little lecture for Luke about the upside of divorce.

FELICITY, GWEN, and Mary Ann were waiting for me in the motel's bar. They looked the same, but not the same. It wasn't so much a matter of clothes. Gwen and Mary Ann were still wearing their safari vests with their jeans and hiking boots; and Felicity, in a navy sweater, was casual enough for any high-country camp. But somehow they looked sleeker, glossier, as if hair spray, makeup, and new earrings had groomed away any trace of wilderness.

They had taken a table by the window and had already eaten lunch. Remnants of their salads lay on their plates. I ordered a double bourbon on the rocks. The mood in the bar was cheery. A football game on the TV made soap-bubble flickers of color in the rows of wineglasses suspended over the bar. The voices of beer drinkers on the stools were jovial.

Gwen had spent the morning on the phone trying to recapture their video from the authorities. Both she and Mary Ann were angry and frustrated. "They can't seem to understand that we've got to have the film back!" Gwen complained. "There's no way we can duplicate those shots, even if we had the money to reshoot."

"It's probably wrecked anyway," Mary Ann said gloomily. She took a swallow from a glass of red wine. "They cut that still out of it—the one they've been circulating."

"Without a credit line," Gwen muttered.

"What, you want it on your résumé? One wanted poster?"

"How was the funeral?" Felicity inquired. She seemed glad to change the subject.

I told them about the procession. "There was no flag on Roland's coffin," I told them. "For some reason, I had the impression he was a vet. Maybe it was that fatigue jacket he wore."

Gwen thought that maybe he had mentioned Vietnam. If he had, neither Gwen nor Felicity could confirm it. I told them about Luke's appearance on the scene. They listened with interest. "Maybe we should try *him* about the film," Gwen proposed. "What's his name again?"

"Luke Donner."

"He actually had the church staked out?" Felicity asked.

"That's what he said. You couldn't tell from looking."

"And you didn't see her there?"

"No."

"I wonder who she was," Gwen said.

"You sound like a broken record," Mary Ann accused. "Let it go."

"You didn't see it," her partner countered. *"I have a message for you,"* she quoted. "Then *thwack, thwack,* the guy's dead. Like she was some kind of nemesis. Maybe she was his long-lost daughter. Maybe he diddled her as a kid."

"It happens to some of the nicest guys," Mary Ann said. "Their mothers made them do it." She polished off her wine.

Felicity said, "Apparently she was at Roland's store, asking after him the day we left. A cousin who worked there told her that Roland had taken off for Lost Pipe Lake. The cousin didn't think anything of it until the cops came in with her picture."

"Where'd you hear that?" I asked.

"The girl at the front desk told me as I was checking out." She glanced at her watch. "We should go." She turned to me. "Gwen and Mary Ann are driving me up to Kalispell to catch my plane," she announced with pleasure.

"What time's the plane?"

"Oh, it's not till tonight. But I heard there were some nice antique shops along the west side of the lake. We thought we'd shop a bit on the way. I'd like to find a old branding iron or a pair of chaps—something authentic for my apartment."

Life goes on, I thought. I took a long swallow of icy bourbon.

"How's Kevin?" Mary Ann asked.

I reported what Luke had told me about Kevin's mother. "But Dolores says he's doing okay, as far as anyone can tell. He's staying with Eddie, but he's been over at Pete's a couple times to visit with the llamas. And play with Paul."

"Who's Paul?" Gwen asked.

"Pete's baby."

"I didn't know they had a baby."

"Yes. He's three. Kevin's very good with him, Dolores says."

We all looked out the window. Beyond the motel's dock, Flathead Lake was rumpled, like steel lamé. Its pine-covered islands were dark as charcoal, and the tops of Missions were shrouded in veils of white fog. I thought about Eddie. What was the "ancient history" that Dolores hadn't wanted me to hear? Was she protecting him in some way? It occurred to me that Eddie had the opportunity to kill Charlie Herron. Eddie had been on the far side of the lake at the time of the shooting. He could have taken the gun while Roland and Charlie were drinking. But if Eddie actually had shot Heron, why would Roland cover for him?

I ordered another bourbon and a club sandwich. Felicity ducked under her chair and retrieved a film-developer's envelope from a Louis Vuitton carryall. She handed a stack of color photos over the table to me. "I got these back this morning," she said. "There's a nice one of you. I'll send you a copy if you give me your address."

I leafed through them and found myself squatting over the salmon steaks I'd grilled on her birthday up at Lost Pipe Lake. A shaft of evening sun pierced the smoke from the pine-wood fire and caught stray wisps of my hair. I looked blonder than I was and a lot more robust than I felt. Not so bad, I thought. I moved on to the others—shots of the llamas, of the lake, of the aster-strewn meadow above it. "These are very good, Felicity," I said, surprised at the quality that emerged from the cardboard camera.

"Oh, I just pointed it wherever the girls were pointing," she said modestly.

I stopped at a shot of the line of tents. Small patches of red, green, and blue against a dark margin of arrowy firs. A wilderness idyll. If you didn't know what was under the blue tarp. Felicity had taken it the morning Roland was killed.

"Mrs. Parsley?" said a familiar male voice behind me.

I looked up from the photos. "Luke!" I exclaimed.

"Yes?" Felicity said.

He included us all in his easy smile. We all sat up an inch and a half straighter. "I'm Agent Luke Donner, Mrs. Parsley. I'm in charge of the investigation into the deaths of Roland Redhawk and Charlie Herron."

"Lee was just talking about you!" Gwen and Mary Ann chorused.

I felt my face turning red and, not for the first time, cursed my thin skin. Felicity looked curiously at me, but Luke didn't notice. Gwen had pounced on him about their film.

"I'll see what I can do," he promised.

"You're investigating poor Charlie's death, too?" Felicity asked.

"Yes, ma'am."

"But why? Roland said he'd done it. And now he's dead, too."

"We're mandated by law to investigate every unnatural death," he droned. "Whether it's homicide, suicide, or accidental, it still has to be investigated." He cleared his throat of officialese. "The sheriff said you were leaving today?"

"Isn't that all right?" she worried.

"No problem," he reassured her. "I just wondered if we could talk a few minutes before you go—maybe out in the lounge?"

"I'll be glad to help out however I can," Felicity consented graciously, "but really, I've already told everything I know."

"I'd like to hear it directly from you, if you don't mind."

"Not at all." She stood up. I handed her photos back.

"May I?" Luke intercepted them. He studied the shot of the tents, then looked up. "I'd appreciate a copy of this," he said. "It might help with our reconstruction."

"Oh my," Felicity said, flattered. "Take them all! I've got the negatives."

They left the bar. I ate two triangles of my club sandwich with my bourbon. Gwen and Mary Ann picked at the others. Voices from the bar rose above the TV. A woman said, "I could recite all the books of the Bible by the time I was three years old." A man said, "So there they were, stranded on this island, and one of them was a doctor, and he said, 'I'll cut a left arm off each of you and we'll eat them; then you can cut off mine...'"

We looked at each other. "I don't think it's an Oscar winner," Mary Ann commented drily.

"Nooo." Gwen said.

We paid the tab and found Luke and Felicity in the lobby. Felicity and I exchanged addresses and hugged good-bye. "If you hear of someone who wants a cook in the Amazon, let me know," I told her.

"Isn't she a dear?" she remarked to Luke, as if I'd said something cute.

Mary and Gwen agreed to meet with Luke the next morning. Then the three of them left.

"What are you up to?" Luke asked.

The bourbon had fuzzed out my edges. "I was thinking about a nap." I met his eyes.

He smiled ruefully. "I'd like you to do me a favor."

"What?"

"They've located Kevin's mother. She was somewhere down in Mexico on a beach with her boyfriend. She didn't expect Kevin back until tomorrow. She's flying into Missoula this afternoon, and I want to interview Kevin before she gets here. I wondered if you'd come along. Might make him more comfortable."

I felt vaguely disappointed. "No problem," I agreed.

SIX

LUKE DROVE US back down 93 in an unmarked Ford. On both radio and cellular phone, he made one call after another. He seemed to be getting nowhere; the patience in his voice had a hard ring, as if it were cast in iron. I drank black coffee through the plastic lid on a Styrofoam cup and read the passing signs for businesses along the highway. Hot tubs, RV parks, and polled Herefords were big. A roadside shack plastered with video posters of leggy blondes in black leather and chains also offered INDIAN "DISCOUNT" GAS. We turned off at a tractor dealership and followed a gravel road between mown hayfields toward the mountains. Luke hung up the phone, exasperated.

"What's the problem?"

"Charlie Herron's jacket."

"What's wrong with it?"

"Someone at the scene removed it. It didn't go to Missoula with the body. The sheriff's people think maybe one of the BLM investigators have it. But all the offices in the tribal complex are closed, due to the funeral."

"You think it disappeared on purpose?"

"If it did, we'll find out," he said evenly.

A hand-lettered sign marked Eddie McNab's driveway. "Eddie's Engine Repair," it said. The shop stood next to the house in a grove of pine trees. The house was a small box with squat windows set in the mustard-colored aluminum siding. The shop was a metal shed whose corrugated roof was littered with dead pine needles. Both the shed's garage doors were closed. Luke pulled in between Eddie's battered pickup and an elderly white Oldsmobile with one maroon fender. He cut the engine, but remained behind the wheel.

"What are we waiting for?" I asked.

"Rule number one: Beware the rottweilers."

"Eddie has rottweilers?"

"That's what I'm waiting to find out. You don't want to get in a position where you have to shoot the family pet." He winced. "Happened to a friend of mine. He'd have been better off shooting the owner, let me tell you."

A door opened in the side of the shed, and Eddie came out in a faded green coverall and the same billed cap he'd worn on our trip. Kevin was right behind him wearing a man-sized blue mechanic's shirt that came down to his knees. No rottweilers. We got out of the car.

"Hey," Eddie welcomed. His lined face still had a yellowish cast, but his skin looked lit from within instead of dully opaque, the way it had on the hike up to Lost Pipe Lake.

"Hey," I said back, grinning. I was surprised by how glad I was to see them both. "How you guys doing?" I asked.

"Pretty fair," Eddie said.

"Okay," Kevin said. The name "Mike" was embroidered in red thread on his shirt pocket. We stood there beaming at each other.

"I'm Luke Donner, Mr. McNab," Luke said, extending his hand to Eddie. "We talked on the phone."

Eddie held up a grease-blackened right hand. "Excuse me, I'm not cleaned up," he apologized. "We're in the middle of a job."

"Looks like you got a good helper there."

"He'll do," Eddie said, but there was pride in his voice.

"Kevin, I'm Agent Luke Donner. I'm investigating your father's death."

Kevin looked at him warily.

"I'd like to ask you a few questions."

Kevin looked at Eddie.

"Take them on inside," Eddie told him. "The man ain't gonna bite. Besides, you've got Lee here to keep him in line for you." He gave Luke a wink and added, "I'd offer you coffee, but they've all gone to the funeral." He sounded jollier than I'd ever heard him.

I puzzled over the relation between no coffee and the funeral as Kevin led us through a cluttered kitchen that smelled of bacon grease and lemon-scented detergent. Had the funeral-goers taken the coffee with them? Did Eddie not know how to work the coffeemaker? Its empty Pyrex pot sat on the kitchen table amid pink foam curlers, supermarket coupons, unwashed mugs, a giant-size plastic bottle of cola. There was no dining room—the house had only four small rooms, including the kitchen—but the living room, despite the presence of a TV, had the formal feel of a parlor. The polished pine floor was bare, save for a small oval of orange shag in front of a sagging plaid sofa. A woodstove sat on a sheet of metal, and a leatherette recliner angled toward the TV. A large carved mahogany dresser—authentically Victorian, from the look of it—took up the rest of the space. Clustered together on its marble top was a collection of family photographs. Most were Kmart-type portraits of children smiling against bright blue backdrops. Although some of the children were darker than others, they might have belonged to any American family. The only obvious indication of their heritage was an old studio portrait propped up against the dresser's beveled mirror. Its pasteboard margins were speckled with brown spots, and the black-and-white tones had faded to sepia. I pulled my half-frames out of my pocket and put them on. The smooth, round face of a young Native American woman sharpened. She wore skinny waist-long braids and a fringed silk shawl that sloped from her shoulders, giving her the shape of a Russian nesting doll. Her expression was stoic, but as I looked at her, I thought I detected a glint of shrewdness or humor in her black eyes.

"Who's this, Kevin?" I asked.

He glanced at the photograph. "Dunno," he said. He picked up a picture of a chubby red-headed child in pink and showed it to me. "This is Lucy when she was little. She's grown up now, but her mom says she's still retarded." He wiped his hands on his shirt and perched on the edge of the recliner. Luke and I took the sofa.

"Whatcha working on out there?" Luke asked him.

"Alvin's cylinder head."

"Who's Alvin?" I asked.

"Some guy."

"I'd like you to tell me what you remember about the night your father was shot," Luke said. "Do you think you can do that?"

"Sure." Kevin tucked his knees up under his shirt.

Luke waited. Kevin hugged his knees and rocked back and forth. "Starting when?"

Luke looked at me.

I said to Kevin, "We had supper, then afterward you helped your Dad with his phone."

"Yeah. He was already pretty bombed. Then he made me go to bed. Pete and Eddie came over with me, and Pete left the lantern. Then I went to sleep."

"And then what happened?" Luke asked.

"I woke up."

"Do you remember what woke you up?"

Kevin shook his head.

Luke took a new tack. "Do you know where your dad's gun was that night?"

Kevin relaxed his hold on his knees. "In Carbon's pannier. Right beside the door of our tent."

"Do you remember your dad getting the gun?"

"I was asleep," he said firmly.

Luke nodded. "No wonder. That's a pretty stiff hike you had that day."

"You were up there with the others?"

"Nope. I'll go up for a look around as soon as I can get things straightened out here."

"You going to take a helicopter?" Kevin asked.

"A helicopter? No way, Jose."

Kevin frowned. "Are you scared of helicopters?"

"You bet."

Kevin popped out of the recliner and walked over to the TV. "I'm not!" he declared. Then he asked Luke, "Are you going to catch that lady who killed Roland?"

"Yessir. Did you see her?"

Kevin shook his head. "We were in the woods with the llamas, waiting for Gwen and Mary Ann to make up their minds. No one let me see anything," he complained. "They wouldn't even let me see the video of her running away. All I've seen is her picture when we went to the supermarket."

"Let's go back to that night again, okay? Good man. So, you

went to sleep in your tent, then you woke up. What happened after you woke up?''

Kevin went back to the recliner. ''Lee came and got me.''

''Fine,'' Luke encouraged. ''I know this isn't easy for you.'' He paused. ''I'm guessing you'll be glad to see your mom.''

But Kevin didn't say anything.

''You like it here with Eddie,'' I said.

''Yeah.'' Then as if to make up for filial disloyalty, he added primly, ''Of course, it is pretty crowded.''

''Where do you sleep?'' I wondered.

''With Eddie and Nona. Agnes and Lucy have the other room.''

''That Lucy?'' I indicated the picture of the little girl in pink.

''Yeah.''

''And who's Agnes?''

Kevin looked at me as if I was retarded. ''Lucy's mother.''

''Ah.''

''She's doing twelve steps. Eddie says he doesn't think she'll make it.'' He pushed himself off the arm of Eddie's recliner. ''Are we done yet?''

''Sure thing.'' Luke stood up. He took a card out of his pocket and gave it to Kevin. ''I want you to call me up if you remember anything else. Here's my number. Will you do that for me, Kevin?''

Kevin nodded solemnly. His neck looked smooth and fragile inside his man-size collar. I stood up and he led us back through the kitchen. ''How's that llama of yours, Ringo, managing these days?'' I asked him.

''He's doing fairly well,'' Kevin said in an adult tone. ''I think he's going to miss me.''

''I'll miss you, too.''

''Ringo has dark toenails,'' he informed me. ''They're the best kind. You don't need to cut them as often as the light-colored ones.''

WE FOLLOWED KEVIN back to the shed. The floor was poured concrete, finished smooth as marble and without a stain. Eddie lay on a dolly under a beige Dodge panel truck. ''Be with you in a minute,'' he said. Red metal tool chests were stacked next to a battered oak schoolteacher's desk. On a clean green blotter, piles of invoices and order sheets were arranged meticulously in a perfect square. Above it hung a calendar whose artwork showed an English setter flushing pheasants from an autumnal field.

"Kevin," Eddie called from under the truck, "get me that nine-sixteenths combination there on the bench."

Kevin trotted over to the workbench and hesitated. Luke joined him. From an array of tools, Kevin picked out a wrench, looked at it, then looked to Luke for confirmation. Luke shook his head, a silent no. Kevin picked a larger one, and at Luke's nod, took it to Eddie. Several moments later, Eddie gave a satisfied grunt and rolled out from under the truck. He handed the wrench back to Kevin who replaced it on the bench. "Boy's a quick learner," Eddie announced. Over at the bench, Kevin grinned at Luke. Luke gave him a wink.

Eddie and Kevin cleaned their hands with pink goo from a tin. Luke said to Eddie, "If you have a few moments, I'd like to ask you a few questions, too."

"Shoot," Eddie said.

We moved out into the daylight and arranged ourselves against the parked cars. "What do you remember about the night of the shooting?" Luke asked.

"I'm not much use there," Eddie said. "Like I told the other cops, I turned in same time as Kevin. I must have dropped off, because the next I knew, gunshots woke me up. As a matter of fact, I was surprised I'd been asleep. Don't sleep too good these days." He scratched the back of his neck. "Never used to have that problem." His intonation was wry, but there was bewilderment and loss in his black eyes.

Luke met them and nodded sympathetically. Eddie went on, "By the time I got my boots on, Pete had come on around from the other side of the lake." He paused, as if he were going over the scene again in his mind. "There wasn't anything to do for it," he concluded.

"Roland Redhawk told you he'd accidentally shot Charlie Herron in a struggle over the gun."

"That's right."

"When you and Pete got to the scene, you found Herron on the ground about twenty feet from his tent."

"Yes."

"And where was Redhawk?"

"Right there beside him. He gave up the gun without a fuss."

"Where was your tent in relation to the others?"

"Didn't use no tent. Just my bedroll. Laid it out back in the woods a fair ways, maybe a couple hundred yards behind the clearing."

"You know anything about Redhawk being sent along on the trip by the tribe?"

"Just what Pete told me."

Luke nodded. A contented masculine silence grew between them. Between the pine branches overhead, the sun was liquid gold. I brushed away a line of rust-colored needles along the Oldsmobile's windshield wiper. "Eddie," I asked, "how come you wanted to come with us to Lost Pipe Lake?"

My question made no ripple in the silence. I began to wonder if I'd said it aloud. Eddie, one arm hooked over the side of his pickup's bed, slowly surveyed the asphalt shingles on his roof, the patched screen on the back door, the unpainted steps, the neatly stacked woodpile covered with curling grey plywood. Luke lounged against the truck's fender, his face relaxed, interested. Kevin scooped a Hackysack out of his pocket and began tossing it in the air.

"It's no secret," Eddie said finally. "My father's buried up there."

Kevin stopped throwing his little beanbag. We all looked at Eddie.

"A friend of mine she's a pretty good healer thought maybe it would help me out to go up there. She gave me some things to do."

Kevin looked perplexed. "Why's your father buried there?"

"He was killed not too far away, down on the east side of the mountain."

"*Your* father was killed, too?" Kevin demanded. "Was he shot?"

"That's right."

Kevin fired off questions. "Who shot him? Was it an accident? How old were you?"

Eddie took the last one. "I wasn't born yet. It was a long time ago. Back in 1919, the middle of October. My mother was about five months pregnant with me. I was born the spring after he died."

Eddie paused, then went on. "My father was killed on a hunting trip. In those days, you didn't hunt for the fun of it, just over the weekend. You went out for six, eight weeks and brought back enough meat to keep you through the winter. My parents took my sister with them. She was six. There was another couple—the Sispels—who had a fourteen-year-old boy with them, and an older couple, Martin One Star and his wife. Martin One Star was too old to hunt—he was almost blind—but he wanted to make one last hunting trip, so my parents agreed to take him along if he would tend the camp for them, watch the horses, cut wood, haul water."

"Like you did," Kevin said. "Only we had llamas. Who shot him? Was it an accident?"

Eddie shook his head. "It was a game warden. He killed all the men in the party. Including the boy."

Kevin's eyes widened. "Why?"

"What my mother told me was, he had no reason." Eddie lifted the cap on his head and resettled it. He told us the story without dramatic inflection, picking his words with care, as if he were building a path with them but wasn't exactly sure where it would end up. If he had told the story out loud before, it hadn't been often.

"The 1855 treaty protected our right to use the old hunting and fishing grounds, even if they were beyond the borders of the reservation," he explained. "So every fall, hunting parties would head east across the Missions into the Swan and Clearwater valleys. The whites in those areas weren't too happy about Indians hunting there. But like I said, it was in the treaty, so there wasn't anything they could do about it if our people had hunting and fishing licenses from the state.

"They had set up a camp near a creek that ran into the Swan River when this game warden from Ovando rode into their camp with a local rancher. My father and his friend—his name was Ambrose Sispel—were out hunting, and my mother and my sister and the two other women were up the river picking berries, so the only ones in camp were Martin One Star and the Sispel boy. The men had left their licenses with the old man, but he didn't speak any English, so the boy had stayed with him to interpret, in case the warden came along. The boy—he was a student at the mission at St. Ignatius—and was fluent in English. He showed the warden the hunting licenses. Then the warden and the rancher searched all the tipis and every pack before they left.

"Next evening, the warden came back again, this time with a German trapper he'd deputized. They asked the men how much game they'd killed. Now my father and Ambrose Sispel could both understand English okay, but neither could speak it too good, so the boy told the warden that Ambrose Sispel had killed two deer and that my father had killed three deer and an elk. The warden told them they'd reached their limit and couldn't hunt anymore. He also said that the old man was hunting without a license.

"Well, the boy explained that Martin One Star couldn't see well enough to hunt. The boy showed the men Martin One Star's permit to leave the reservation—in those days you had to get permission from the Flathead agent to travel off the reservation. And the warden took Martin One Star's permit and crumpled it up and threw it in the fire. The warden said if the party didn't leave, he'd arrest them and haul them into the magistrate in Missoula.

"So that night they sat up trying to figure out what to do. Sometime before dawn, they decided to leave and go back up over the mountain onto the reservation. They took down the tipis in the dark, but a couple of the horses had gotten loose, and they didn't find them until late in the morning. They were all saddled up and ready to go when the warden and the German man came out of the brush with rifles. The warden said he'd come to arrest Martin One Star. My father had harsh words with the warden and grabbed him by the throat. Then the shooting started. The horses and dogs scattered and ran into the brush. My father fell backward over a pile of tipi poles before he could get off a shot. My mother said when she lifted him up, blood squirted all over her face. His last words were 'Run for your life.'

"So my mother and my sister started running, and while they were running, my mother looked back and saw the warden aiming at them. She pushed my sister under a fallen tree, then pulled her blanket up over her head and ducked down over my sister and heard the bullet hit a tree beside her head. Then the shooting stopped and the women came out of the brush and started to check on the men. Martin One Star was lying with his head in the fire pit where he'd smoked the meat for them, and my father's friend, Ambrose Sispel, was dead, too. Their guns were leaning against a tree. The Sispel boy was crumbled on top of his gun. He had holes in his heart and also in his hat. The warden was lying on the ground, moaning. The boy had hit him in the stomach.

"My mother heard Mrs. One Star call out in Salish that the warden was getting up, trying to reload, so she rolled my father off his rifle, took it out of its leather scabbard, and ran over and shot the warden point-blank in the chest. She told me he didn't see her coming. She right ran up to where he was kneeling. She figured out where his heart was and put my father's rifle right up against it and pulled the trigger. She said it took him a long time to fall backward.

"Then she reloaded and ran a circle around the camp, looking for the German man, but he'd run off. The women laid out the bodies of the men side by side in the old way. Then my mother tracked down a horse and galloped off to find another Flathead camp. It started snowing, so she didn't get back with help until the next morning. The Salish men were worried about the German deputy coming back with a posse of ranchers, so they left the warden there in the snow and packed the four bodies of their own dead onto horses. They carried the bodies back up over the mountain, crossing onto the reservation above Lost Pipe Lake, and buried them there, all four of them in the same grave."

Eddie looked at us. His eyes were bleak. Some stories don't improve in the retelling. Overhead, a bulked-up cloud muscled away the sun. I zipped up my jacket. "Is that a picture of your mother in the living room?" I asked.

He nodded. "I found it in a box along with an old newspaper

she'd saved. The headline said SQUAW KILLS WARDEN. I reckon she must have been proud of it.'' He allowed himself a small ironic smile. ''The newspaper talked about the Indian wars starting all over again. Feelings were pretty high.''

''What happened to your mother?''

Eddie shrugged. ''She found a good man and had three more children.''

''I mean, was she prosecuted?''

''There was some kind of hearing but it didn't lead to nothing. The German never showed up to testify. And then some of the whites over there in the Swan valley took my mother's part. They didn't think too much of the warden. Turns out he'd arrested a couple of them for hunting out of season. Back then no one worried too much about what time of year you shot game, if it was the meat you were after.'' Eddie turned to Kevin. ''I've had a good life,'' he said firmly. ''I'm sorry about your dad. But you can still have a good life.''

Kevin looked at Eddie, then spun away. ''It's not the same!'' he burst out angrily. ''It's not the same! You weren't even born. You couldn't do anything to stop it. It wasn't your fault!''

''Kevin!'' I objected, shocked. ''You don't think—''

Luke's hand shot up in warning. I shut up. Kevin's back was toward us. The slender cords in his neck trembled, like cables under tension.

Luke asked quietly, ''Do you think your father's death was your fault?''

Kevin was tossing his Hackysack from one hand to the other.

''Why?'' Luke asked. There was genuine interest in his voice. ''You think you could have done something to stop it?''

Kevin turned back to Luke. ''I saw it,'' he answered.

I realized I'd been holding my breath. I let it out slowly.

''You saw it,'' Luke repeated. ''What did you see?''

''My father getting shot, dork-brain!'' Kevin flashed. He tossed the Hackysack high over his head and caught it. In a more casual voice he added, ''It was sort of like a cartoon.''

Luke thought about it. ''Like Power Rangers?''

Kevin shook his head. ''I mean an old one. Like Mickey Mouse in black-and-white.''

"Where were you when you saw it?"

Kevin rolled his eyes around in exasperation. "I already told you. In my sleeping bag."

"Do you think you could have been dreaming?"

"I was awake."

"Was there a sound track?"

"Dad was saying something about a favor."

"He wanted a favor?"

"It was like when he talks on the phone."

Luke nodded. "Like he was doing business?"

"Yeah."

"You think maybe he wanted a favor from Roland?"

But Kevin rushed on. "Then bang, bang, you're dead, *thud*."

Luke waited for more.

"Something woke me up," he said. "I thought it was, like, a bear. I was so scared I didn't move, but it was probably just Dad, getting his gun. If I'd gotten up to go to the bathroom, maybe they'd have stopped it."

"Maybe," Luke said. "And maybe not. You might have been the one to get shot."

Kevin looked startled. Then he hurled the Hackysack at Luke. "Catch!" he challenged, his voice suddenly boyish and free. Luke plucked the beanbag out of the air and tossed it back over Kevin's head. Kevin ran for it, his shirt flapping, and returned it with the side of his sneaker. "Aha!" Luke cried, jumping for it. The interview was over. Eddie and I stood together watching them play. Kevin had some impressive moves, but Luke was a match for him, even in his dress cowboy boots. The two of them seemed luminous with energy. They darted and dove and jumped in the shifting autumnal light. Suddenly I felt my own tiredness. It pulled at me like a slow, salty tide.

A NONDESCRIPT grey sedan bristling with four short antennae stopped the game. It rolled hesitantly down the dirt driveway. Luke waved it on up behind his Ford. The driver, a compact man in jeans and a windbreaker, got out of the car and crossed to open the passenger door. Mrs. Herron didn't wait. She flung open the passenger door and popped out. She steadied herself on the open car door and looked around. She was wearing widow's weeds a la Michael Jackson: black jeans, an oversize black silk blazer with the sleeves rolled up, black sunglasses. She had tied a sheer black veil over her blond hair and the frizzed tresses that escaped were the same color as the small gold buttons on her jacket and the large gold buttons on her earlobes. A younger man, early twenties at most, preppy-looking in baggy khakis and crew-necked sweater, got out of the backseat.

"Who's that with your mom?" I asked Kevin.

"Jack. Her boytoy." For an eerie second, I could hear the sharpness of his dead father's voice.

His mother spotted him, "Kevin!" she wailed. She sailed over to us, the black gauze of her scarf trailing theatrically behind her. Kevin stepped forward. She clasped him to her gold-buttoned breast. "Kevin, oh Kevin!" she sobbed.

He stood as rigidly as a wooden post. "*Mom,*" he objected.

She gulped air and released him. "Sweetheart, I was so worried! Are you all right?"

The driver ambled over. Luke raised a questioning eyebrow, and the driver answered with a slight nod. "This is Agent Chapman," Luke said to us.

We said polite hellos.

Mrs. Herron looked up, aware of her audience. "Oh God, I must look a mess!" she exclaimed. She took off her shades and smeared away her tears. Her eyes were red-rimmed and swollen. Luke made introductions, but she was distracted. She scanned the house, the dirt yard, the dusty pickup. She latched back onto Kevin. "What have they been feeding you? And what on earth are you doing in that shirt?"

"Mom, nothing."

"I just can't believe your father did this to us!" She dove into her purse for a Kleenex and blew her nose angrily.

For someone just back from a Mexican beach, she was pale; and although her eyes were puffy, the rest of her face had a pinched look. Maybe it was plastic surgery. Maybe it was the shock of sudden death. She blew her nose again and told us to call her Celia. She tried to press a fistful of bills into Eddie's hand. "For your trouble," she said.

"He was no trouble," Eddie said. "He's a good kid."

"Go on, take it," she urged. She gave Eddie a sorrowful smile. "I'm sure you could use it."

"No, thank you," Eddie said with authority.

"Oh, for heaven's sake," she said crossly. She shoved the money back in her purse, then burst into tears again. "I don't know what to do," she sobbed. "Oh shit, I'm sorry. I just don't know what to do. Poor Charlie, he did everything for me. He took care of everything. My husband was crazy about me, you know. In spite of everything." She waved a despairing hand in Jack's direction.

Jack ignored her. "Come on, Kev," he said, "I'll help you get your stuff."

She turned to Luke and Agent Chapman. "Charlie was just crazy about me," she told them. It sounded like a boast.

SEVEN

DRIVING BACK UP to Polson, the late-afternoon weather moved around us, spectacular as a three-ring circus. Dark blue storm clouds, their insides flashing, labored up against the mountainsides; shafts of sunlight slid like spotlights across hay fields; curtains of white rain blurred the tin roofs of barns and left roadside fence wires dripping with sequins of gold light. I found it hard to enjoy the show. My mind kept going back to Eddie's.

"Did you ever think you'd been born into the wrong family?" I asked Luke.

The question surprised him. "No. Did you?"

"I was thinking of Kevin. His mother was"—I hunted for the right word—"stunning," I decided.

Luke made a small grimace. "I wouldn't go that far."

"I mean literally. She absolutely stunned me. It's hard to believe she's his *mother*. I keep thinking he'd be better off with Eddie and his family."

"Hm."

"You don't think so?"

"She's a victim, Lee. Same as Kevin. He's lost his dad. She's lost her husband."

"Estranged husband. Don't forget the boytoy. Though he seemed nice enough, poor kid."

We drove into a patch of rain. It hammered loudly on the roof, making conversation difficult. Then suddenly the road was dry.

"She was appalling," I said angrily. "All she could think about was herself."

The windshield wipers began to squeak. Luke turned them off. "Grief's a self-centered business," he observed philosophically. "I try to think of it like a dozer suddenly crashing through the victim's front yard. All the nice green grass gets torn up. Maybe the septic line gets broken. Maybe a foundation wall caves in. You go in there, you got to watch where you step."

"Homey metaphor," I remarked sourly.

He shrugged, unoffended. It occurred to me that Luke's job went beyond fitting grim clues together into a picture that would convince a jury. His work also entailed navigating through the swamp of human loss. How much of my anger at Celia Herron came from my own loss? How much did I resent the fact that she had Kevin and I no longer had my daughter? I looked over at Luke. "Are you saying I've got shit on my shoes?"

He wrinkled up his nose and sniffed theatrically.

"And moving quickly along here—where were we? Oh, yeah, Kevin. What about that Mickey Mouse stuff? You think he was dreaming?"

"No. He said he was awake. I believe him. Kids are often more reliable witnesses than adults. They don't have a lot of preconceptions like we do. The trick is to figure out where they're coming from. Kevin obviously saw and heard something. The question is what. I didn't want to push it. I was afraid he'd close down."

I glanced out the window. An enormous rainbow, the largest I'd ever seen, arched over the cloud-shrouded mountains. It was garishly perfect, each band of color distinct as a neon tube. "Will you look at that!" I exclaimed. Then I saw the second arc, a fatter, paler ghost of the first. "A *double* one!" I felt as if fate were blessing us as we rolled down the highway. "Hey, is that a good omen or is that a good omen?"

"It's the season for them." His voice was matter-of-fact.

I looked at the rainbows, then back at Luke. "Did anyone ever tell you that women find evasiveness a particularly endearing quality in a man?"

He almost smiled. Five miles later, he asked, "How long are you going to be around? I'm thinking I'd like you and Pete to come back up Lost Pipe Lake with me and set up camp for the crime-lab team."

"With the llamas?"

"Yeah. We'll pick up the tab."

"You miss my cooking," I teased.

"More than that." His eyes were firmly on the road.

"I'll talk to Pete," I said, keeping my voice casual. "How ong are you going to be up there?"

"A couple of days, at least. Depends on the weather, on how nuch has been wrecked. A reconstruction takes a lot longer than rocessing a scene at the time. There'll be four of us—Webb and ne, and two lab people."

"Webb?"

"Agent Chapman. You met him at Eddie's. He picked up Mrs. lerron at Kalispell, interviewed her on the way."

"Tell me something. How come you guys don't say, 'Special gent,' like on TV?"

"Only FBI agents are 'special.'"

"Agent Donner, do I detect a sour grape in the hierarchy?"

"Special, as in 'Special Olympics.'" He grinned.

"Watch yourself, bud, or the PC police will come and take you way."

"Yessir, officer," he promised with the sincerity of an offender ho's been let off the hook.

We passed a roadside museum called Miracle of America. I ent back to the Mickey Mouse puzzle. In black-and-white, evin had said. "Those old cartoons," I said to Luke. "My other used to rent them for our birthday parties. I remember opguns—the kind where a cork popped out on a string—and lmer Fudd had a shotgun, but I don't remember revolvers. I ould check it out," I offered.

"First things first," he said. "I want to get the team up to Lost ipe Lake tomorrow, if possible. Mickey Mouse can wait. Intersting, though, what the kid said when I asked about a sound ack: 'Bang, bang, you're dead, thud.' Like he heard two shots, en heard his father falling. But across the lake, your group heard ve shots. Two, and then three more."

"Right. So what does that mean?"

He shook his head. "There were two slugs in the body. If the cket turns up, we can run a GSR on it. That should tell us omething."

"GSR?"

"Gunshot Residue test. If Herron was shot as Redhawk aimed, at close range in a struggle, there should be unburned powder on Herron's jacket." He let out a sigh of frustration "And if we can ever get back up there, we might be able to fin the casings."

He let me out in the motel parking lot. "I've got a couple thing to do. Are you free for dinner?"

"Sure. What time?"

"Seven, seven-thirty? Meet you here, in the restaurant."

"Great." Boom, boom, went my heart.

THE RED DIGITAL NUMBERS on the clock radio in my room rea 5:32. The red light on the phone was blinking. I had two mes sages. One was from Dolores. I got out my phone card and m half-frames and started punching numbers. Pete picked up. I tol him that the state of Montana wanted to hire him.

He wasn't delighted. "I'm going hunting tomorrow. I'll b gone for the week."

My heart sank a couple of inches. "I should tell Luke nc then?"

"Tell you what. You take them up there."

"Wait a sec. I don't know diddly about llamas."

"You'll do fine. Just make sure they don't get overheated."

"What happens when they get overheated?"

"They'll quit on you. Their muscles give out."

"What do you do then?"

"Wait for them to cool back down."

"And how long does that take?"

"A good long while."

"Pete, I feel as if I'm pulling molars! Exactly how long is good long while?"

"Oh, it can take twenty-four, maybe thirty-six hours befo their temperature comes back down to normal. Don't worry abo it. There's supposed to be a cold front moving down from Canad You'll probably get some snow up there."

"Oh goody."

"Hang on, Dolores wants to talk to you."

Dolores told me that Charlene Redhawk, Roland's widow, ha asked why I hadn't come by after the funeral. "She seemed t want to meet you," Dolores said.

"Me? Why?"

"I don't know. Maybe because you were there when it happened."

"You think I should go see her?"

"Might be a good idea."

"I take it this is a command performance."

"You could drop by the trading post," Dolores said. "She said she was going to open shop tomorrow."

"Luke wants to leave tomorrow," I told her. We went back and forth on the logistics of provisions and transporting llamas. In the end, I agreed to visit Charlene Redhawk. I hung up. Not fun, the idea of sitting down with Roland's widow and rehashing the details of his "unfortunate death situation" to borrow a euphemism from the O. J. Simpson defense team.

The other message was from my mother. I dialed my mother's number reluctantly. We had already talked on the phone. Three times. The last time had not been successful. I hadn't really wanted to talk about Lost Pipe Lake anymore. Moreover, my mother's calculated silences had gotten under my skin. Face to face, I'm usually able to ignore them as an unattractive trick of her trade. But at long distance, her pauses seemed to carry fat electrons of disapproval across the continent, as if my presence at two killings was something I had *chosen.*

Her phone rang twice, then she answered. "Lee, darling!" she exclaimed happily. "I'm so glad you called! How *are* you?"

"Fine." I told her about the plans to go back to Lost Pipe Lake.

"So you are going off again into the wilderness?" she said, interested.

"Yeah. We'll probably leave tomorrow. I'll be out of reach while we're up there."

"Yes, yes, of course. Thank you for telling me." She sounded distracted. In the background, I heard kitchen noises. I remembered it was eight o'clock in D.C.

"Are you in the middle of dinner?" I asked.

"We are just about to sit down," she said. "I won't keep you." She paused, then went on. "I called you because I keep thinking about that girl's bow." Her voice was warm and encouraging. It also carried a slight Old World inflection. Those who didn't know my mother assumed she had inherited her "accent" from her Romanian mother. They found it charming and aristocratic. In fact, she had assimilated the intonation from her Viennese-born analyst and mentor, Dr. Ludmilla Katzen. When "Ludi" appeared in my mother's voice, it was a sure sign that she had shifted from her maternal mode into the Great Collective Unconscious.

"Yes?" I said, warily.

"You said the killer used a bow and arrow."

"Right. Two arrows, actually."

"I am thinking you have had an encounter with Artemis."

"Far out."

"Lee, it is important to be attentive to these matters."

"Mom, spare me the Goddess-Within stuff. Please."

"You are always going off into the wilderness. You tell me you want to feed your soul. But you will be always hungry, unless you can accept your own wilderness."

I shut my eyes, took a breath, then opened them. "I think that is an *extremely* presumptuous statement."

"You are my daughter. I love you very much. I feel you are in a dangerous place."

"The killer girl is long gone, Mom. They've had search teams combing the mountainsides for the last five days, they've brought in K-9 teams, helicopters equipped with heat-sensing devices, they've checked every bus depot in the state, every trucking line—"

"I am not talking about the girl," my mother interrupted. "I am talking about you. Now I must hang up. Dinner is ready. Tommy has made the most beautiful lasagna verde!"

Tommy is one of my mother's three housemates, an "alternative family" she collected after my father died. I try not to be too skeptical about this arrangement, but it is hard not to see her friends as a trio of lame ducks. Tommy, for example, is a diagnosed schizophrenic living on disability and rarely can manage a share of the rent. On the other hand, he is a licensed masseur whose ministrations, my mother claims, helps her arthritis. He also happens to be a willing and talented cook. "Bon appetit," I told my mother.

I hung up the phone, poured two fingers of Jack Daniel's from my flask into a motel glass, and took it out onto the mini balcony that overlooked Flathead Lake. The mountains on the far side were still shrouded in clouds. A cold breeze puckered the grey water. The other balconies were empty, and there were no boats tied up at the docks below. Saturday evening, off-season. I had the lake to myself. I sipped whiskey, felt the clean burn of its amber fire, and considered Roland's killer in the guise of Artemis, virgin goddess of the hunt.

Now that my mother had so irritatingly pointed it out, the connection was obvious. Even more irritating, however, was the way her suggestion had immediately ingratiated itself into my memory. Suddenly, thanks to my mom, the dirty, young woman who had smelled of wood smoke was now bathed in a mythological glow. Her awkward bounds across the rocks were now graceful as a young doe; her concentration as pure and icy as a mountain creek.

I must say I don't have much affection for Artemis—at least not the Artemis I encountered in schoolbooks. What with the way she flitted through the woods of Attica in a floaty little tunic carrying a bow barely big enough for Bambi, she seemed silly, rather than powerful. Her one claim to fame was loosing her hounds on a Peeping Tom who had hidden in the bushes to watch her bathe. The dogs savagely tore the unfortunate admirer to pieces, a punishment which had always struck me as extreme—until I had a run-in with a Tom of my own.

If I had to pick a goddess, I suppose it would be owl-eyed Athena, not only because she sprang full blown from the head of Zeus—no doubt taking the better part of his brains with her—but because she wore golden armor and carried a mean-looking spear. (Perhaps I've never gotten over my fifth-grade jealousy of Marsha Buccellini, the smartest girl in the class, who, despite the fact that I was the tallest girl in the class, won the part of Athena in our spring play and, to my mind, looked far more like a frog in gold wrapping paper than a Homeric warrior goddess.)

I pushed Hellenic goddesses aside and fixed on the girl's tattered red sneaker with its dark drip of Roland's blood. Why had she pulled the one arrow out of his chest and left the other? Was it a souvenir? Or a matter of survival? There had been no other arrows in the narrow nylon bag slung over her shoulder. Perhaps she had wanted to keep one steel-tip for hunting—or for self-defense. On the other hand, she may have grabbed it for no reason at all, the way people rescue peculiar objects from a house on fire.

I took a swallow of bourbon. Out on the lake, another rainbow appeared, this one a faint arc over the water. I watched it grow larger and stronger, as if it were sucking color out of the gray water. A white gull flew under it. "The season for rainbows," Luke had said. I finished my drink and went inside feeling hopeful.

I WAS IN the restaurant by seven-fifteen, napped, bathed, and wearing an indigo blue sweater that tends to draw compliments on the color of my eyes. Only two of the tables were occupied. A grey-haired couple in pastel polyesters sat at one. A trio of businessmen in sports shirts sat at the other. I took a table by a window with a waterfront view. In the dusk, the town's lights made fat orange-and aqua-colored paths on the grey water.

An hour later, the water was inky black and the reflections had sharpened into daggers. Luke didn't show. I ordered a glass of red wine and a plate of fettuccine Alfredo. It tasted like kindergarten paste. I ate slowly, washing it down with sweetish wine, then went back to my room, hoping to see the red light on the phone blinking. There was no message waiting for me. I walked back to the lobby and checked at the front desk. No message.

I should have gone back to my room, taken out a pad and pencil, and started working out menus and grocery lists for the trip up to Lost Pipe Lake. By this time, however, I was ready to dump the expedition and Luke with it. I walked out the lobby's glass doors and followed the blacktopped driveway around the buildings to the resort's docks. The night air was crisply autumnal and carried the faint tang of highway exhaust. Lake water lapped peacefully against the pilings. I walked along the shorefront to the town landing ramps. In the parking lot, maybe a dozen cars, none with boat trailers, faced the lake. The bass on someone's stereo beat like an invisible heart. A lit cigarette, ejected from a window, cut a brief arc in the night. I quickened my step, cut through a park named Sacajawea, and emerged onto the town's main drag.

A Jeep Cherokee pulled up in front of a bar that advertised karaoke, and a group of three women and one man got out. They were older, in their sixties perhaps, and looked as respectable as Rotarians. I followed them into the bar. The light in the place was red, and the quilted leatherette booths were black. There was a stuffed wolf mounted over the back bar, and a big-screen TV monitor facing tables around a little dance floor. The Rotarians took a table. I slipped into a booth at the end of the bar and ordered from a waitress in a white uniform and white shoes. She was middle-aged, blond with dark roots, and employed a nurselike royal we: "What are we having tonight, hon?"

"Rainier," I told her.

A decent number of the tables were taken, but it was still early, and the drinkers only smiled politely when the karoroke DJ tried to coax them up onto his stage. He brought his mike down to the tables and encouraged people at the tables to sing along with his videos. Whatever the song, be it "Red River Valley" or "Great Balls of Fire," the accompanying video featured a grassy hillside, a clean-shaven cowboy in a white hat, and a long-haired shampoo model in cutoffs.

The DJ announced a break and switched off his system. In the sudden quiet, you could hear his boots echoing on the dance floor as he crossed to the bar. Then conversations resumed. Ice clinked in glasses. A chair scraped. At the bar, two men flirted with a sassy-looking girl in pink jeans and a calico blouse. One of the men wore black leather chaps studded with silver. The other wore a black T-shirt that revealed tattoos on his skinny forearms. The men laughed. The girl looked pleased. Then, somewhere behind me, a male voice surfaced above the general chatter and I caught the words, "...this guy Donner's okay."

I froze at the mention of Luke's name, strained to hear more.

"...Said he wasn't going to start till everyone was there, and that meant the sheriff, too," the voice went on. "We was all waitin' there the better part of an hour, and he never even peeks at his watch—just sits there on the desk with his arms crossed and his mouth shut tight. Well, the sheriff was at his supper,'' the voice drawled ironically. ''Finally one of the deputies goes to get him. Sheriff walks in and Donner says, sweet as you please, 'Thank you for joining us, Sheriff.'''

The nurselike waitress stopped at my table. ''How we doing?'' she asked, her voice full of sympathy. If I'd had a pillow, she would have fluffed it up.

''Fine, thanks.'' I slid around the semicircular banquette for a look at the group behind me. Two heavyset men in work clothes had swiveled on their stools and were facing outward. One wore glasses under his billed cap. Both had broad Indian faces. The speaker stood with his back toward me in the aisle between the bar and the booths. He was thinner than the other two and hatless. His black hair skimmed the collar of his twill uniform shirt. I couldn't make out the patch on his sleeve; the light from the red globes hanging overhead was too dim. One stool over, a large woman in a purple sweat suit was sipping beer and listening with interest to the speaker in the aisle.

He was still talking about Luke's meeting. ''So Donner says, 'I see we got a mix here, Indian and white. Anyone got a problem with that?' Well, you coulda heard a pin drop, every one wondering who let the cat out of the—'' He stopped and turned to the woman in purple. ''You can't write any of this, Patty,'' he warned.

''Hey,'' she appealed to the two other men, ''have I ever screwed you guys?''

They grinned.

''Seriously.'' She turned to the speaker standing in the aisle. ''I always protect my sources, Claude,'' she declared with the solemn dignity of a queen.

One of the men on the stools nodded to Claude. He picked up his story. ''So Donner says, 'Have we got a problem here? 'Cause if we do, let's put it aside. I don't have time to deal with racist crap. If I hear any of you got a problem, you're outta here.' And he looks right at the sheriff. 'I ain't no miracle worker,' he says. 'I can't wave a magic wand and solve the case. It's going to take teamwork.'''

Patty in purple caught me staring. She leaned over the empty stool between her and the two men and said something to them. Claude, the speaker, turned and glanced at me. He had a young, narrow face I'd never seen before. He hadn't been up at Lost Pipe Lake with the troops. He hopped onto the empty stool and all four of them swiveled back to the bar.

The DJ escorted the girl in pink jeans up to his mike. Her ass was as perky as a pair of new tennis balls. The opening bars of "Crazy" blared from the amps, a white cowboy hat appeared on the screen, and the girl's bounce evaporated. She held the mike as solemnly as an acolyte holding a candle, and sang without moving an inch. Her voice was pretty enough, but thin—more evocative of a choir loft than Patsy Cline's roadhouses. The audience was not impressed—there were one or two polite claps—but she sashayed back to her friends at the bar with a smug "I told you so" expression on her face.

The waitress in white brought my beer, and Patty in purple slid off her stool. "Hey, Fern," she said to the waitress, "how's it going?"

"My corns are killing me," Fern said. She lowered her voice and made a crack I couldn't hear. Patty laughed a deep laugh. Fern winked at me and moved on with her tray. Patty stepped over to the table of my booth. "Didn't I see you at the funeral?" she asked.

"Yes," I said. "I was there."

She must have been six feet tall and close to two hundred pounds. Her size was intimidating, but her voice was friendly. Her light brown hair was wavy and under her bangs, her dark eyes were mournful. "Are you the one with *Newsweek?*" she asked.

"Nope."

She looked puzzled. "I'm Patty London," she said.

"Lee Squires," I reciprocated.

"Your name sounds familiar." She lowered herself into the opposite side of the booth. Maybe on a more secure day, I would have felt sylphlike sitting across from her. As it was, I felt measly. It was hard to tell how old she was; the red lighting made her age as hard to read as the dog-eared song menu the DJ had put on each table.

"I work for the tribal paper," she said.

"Are you, uh, a member of the tribe?"

She gave me a wry smile. "No. I'm not Native American. I got the job because I was the only applicant with a degree in journalism. Ohio State," she added. "I came out here eight years ago. I love this country," she burst out, as if I might doubt it. "I love being out here. There's so much space, it makes your problems seem small. Know what I mean? Like, it changes your perspective on things." She shook her head disapprovingly, and went on, "All these fun hogs trooping in from California, they're going to subdivide the place to death. You're not from California, are you?" She didn't wait for an answer. "Maybe I shouldn't say it, but I'm not crying any tears over that developer Roland shot."

"You knew Roland?"

"Oh sure." She peered at me. "You know, I'm sure someone told me you were with *Newsweek.* Or is it *Time?* You've got that sophisticated kind of look, like you could interview some world leader in French."

I laughed. "Thanks very much. But I'm afraid no amount of soft soap's going to turn me into a journalist. I'm working for a friend's outfit. Pete Bonsecours."

She frowned, trying to place the name.

"We were up at Lost Pipe Lake."

"Oh. Oh!" Recognition dawned. "Hey, guys!" she called excitedly to the men at the bar. "This lady's a friend of Pete Bonsecours! You know, the guy with the llamas. She was with him up at Lost Pipe Lake when Roland was killed."

The men were noncommittal.

She turned back to me. "I did a piece on Pete right after he started up the business," she said cheerfully. Then suddenly she changed gear, downshifting into sympathy. "Hey, I'm sorry. I bet you had a rough time, huh? You want to do an interview with me?" There was a pleading note in her voice that was almost childlike disconcerting in someone who'd been a reporter for eight years.

I smiled. "No, thanks."

"I don't blame you," she said sincerely. "Hope you don't mind that I asked?"

For her sake, I hoped her submissive approach worked better with her tribal subjects than it had with me. We ordered another round from Fern and listened companionably to two young women—from Spokane, the DJ announced—sing "These Boots Were Made for Walking."

"Now they're smart," Patty approved. "It's much easier to do the fast ones. You sing?"

"Nope," I said firmly.

In the next breath, out of nowhere, she asked, "You know that Eddie McNab's father was buried up at Lost Pipe Lake?"

"Yes," I said, surprised. "He told me. Is it general knowledge around here?"

She thought about it. "No," she said slowly. "I wouldn't say so. I came across the story in a state historical magazine, and it kind of caught my interest. I wanted to do a feature on the seventy-fifth anniversary of the massacre, but I couldn't get it approved. I guess the tribe didn't want to open up old wounds. Did McNab say anything about why he went up there?"

"He said a healer suggested it."

Her eyebrows shot up. "Oh. A healer. Did he say which one?"

"No," I told her. "What about Roland Redhawk?" I asked. "What was he like?"

She took a swallow of beer. "Well, he was thick with the cultural committees."

"Cultural committees?"

"They're supposed to help preserve the tribal languages and traditions—you know, the old dances and ceremonies. There's a Salish committee and a Kootenai one. They're kind of a power behind the throne—or I should say, behind the tribal bureaucracy. Roland was in with both committees. That's how he got his museum going at the back of his store. He and Charlene got into collecting old beadwork. The elders on the committees gave him leads on who had what—I guess they figured better him than some outsider. At least the stuff stayed on the reservation, and I heard he paid top dollar for it. You been in there? It's pretty impressive. He was also real active in environmental issues. He did a lot of work for Bernadette Walker during her election campaign."

"She's the council member?"

"Yeah. The council rules the tribes. They used to be governed by their chiefs, but back in the thirties, Congress ordered them to get democratic, so they switched to a ten-seat council. Anyway, Bernadette Walker got seated two years ago." She hesitated, then leaned toward me, shelving her breasts on the tabletop. "Rumor has it that she gave Roland a contract on the developer."

I met her gaze. "You buy it?"

"I've heard weirder. Roland used to be AIM. They were pretty heavy-duty, those AIM guys. He told me he was at Wounded Knee, back in the seventies."

"Really?"

"That's what he said. I was doing an interview with him last year. There was this big debate about land use going on. Anyway, I was talking with him and he told me, off the record, that he'd been part of the action at Wounded Knee—like he was right-hand man to Buster Littlepond."

The name was supposed to impress me. "Who was Littlepond?" I asked.

"One of the big honchos. Afterward, he was tried for conspiracy, along with Russell Means and Dennis Banks. I forget who the others were."

"Was Roland one of them?"

She shook her head. "He said he escaped through the lines and went up to Canada. He wouldn't say any more. It was like he was bragging, like he got a kick out of being Mr. Mysterious."

I thought back to our trip and the way he always managed to avoid the filmmakers' camera. "He told us he wasn't Salish," I said. "But he never said what he was."

Patty shrugged. "Some people get kind of touchy about lineage questions. Like, what makes someone Indian? Is it the kind of language you speak, the dances you dance, the songs you sing, or is it a certain quota of blood?"

I went back to Bernadette Walker. "You really think she hired Roland to take Herron out?"

"She's a strong woman," Patty speculated. "She doesn't take shit from anyone."

"That doesn't make her a murderer."

"No," she agreed. Then she added, "She's a grandmother."

"Grannies don't kill?"

"Excuse me?"

I didn't want to backtrack. "Do you know if Roland had kids? I didn't see any at the funeral."

"They had three. Two were Charlene's. The youngest was his." She took a swallow of beer. "They're all dead."

"My God," I said, shocked. "How?"

"The usual. Alcohol. One OD'd on a booze-and-pill combo. The other two were killed last year in a car wreck. The kid driving had just turned fifteen."

"Fifteen?"

"Fifteen's legal in Montana. His speed was legal, too. They figured he must have been going close to a hundred. What wasn't legal was his blood alcohol." She paused. "The interview I did with Roland last year? He told me that if he'd been able to get his kids connected to the wilderness, they might still be alive."

"But he drank," I protested. "He and Herron were pouring it down."

She gave an ironic shrug and lifted her glass, as if to toast human frailty. Then she drained it. "One more and I'll be drunk enough to sing," she observed amiably. "Come on, how about a duet? Do you know 'Your Cheatin' Heart'?"

EIGHT

I DIDN'T STICK AROUND to hear Patty take the mike. I walked back to the motel along Main Street. Its orange streetlights robbed color from the displays in store windows and erased shadows on the empty sidewalks. No cars passed. I felt as if I were walking through a dream about the last person on earth. A chilly dream. My breath made ragged puffs of orange steam.

Under the door to my room, I found Luke's card, a crisp white rectangle on the carpet. The state of Montana's seal was printed in blue in the upper right-hand corner. On the back, he'd written, "Sorry. Call me here when you get in." Not for the first time, his handwriting disconcerted me: the letters struck me as too round and soft for someone so angular.

Below the message, there was a three-digit number. It took me several moments of study to realize that the number belonged to a room in the motel, not a telephone extension. I looked at my watch. It was eleven-forty. Then I looked in the mirror. My eyes were pink and watery. I used some eyedrops, brushed my teeth, then picked up my key and went to find Luke.

His room was in a wing on the other side of the lobby. I knocked softly on the door and waited. Maybe he was asleep. I was about to go back to my own room when he opened the door. He was wearing a white T-shirt that sagged at the neck and old jeans. Behind him, every light in the room was on. He looked at me with the wariness of a man expecting a woman to explode. "Evenin'," he said.

"Good evening," I said back.

His eyes were as bloodshot as mine, and it wasn't from barroom beer. He'd been drinking Coke. There was an empty can on the dresser beside his holstered gun and a half-beaded can beside the phone. Files and computer printouts were strewn across the beds. "Step into my office," he said with a courtly sweep of his arm. "If we're still speaking."

"We weren't for a while there, I can tell you."

We hugged, firmly and briefly, like old friends. "You've shrunk," I noticed.

"Took my boots off." I looked down. He was wearing faded navy blue socks. "Lee, I apologize," he said sincerely. "I got held up."

"I heard. At least the sheriff got *his* supper."

His head made a small jerk of surprise.

"News travels fast around here. There I was down at the local saloon, drowning my sorrows in brew, and I heard your name across a not-so-crowded room. Sounds like your stock's on the rise at least among a certain group of barflies."

"Really?"

I told him what I'd overheard. "You could have called while you were waiting," I rebuked him.

"No," he said. "I don't think so. Not without ruining my mystique."

"You're serious."

"You bet. Gotta keep my edge."

"Oh, the games you boys play."

"Your maturity is irresistible."

I laughed. Despite his prematurely receding hairline, Luke was six years younger than I. The difference in our ages had been a running joke. The fact that it was still jogging along gave me a boost.

"Believe it." He said it lightly, but the look on his face made something plummet inside me. Maybe it was my heart. I glanced around, looking for an anchor, and was confronted by the sight of a blood-soaked jacket draped carefully over the back of a chair. The large maps of blood on the pale grey fleece were still bright. "That's not *yours,* is it?" I demanded. I scrutinized his T-shirt for signs of blood, for a bandage underneath.

"It is now. Herron's jacket turned up. Someone stuck it in a plastic garbage bag."

"Jesus. Stick it back in."

"It's got to air dry. Then it goes into a *paper* bag. Otherwise it will rot." He shook his head in annoyance. "The trouble with amateurs is they want to wrap everything in plastic."

Inwardly, I winced. Pete and I had taken pains to wrap Herron's gun in plastic. I decided not to mention it.

"Have a look at this." He picked up a pencil, walked over to the jacket and, using the pencil, lifted the back of it up into the light. Six inches above the hem, there was a small three-spoked design stamped into the fleece. It was no bigger than a quarter. Each of the three spokes was the same length.

"What does that look like to you, a peace sign?" Luke asked.

On a motel pad, I drew the old symbol from my Vietnam protest days.

Luke studied it with interest. "But there's no circle around the mark on the jacket."

"No," I agreed. "What do you think it is?"

"I don't know. It looks like a crow's foot to me."

We peered at the imprint. "A baby crow with fat toes, maybe," I said dubiously.

"Weird," Luke said.

Suddenly, standing there beside him, something shifted. Everything seemed to have a resonance; the wicker back of the chair, the yellow pencil in Luke's tanned hand, the way the worn cotton of his T-shirt lay thinly over his biceps. I had a sense of molecules arranging and rearranging themselves, as if suddenly things no longer had the barrier of surface.

Using the pencil, Luke carefully redraped the jacket then tossed the pencil back onto the bed. It thwacked on a manila file. He massaged his temples as if trying to rub away his fatigue.

"Did you know Roland was AIM?" I asked.

He looked up. "No."

"The reporter I met in the bar said Roland told her 'off the record' that he had spent some time up in Canada. He gave her the impression that he'd been a fugitive."

Luke frowned. "He didn't turn up in the computer."

"Patty said he was at Wounded Knee. That was back—"

"Before my time." He grinned. "But you're in luck. I was an American Studies major."

"Really."

"Yeah. I thought I wanted to be a history teacher. Then Barb got pregnant and I dropped out."

"When was that?"

"End of my junior year. We were high-school sweethearts—did I ever tell you that?"

"More than once. You were married on the day after your high-school graduation."

"Turned out she wasn't pregnant." His voice was flat. "It took us almost ten years before we got around to Jason."

"How's he doing?"

"Good," Luke said with automatic cheerfulness. "Good," he repeated to himself, as if he needed reminding.

I changed the subject. "The reporter in the bar? She said at Wounded Knee, Roland was close to a guy named Buster Little-pond."

"I'll look into it," he said. "Thanks."

We moved on to the trip up to Lost Pipe Lake. Luke had decided to postpone departure for a day. Instead of leaving the next day, Sunday, we would leave Monday morning. Apparently, several of the state crime lab's technicians had gone to a conference in Frankfurt, Germany, leaving the lab shorthanded. Luke was clearly frustrated by the delay, but I was relieved to have the extra day to organize provisions.

"See you in the morning, then." I moved toward the door.

He moved with me. A moment later, we were kissing. His beard was sharp. I could smell the chemical spices of his deodorant.

"Stay," he said.

I felt his breath stir my hair. "What about Barb?" I asked. My voice sounded oddly ordinary.

"Barb is Barb," he answered finally. We looked at each other. His hazel eyes were soft, with a quality of sadness, like dappled autumn sunlight.

"Okay," I said.

He closed his eyes, let out a long breath, and pulled me hard against him.

"But get rid of that bloody jacket," I stipulated.

His eyes snapped open. "I'll hang it in the bathroom."

"Not until after I use the shower."

He smiled lazily. "Anything else?"

I smiled back. "Now that you mention it," I said.

LUKE WOKE ME, shifting his shoulder under my head. "You're snoring," he said.

"Sorry," I said. I rolled onto my back, releasing his arm. The sheet felt icy against my skin. The room was dark and smelled of lake water. We had turned out the lights, opened the curtains and the windows to let the night in. A greenish reflection trembled on the ceiling. "What time is it?" I asked.

"About two."

I fished around for the covers, found a piece of blanket, and pulled it up. "Want some?" I asked.

"No, thanks."

Sleepily, I ran my hand down his torso. His skin was silky and hot. "You still feel like a furnace," I said. "Doesn't your metabolism ever quit?"

He didn't answer.

"What's the matter?"

"That mark on the jacket. It's bugging me."

"Your baby crow's foot?" I drew it in his pubic hair.

"Don't." He took my hand, moved it back up to his chest, and laced his fingers through mine, imprisoning them. "I know I've seen it—or something like it—before, but I can't think what it is."

I wasn't very interested. "Maybe it's some kind of rune," I suggested without thinking.

"A rune?"

"A kind of scratchy-looking letter. Part of an old Anglo-Saxon alphabet." I yawned. "Used to be only Beowulf scholars paid any attention to them. Then they enjoyed a moment of chic as a New Age toy. You could buy a little leather sack full of runes engraved on stones and do magic with them."

"What kind of magic?"

"I don't know. If you like, I'll call up my mother, the Great White Witch, and ask."

I could feel him smiling in the dark. "Sure," he said. "Can't hurt to have a witch on the team."

"I don't know about that," I said gloomily. A draft of cold air stirred the curtains. Luke retreated into a preoccupied silence. I thought about getting up to go to the bathroom and instead began to drowse under my piece of blanket.

"If it's some kind of emblem," Luke announced, "it's in a strange place—over the right hip. You awake?"

"Half."

His fingers tightened around mine. I woke up some more. He tugged at my hand and I rolled toward him.

"What about a right hip?" I wondered.

"Nothing," he said.

NINE

I WENT BACK to my own bed about four, poured a snort of Jack Daniel's, and forgot to drink it. When the alarm woke me at seven in the curtained dark, my first awareness was the scent of bourbon wafting out of my glass on the bedside table. On any other morning-after, my stomach would have rolled over. On this particular morning, however, the liquor actually smelled sweet. I didn't want to drink it, any more than I would have wanted to drink Chanel No. 5, but I felt no need to immediately get rid of it. Instead of fumbling around for one of my paperbacks to cover the glass, I found myself interested in the complexities of the bouquet. I realized I'd escaped a hangover. Moreover, by the time I'd showered, dressed, and opened the curtains on the morning, I was beginning to think that perhaps I'd also escaped the heavy-duty arm of my conscience.

People often speak of "the clear ring of conscience," but mine tends to assert itself with depressing thuds, and on the occasions when I break one of my own rules—in this case, Thou Shalt Not Sleep with Someone Else's Husband—I usually end up in a foggy low. But I didn't feel anywhere near low. Maybe it was too early. Maybe I hadn't yet finished sinning with Someone Else's Husband.

I stepped out onto my balcony. The peaks on the far side of the lake were still hidden in clouds. The air was cool, but there was no breeze, and under the grey ceiling, the water was glassy. Formations of swimming ducks incised dark vees into the lake's pale surface. Overhead, the wispy edges of clouds caught cream-colored light. I watched them slide apart, revealing a slice of blue. The blue grew into a patch big enough for The Last Judgment. I waltzed off to find a cup of coffee.

Luke and Agent Webb Chapman were in the restaurant eating breakfast. Luke was concentrating on steak, homefries, biscuits and a pair of fried eggs. Agent Chapman was working on pancakes cut into neat syrup-soaked stacks. He was about Luke's age, but more thickly built. He had a square face and pink skin that showed the shadow of his beard, even after his morning shave. His hair, slicked back with water, looked black, but his lavish sideburns were brown and frizzy. "Hi, guys," I said.

Luke straightened up. "Hello there!" he said. "And how are you this morning?"

"Fine. And you?"

"Magnificent. As usual." Luke's smile kept on going, its crinkles deepening, his eyes almost disappearing on either side of his large, dented nose—the dent a souvenir from his college rodeo days.

Webb regarded me with interest over the rim of his coffee cup. "You must be Lee," he said in a pleasant baritone. "Luke told me about you."

Oh? I wanted to say. Instead I dove into my Capable Cook mode and announced to them both, "I'm working up a shopping list for your trip. If you've got food preferences, now's the time. I don't want to hear you guys bitching because I forgot the calamari."

"What's calamari?" Luke said.

"Salami," Webb answered with authority.

"Squid," I corrected.

Webb's eyes widened, then flashed with humor. "Exactly. We love it. Bring lots. And raisins. Put raisins on everything."

Luke said to me, "Don't mind him. He's just jealous because he doesn't get to come. He's going be coordinating things down here."

"Ah," I said. "So what's the head count?"

"There'll be three of us—me and two technicians." He raised an eyebrow. "And thou."

"Smooooth," Webb commented. "Watch out for yourself. Professor," he added with a wink.

"I appreciate the tip. Detective." I smiled.

He turned to Luke. "Now I *am* jealous."

"Eat your heart out."

"So what's with raisins?" I asked him.

"I *hate* raisins." He sounded about four years old.

Webb burst out laughing.

I took coffee and an English muffin back to my room, and on the way, I stopped at the front desk and asked for a dictionary. It seemed as good a place as any to hunt for runes, but I had the feeling that a request for a condom would have caused less commotion. Two people came out from the back to join the desk clerk. A dictionary? They shook their heads gravely.

"My mother has one," said the desk clerk, a young man wearing a kelly green polo shirt embroidered with the resort's logo.

"Maybe the library's got one," another green polo shirt suggested. "You could try there. It's just up the street. But they might be closed on Sunday."

"There's a spell-check on the computer," offered a woman in a white suit blouse. "What word did you want to look up?"

"Actually, I'm looking for an alphabet." Their faces were curious. "Thanks, anyway," I told them.

I SPENT THE NEXT hour with a lined yellow pad working out another puzzle: what to feed the Law up at Lost Pipe Lake. Somewhere beyond raisins lay the way to Luke's heart. (How could the man not like *raisins!*) I called Dolores to consult, and she offered elk and trout from her freezer. She said that Pete had left early that morning on his hunting trip, and that she'd arranged to have her brother truck the llamas to the trailhead for us. "I wish I didn't have to teach," she said wistfully. "I'd put Paul on Ringo and come up there with you."

"Do it."

"I can't. Tuesday I'm taking thirty little monsters on a field trip. Stop off here before you go to the supermarket, and I'll give you a check. And Lee? Don't forget to drop in on Charlene."

"Oh yeah."

"You *did* forget," she chided.

"I was working hard at it."

I HAD NO TROUBLE finding Roland and Charlene Redhawk's Trading Post. It was located on Route 93, the main artery through the Mission Valley. I had passed it on my trips up and down the reservation and ignored it as yet another tourist trap selling "Genuine Turquoise Jewelry," huckleberry chocolates, and gag Montana postcards. (Sample gag: Group photo of grotty-looking mountain men sporting bandages and slings. The caption: Grizzly Bear Artificial Insemination Team, Montana.)

The highway billboard for "Redhawk's Historic Trading Post" was larger than its buildings, a trio of small log cabins joined by a wooden walk. One of the cabins housed Roland's "Flathead Beadwork Museum." Another was a convenience store that sold soda, baloney, and disposable diapers inside and two grades of gas out front. I filled Pete's van at the high-test pump, paid up, and was told I could find Charlene next door.

The trading post's "historic" tag was more than hype. It was authentically dark inside. The logs were age-blackened, and the pair of dusty-paned windows were too tiny to let daylight penetrate. Low-watt bulbs hung from the ridge beam and a gooseneck desk lamp, circa 1950, sat on top of the counter. Behind the counter, a pair of solid-looking young Indian women sat glumly on stools. Relatives, maybe?

Over at a display of beaded earrings, Charlene was waiting on a customer—a chatty woman with a North Carolina accent. Charlene was wearing jeans, an olive green wool cardigan, and a large earrings of old Navajo silver. I wondered if the sweater was Roland's. She stood with it pulled around her as if she were cold, but her back was ramrod straight and her thin, steely braid hung true between her shoulder blades.

Her customer held up a bead-encrusted hoop. "And what are these ones, again?"

"Peyote Stitch," Charlene said.

"No, I mean, what tribe?"

Charlene frowned. "Chippewa-Cree, I think," she said. She turned to me. The strong bones of her face had a flattened look, as if fate had fed her through a wringer. "Be right with you," she said.

"No hurry." I put on my half-frames and examined a display of beaded medallions: elk heads and candy-box roses, American flags and saddle ponies, even a likeness of Donald Duck. I spotted the Sacred Heart of Jesus realistically rendered in tiny red and orange crystals. The curves of the heart glittered wetly.

I moved on to safer browsing—a bookcase full of pamphlets and craft books—and picked up a scholarly-looking reprint titled, "Warfare Practices among North American Indians." The first paper was an abstraction of a German Ph.D. dissertation ("Doktorwurde") written in 1906. I read:

> To the eastern Indian, the scalp lock was visible proof of personal bravery; it was like a war medal gained honorably from his enemies.... In its pure form, scalping could be performed only on an enemy and was an act of national significance, a manifestation of a state of war.

I flipped to the second paper, an examination of scalping techniques written in 1940 by a Massachusetts M.D. It was illustrated with an old news sketch that showed an inky-skinned Indian scalping a little white boy while his mother cowered over her babies. The drawing had all the inflammatory flair of a contemporary supermarket tabloid. The caption instructed: "The Indian (a) has already incised the skin around the head with his knife, (b) is now prying off the edge of the scalp with the tip of his thumb, and (c) will finish the mutilation by grasping the skin to strip it off."

"I always wanted to run away and go live with the Indians," drawled the North Carolina customer.

Startled, I looked up from the scalping primer. "Like Sam Houston," the woman rattled on. "As a child, I was inspired by his biography. I remember it had an orange cover and silhouette-type illustrations. I thought, how *won*derful to be adopted by Indians!"

I couldn't see Charlene's expression. Her back was toward me. But she seemed to take no offense. "You know, there's lots of accounts of white women and children being captured by Indians and taken into their tribes. The majority of them refused to go back to civilization." She paused, then added ironically, "Civilization didn't agree much with the Indians, either."

The woman held up a fringe of pale blue and white beads. "Look, Chapel Hill colors!" she exclaimed. "I could wear them to a gay-aim! Aren't they darlin'."

I turned back to the German doctor:

> The Indians of the West never scalped a suicide, and, according to Major Dodge, they never scalped a negro; the eastern Indians were in the latter regard, it seems, less particular, for the writer came across two records of the scalping of negroes.

I wondered if the Indians had bothered to scalp women. I replaced the pamphlet. The title of another booklet made my own scalp crawl: "How to Make a Primitive Bow."

> Step one: Cut down your tree.

Okay.

A grainy photo showed the author's hands wielding a handmade stone ax. Had Artemis made her own tools? If her store-bought arrows were any indication, probably not. I skipped over illustrations of hands splitting the tree with a stone wedge, scraping off bark with a stone flake, and read about "curing." Depending on the wood used, a "quickie" bow could take from several days to more than a week to dry. More photos showed a crudely hewn "green" bow. It was white and hairy. The finished bow, however, had dried for a week in a warm basement and been worked into a smooth, graceful arc. Clearly, the girl's bow had been finished.

I felt a surge of excitement. Artemis had not made her bow at Lost Pipe Lake. There had not been time. In the space of two days, she had arrived at the trading post, learned Roland's whereabouts, hiked up to the lake, and killed him. A bow like the one she carried had not been made in two days.

How long had she been on the reservation before the murder? Had she made the bow at a hidden campsite? Or had she fashioned it in another time and place—in a city apartment, a suburban garage? Wherever she had made it, she had carried it up to Lost Pipe Lake. Did she carry it back out with her?

Had Luke thought about the bow? Newspapers and TV stations had run the girl's picture. Detectives had been canvassing the reservation with it. Luke also ordered it posted in every bus depot in the state. So far, no one had recognized her. But faces are elusive. If she had taken a bus or hitchhiked with a handmade five-foot-long bow, someone might remember.

Another possibility occurred to me: Artemis hadn't made the bow. Suppose it belonged to someone else. Suppose she had stolen it. Maybe Luke should find out if anyone on the reservation is missing a bow.

I felt the urge to jump back in the van and find a pay phone.

Good thinking, Squires. Call the man up and tell him how to do his job. He'll love you to death.

I put the pamphlet back on the shelf. Then I picked it up again. I took it over to the two women behind counter, paid for it, and stuck it in the day pack I was using as a purse. The North Carolina woman decided on a pair of porcupine-quill earrings. They were for her daughter, a student in Missoula. The mother had driven out to visit and was spending the day touring on her own. "It's been a kinda long visit, if you know what I mean," she confided to Charlene with a little laugh. She paid for the earrings and left.

Charlene looked at me expectantly. I took a deep breath, introduced myself, and offered condolences. The young women behind the counter listened without expression.

Charlene digested my attempt at comfort. Then she said brusquely, "They said you were there with him when he died."

"Yes," I said. "Gwen Mears—the filmmaker? She was there, too. There wasn't anything we could have done to—"

She waved away my guilt. "Did he say anything?" There was a note of hope beneath her gruffness.

I shook my head. "No. Sorry."

"I was just wondering."

"When the first arrow hit him, he let out a kind of roar and got to his feet. He was angry and surprised. Then the second one got him. He didn't make a sound. He must have died instantly. He had no pulse by the time we got to him."

She stared out the dusty little window. Silvery daylight outlined her profile.

"How long were you married?" I wondered.

"Eighteen years last July," she said. "Roland came down here from Minnesota just after my first husband got himself killed in Vietnam. The twins were just babies." She turned away from the window. "I married two warriors," she said, more to herself than to me.

"Roland wasn't in Vietnam, was he?" I asked.

"No."

"But he was involved in AIM?"

"That was a long time ago," she rebuked me sharply.

I nodded. "Well," I said awkwardly, "I've got to be going." I met her eyes. "I'm sorry, Mrs. Redhawk."

She let out a sad snort. "Did he go on about it up there? Pete said he got loaded drinking that man's Scotch."

"Go on about what?"

"That AIM occupation at Wounded Knee. The people didn't have no food there, no electricity, no sanitation. But when Roland was drinking, to hear him talk, those two months were, like, the high point of his life."

"Were you there?"

"Me?" She sounded incredulous. "Not me. I made him give up all that protest business before we got married. I had Roland baptized at St. Ignatius. He was a good Catholic husband and father," she declared proudly. "He did a lot for the tribe. He was a fighter. It was in his nature. He never could resist a battle."

A movement in the doorway made us turn. "That was Roland, all right." A short, bulky woman in glasses stood on the threshold. I wondered how long she'd been listening. Her black hair was spiky in front—a cut that looked a lot younger than her old-lady knit slacks and ruffled polka-dot blouse. Against the light, she looked turnip-shaped. Her wide shoulders and large breasts tapered down to little feet in black Nikes. Her voice was frank and good-humored. "Just stopped by to see how you were doing," she said to Charlene.

Charlene didn't answer. Her eyes were wary.

The woman stepped into the room and went on cheerfully, "I heard you were back in harness already." She raised a questioning eyebrow.

"I'm better off busy. Like they say, you can't keep trouble from visiting, but you don't have to offer it a chair." Charlene made it clear that she didn't want to offer the woman a chair, either.

But the woman seemed not to hear her hostility. She grimaced sympathetically, and took another step into the shop.

Suddenly Charlene seemed to warm to me. "I'd like for you to see Roland's collection," she told me. "He was real proud of it. We had one man come all the out from the Smithsonian museum in Washington, D.C., just to see what he had." Then she turned to the turnip woman and introduced us. We recognized each other's names. She was Bernadette Walker—the councilwoman who had sent Roland up to Lost Pipe Lake.

"You'll have to forgive me," Charlene announced briskly, "but I've got some things that need tending here. Bernadette, would you take Lee here over to the museum?"

Bernadette took the brush-off with good grace. We walked outside. I felt another postfuneral urge for a cigarette but Bernadette didn't whip one out. Her car, a new dark maroon Lincoln, gleamed in the sunlight. She had pulled up to the wooden walkway at a careless angle, commandeering enough space for three cars. The Lincoln's shiny chrome grill nosed a nail keg full of frost-blackened marigolds. She glanced back at the door of the trading post. "I suppose she blames me," she said.

"Is she the only one?"

She gave me a speculative once-over. Then her eyes went back to the trading post. "Charlene and Roland moved this building up from the Bitterroot," she told me.

"Huh," I said politely.

"The Bitterroot Valley was our homeland, before the United States government ordered us out of it. My family was one of the ones with Chief Charlo who refused to leave. When the U.S.

Army finally forced us out, we moved up here. On the last day of the march, the braves took the lead. They put on red war paint and their finest tribal dress and came galloping up to the church at Jocko, firing their guns in the air. The women came behind, crying."

She paused, then smiled wryly. "The people at the church thought they were under attack." Then, dismissing the church-goers with a small gesture, she made her point: "If I'd been with my great-grandfather, I'd have wanted to be up front shooting, not wailing at the rear with the women. I'm an activist. Center stage agrees with me, and I make no apologies for it." Her chin went up defiantly; behind her glasses, her eyes flashed. Unchallenged, she settled back into cheerfulness. "There's just one big problem with the spotlight," she observed. "It makes you an easy target."

I realized I was wrong. There was nothing turniplike about her. With her round glasses and her spiky hair, she looked like an owl. A plump owl with sharp talons hidden under her feathers.

Abruptly, she changed tack. "I hear you're good friends with the hotshot the state sent in."

Her statement caught me off balance. For a second, I felt a rush of panic. Did the woman have spies in the motel? Had anyone seen me coming out of Luke's room? But there was no hint of innuendo in her voice. "We're friends," I said.

"We Salish are a practical people," she told me. "Our medicine men used to pray and fast for visions to locate buffalo. But they also sent out runners. You could say Roland was one of my runners. I asked him to go along with you to find out what Herron was like as a person. That's all. The rest is just a lot of noise, people trying to make me out as some kind of Lucrezia Borgia." She watched my face.

"Hm," I said noncommittally.

"I've got an election coming up. I'd like to see these killings cleared up. I'll do whatever I can to help. You can tell your detective friend." It sounded more like an order than an option. She glanced at her watch. "Come on," she said. "I'll show you Roland's collection."

I followed her into the "museum" cabin. It was no bigger than the trading post and its logs looked as old, but a battery of fluorescent fixtures flooded the interior with a cold light. Three walls were lined with glass cases of brilliantly colored beadwork. There were a few moccasins, and one exquisitely embroidered vest, but the collection was mainly rectangular-shaped bags completely covered with beads. Unlike the medallions for sale in the trading post, however, the bags were not kitschy. The floral designs had a formal symmetry that reminded me of old quilt appliqués. The ones depicting animals had the directness of folk art. There were no cuddly Pooh-bears here. "Roland had good taste," I complimented.

Bernadette seemed amused. "That's what the experts say."

"You don't think so?"

She shrugged. "These things—they're us. They're who we are part our life, part of our wholeness. To me, that's what's beautiful about them. But Roland looked at them differently."

"How's that?"

"He saw them as works of art. 'Pieces,' he called them. He kept buying and selling, trying to 'upgrade.' I offered to give him a bag my mother made—told him he could have it but he didn't want it. You know that picture of The Last Warrior—the one with a defeated brave on his horse? My mother copied it, bead by bead. It was perfect.

"See this one?" She pointed to a bag with a stylized plant motif worked in orange and green beads. "This was the kind of thing he liked. It's an old contour bag. Look at the background."

I peered at the pale blue beads. They were sewn in curving lines that outlined the plant.

"You notice how the lines make a kind of halo around the leaves? Roland said it was the work of an artist expressing the spiritual power of the plant. To me, it looks like a kind of natural way to fill in the background."

"Your practical nature, maybe."

She looked at me, surprised, then smiled. "Maybe."

"I write poems," I told her. "I'm not going to call them works of art. But sometimes the thing made goes farther than its maker. People find things in my poems I didn't know were there." I studied the bag. The more I looked at the background, the more the beads resembled a energy field around the plant.

Restless, Bernadette moved on to the next case.

"When we were up at Lost Pipe Lake," I told her, "Roland got pretty intense about Native American religion. We were sitting around the campfire after dinner, and Charlie Herron made some dim remark about sweat ceremonies. Roland let him have it. Of course, they were both half in the bag by that time, but I remember being surprised—Roland had been sucking up to Herron all day."

She was interested. "What did he say?"

"Herron? He thought après-ski sweats would be a nifty promotional tool for his resort."

She said nothing. I wondered where she stood on the issue of traditional religion. For all I knew, she could have been a Jehovah's Witness. I'd driven past a Kingdom Hall on 93. Moreover, the directory in my motel room listed a dozen other Polson churches, from Episcopal to Pentecostal.

"I don't remember Roland's exact words," I said. "But the idea was that Native Americans didn't have a cafeteria plan, that Herron couldn't take a religious ritual and leave, say, the economic welfare of the tribe. That being Indian was the whole ball of wax—if you'll forgive the unpoetic metaphor."

She let out a little grunt. Her eyes didn't move from the display case.

I took a breath and plowed on. "I don't know how close you were to Roland and I don't want offend you, but he didn't practice what he preached."

She looked up.

"He used the cafeteria plan here." I gestured around the room.

"What do you mean?"

"Look around. He's got plant auras. Magical bears. Eagles. But No Last Warrior. No Snoopy. Roland took want he wanted—just like Herron."

She thought about it. "Maybe that's why he got angry at Herron." She sounded resigned.

"Angry enough to kill him?"

"I don't know." She sounded sincere. I wondered if she was lying.

She glanced again at her watch. "Let me tell you a story about Roland. It was going around here after he came down from Minnesota. Hearing Charlene talk about Roland being at Wounded Knee reminded me of it."

She paused, as if going over it in her head. Then she said, "Wounded Knee was a classic siege. Several hundred Indians from all different tribes dug in behind barricades and held off the FBI and the National Guard for two months with deer rifles. They had one AK-47, and it was shown on network TV as proof of communist ties. It had been captured in Vietnam by a Native vet. But he had no bullets for it.

"Roland was one of people who risked going out at night to bring food back through the lines. Well, toward the end, I guess things got pretty basic. A transformer was shot out, and there was no electricity or water for personal hygiene. And one of the women noticed that Roland had been dyeing his hair black. I guess his roots were growing out. Of course, they teased him about it. And he blew up, told them to go get their own food."

I looked at her. It was the end of the story. I didn't get it. "You're saying he was vain?"

"Could be that's all it was. Just another More-Indian-Than-Thou squabble. But the way I heard it was, a lot people thought he wasn't any kind of Indian at all. The rumor was that he was an FBI plant. Which would explain why he'd been able to get through the lines without trouble."

"So what happened?"

She frowned. "What do you mean?"

"They didn't kick him out?"

"I doubt it. Roland was up there in the AIM hierarchy. At least, that was my impression. I understood Roland was Buster Littlepond's right-hand man."

The tour was over. She moved toward the door. "Your agent friend—what's his name?"

"Luke Donner."

"He might want to talk to Littlepond," she suggested.

"Would Littlepond want to talk to Luke?"

She thought about it. "Let me ask around. I think I heard Littlepond was back at Pine Ridge. Running a substance-abuse program for kids. Something like that."

"Where's Pine Ridge?"

She gave me an odd look. "South Dakota. Pine Ridge is the name of the reservation. Wounded Knee is one of the towns there."

I winced. "I'm an East Coast provincial."

But she was more curious than offended. "Is this the first time you've been on a reservation?" she asked.

"Yes."

"Most of them aren't like this one." She snapped open her patent-leather purse and handed me a business card. "I'll see what I can find out about Littlepond. Have Agent Donner give me a call."

She left.

I spent another half hour looking at Roland's collection. There was something else missing besides contemporary kitsch. The American flag.

For some unfathomable reason, despite Wounded Knee I and Wounded Knee II, despite the long history of wrongs inflicted on native peoples by our government, the American flag has been and still is a popular Indian motif. There were plenty of beaded flag medallions for sale in the trading post. But Roland's collection boasted no Stars and Stripes.

TEN

THE COLD FRONT Pete promised must have stalled somewhere up over Glacier—the afternoon was warm and hazy. At St. Ignatius swallows dove around the church bell tower as if saying a last goodbye. The air felt soft for Montana, redolent of Keatsian "mists and mellow fruitfulness," but the town's empty streets were bleak enough for a Richard Hugo poem. (Hugo was no less melancholy than Keats, but his imagery was a lot starker: his "black blue" Mission range climbed the sky "like music dying Indians once wailed.")

The main drag in St. Ignatius dead-ended into the high school; mountains staggered above its flat roof. The cutest building on the strip was a snug little board-and-batten law office. A windowless video emporium took up half a block. A lumber company's prefab warehouse took up a whole block. The supermarket took up another one.

I tried the video store first. I found the Mouse in the Family Viewing section between two other old-timers, Huckleberry Hound and The Muppets. There were three tapes of Mickey cartoons. Two of them were all color. The third, a "Limited Gold Edition" promised fifty-one minutes of color *and*—thank you, Dr. Watson—black-and-white. Renting it cost a dollar and two cents. A bargain—if you belonged to the store's "video club." Membership was another twenty bucks. I came, I saw, and Curiosity conquered.

Over in the supermarket, I was the only shopper. I rolled through my list in record time. I have to tell you that arugula, as much as I love the leaf, was not on my menu. On the other hand, I was hoping for something a bit more glamorous than iceberg. But the Sunday pickings in the produce section looked as sad as an old dog. I ended up with a head of iceberg and a cabbage, both as pale as moons. My cart looked like a time machine headed for 1950. All I needed was a couple packs of Jell-O for a congealed "salad" and no doubt I'd remind Luke of his mom.

Mom's Jell-O in the wilderness?

Brilliant. Mold it in a deer skull, set it in snow, serve with wild berries. You'll be a legend in your own time.

Meanwhile, bits and pieces of my conversation with Bernadette Walker kept elbowing my Martha Stewart fantasies. Who was Roland, anyway? Killer or warrior? Indian activist or white snitch? An art collector with a taste for the mystic or a hustler hawking kitsch to tourists? My picture of Charlie Herron was fuzzier, but no less contradictory: a wilderness-loving developer (an oxymoron if there ever was one) who packed a gun and talked compost toilets; a man dumped by a spoiled wife but still in love with her—if Mrs. Herron's boast was true. I wondered what number wife she was. Did Kevin have older stepbrothers and -sisters?

No one on our trip had traded any personal information. It was as if in venturing up to Lost Pipe Lake, we had shed our day-to-day lives, wriggled out of them and left them along the side of the trail. We were content with the moment, with the novelty of the llamas, with the demanding beauty of the mountains. The complex particulars of our "down below" pasts were irrelevant. Felicity's work as a high-end travel agent mattered no more than my ragged succession of house-sitting and teaching jobs. No one had bothered to ask about Charlie Herron's past projects or Gwen's and Mary Ann's previous films. Had we had more time before the trip crumpled, no doubt details would have surfaced, been passed around like curiosities discovered on a walk—a brittle bone, a bright feather.

As it was, however, the only thing I knew for certain about Charlie Herron and Roland Redhawk was that they were both dead. Roland's fingerprints had not turned up in the police computer. But according to Patty, the reporter in the karaoke bar, he had been a fugitive. Moreover, if—as Eddie had pointed out—a number of former AIM leaders now enjoyed fame as movie stars, Roland had taken pains to avoid Mary Ann's camera.

"I never forget a face," Charlie Herron had said, trying to place Roland's. Had Charlie been mistaken—or had he crossed paths with Roland before?

Leave it to Luke, I told myself. I loaded my groceries into Pete's van and headed out of town. The tree-lined residential streets were as empty as the supermarket: no kids on bikes, no homeowners raking leaves. Back in Washington, on a fall Sunday like this, half the city would have been out jogging or roller-blading along the Potomac's bike paths. Was St. Ignatius a town of couch potatoes? The more-prosperous blocks had small ranch houses and Victorian-type cottages trimmed in mauve and fuchsia. Their yards were tidy, their woodsheds full, their cars and pickups sheltered in carports. Yellow *Missoulian* tubes stood beside mailboxes. On poorer streets, however, camper tops and harrows rusted in weeds, gutters sagged, porches listed. Nothing was square. Even the trailers looked as if they were sitting on bumpy ground. If these homes were Indian, Pete's place—at first glance—fit the label.

His new llama business was located a couple of miles outside of town in open farmland. Winds had scoured most of the paint off the house, a two-story clapboard punctuating the end of a long straight driveway. The first-floor shutters were all missing, and one upstairs window was boarded up with plywood. The farm machinery in the yard looked antique, if not primitive, and the barn out back, a magnificently huge log structure, had a gaping hole in its frail, shingled roof. On second glance, however, you noticed that the gravel popping sharply under your tires was new and so was the big white tank of propane at the side of the house. There were new llama sheds, new rail-and-woven-wire fencing. It was a place on the way up, not down.

The llamas in the paddocks were all attentive as I got out of the van. A dozen heads with banana-shaped ears swiveled serenely, tracking my movements in unison. Only Jake, my kitchen llama, was uninterested. Head down, he nibbled at a bleached tuft of grass. Ringo and another llama I didn't recognize struck princely poses atop of a three-foot-high hill of "beans"—aka llama droppings. (In their home pastures, llamas defecate in the same spot, building up a communal "toilet." This sounds messier than it is: their mound looked and smelled no worse than a pile of dirt.)

Dolores came out to help me unload the van and carry the

provisions into the kitchen where Rose, her mother, was watching baby Paul and a batch of pumpkin bread in the oven. The smell of it, buttery cinnamon and clove, gave me the first real scratch of hunger I'd had since the murders.

Like the outside of the house, the kitchen was in process. The countertops were new yellow Formica, but cabinets were still somewhere up the road ahead, and Dolores had made red calico skirts to screen cardboard boxes packed with pots and pan, empty oleo tubs, and rolls of paper towels. The Mr. Clean and other hazards to Paul's existence were locked in the bottom half of an reproduction Colonial hutch. Face and fingers smeared with batter, Paul stood on a chair at the kitchen table, licking a dented metal mixing bowl. Soup cans, empty freezer containers, and plastic trucks littered the faded linoleum rug. "Watch your step," Rose warned.

We stowed the perishables in the refrigerator and carried the rest of the groceries into what was originally a dining room but now served as an expedition pantry/gear storage room. Working from my menu lists, Dolores and I packed and weighed the dry-goods panniers. Normally, for a pack trip, I would have spent a day or two precooking and freezing meals—a tactic that, after a day on the trail, ensures supper before midnight for hungry campers. Working for Pete and Dolores, however, I had access to their frozen stockpile. If the end-of-the-season selection was limited, I wasn't complaining. Moreover, on this particular trip, I wouldn't have to worry about scrambling every evening to get my kitchen set up and dinner under way. Once we got up to Lost Pipe Lake, our camp would be stationary. While Luke and his team hunted for evidence, I'd have all day to simmer a stew or bake bread. I found I was looking forward to it. I added extra Ziploc bags of flour and cornmeal to a pair of panniers, then hefted them on a hand-held spring scale. Thirty-two pounds each. Still under the eighty-pound limit. (A full-grown llama weighs around 400 pounds and can carry one-quarter of their body weight over long distances—i.e., about 100 pounds. Pete, however, worked with a wide margin of safety: if a llama balked or was injured on the trail, its load could be redistributed among the others in the string.)

"Can I take a Dutch oven?" I asked Dolores. "I mean, a real one one of your old ones. I don't really go for this new aluminum ware you're using."

She frowned. "It saves a lot of weight. What, you worried about Alzheimer's?"

"I just think food cooked in cast iron tastes better."

"I suppose it depends how much gear the lab people are bringing. Take the scale back to the motel with you and weigh their stuff tonight, if you can. Give me a ring before eight."

"What happens after eight?"

"I turn into a pumpkin."

"Speaking of which," I said with a nod to the kitchen, "your mom's bread is making me drool." I made a convincing slurping sound.

"Is that a hint?"

"Oh, no."

ROSE CUT US warm slabs. Maybe it was their mulled-cider-Halloween-and-pumpkin-pie aroma. Maybe it was Rose's indulgent maternal hand. Whatever it was, I suddenly felt undone. A lump of the sweet bread stuck in my throat. Tears welled up into my eyes. I took a bracing swallow of black coffee and scalded my tongue.

Get a grip. "I was out at Eddie's place yesterday," I said. They were interested. I described Kevin's mother and her boyfriend, and they shook their heads. "Eddie told us about his father being killed up at Lost Pipe Lake."

Rose studied the kitchen table's chipped enamel top.

"Look at you," Dolores said to Paul. His fuzzy black hair was matted with pumpkin batter.

"No," Paul said. He dove back into the bowl.

"He's going to make himself sick," Dolores complained to Rose.

"I doubt it," Rose said.

"Eddie said it wasn't a secret," I said. "How come you didn't want me to know?"

The late-afternoon sun coming through the window over the sink brushed Dolores's dark hair with orange light. "You are our guest," she said with dignity. "I didn't want to make you uncomfortable."

"But why should it make me uncomfortable? It's a dreadful story, but—" Then it dawned on me. "Wait a sec. You mean, because the warden was white?"

She looked away.

I suppressed a flash of annoyance. "So the man was not a credit to his race. What else is new? Dolores, there's bad guys in this world, and there's good guys. We're the good guys." I stopped and looked at her. "Aren't we?"

She gave me an twisted little smile. "Sure."

"You don't think so?"

"Of course I do. But what about the rest of the world? How do you tell the sheep from the goats?"

"What do you mean?"

"I bet that game warden thought he was a good guy."

"How about 'By their fruit, ye shall know them'?"

Rose grunted, as if the matter were settled, Paul was squirming in his chair. His bowl clanged to the floor. "All gone!" he announced.

Rose picked it up. "All gone!" she echoed.

Dolores said, "By the way, your filmmaker friends called. They say they can't get their original footage back until after there's a trial or the case is closed. They wanted me to get them back up to Lost Pipe Lake with the llamas."

"What'd you say?"

"I said the llamas were going back up with the cops, and they could talk to Pete about it at the end of the week. They said they didn't have a week."

Rose gave Paul her coffee spoon. He threw it on the floor.

Dolores let out a weary sigh. "Time to get you cleaned up, mister." She scooped him up and carried him off under her arm like a small keg. His howls of outrage trailed after them, only slightly muffled by the house's old plastered walls. I remembered my own wars of will with my daughter Rachel. It wasn't the part of motherhood that I missed. Then, abruptly, the screaming stopped. A pipe groaned; upstairs, a bath was running.

Rose refilled my coffee and cut me another slab of pumpkin

bread. Now undeterred by her daughter, she leaned back in her chair and asked, "So what did Eddie say?"

I told her about the old killings at Lost Pipe Lake. She listened without asking questions, her broad face attentive. She and Dolores had the same flattish triangular nose, but Rose's skin was lighter and dusted with freckles. She looked somewhere in her late fifties; there were navy blue circles under her eyes and deep lines at the sides of her mouth that gave her an air of disapproval when she wasn't smiling.

When I had finished, we sat in silence. Rose pushed her chair back, reached into the drainboard in the sink and retrieved an ashtray made of molded avocado green plastic. Then she took a pack of Kools from the pouch pocket in her sweatshirt and lit up, leaving the pack at a friendly angle on the table between us. "I wonder what Eddie was after up there," she said, exhaling.

I took a swallow of coffee. It had gone lukewarm. "I didn't quiz him on it."

"No," she agreed. "I was just wondering. When my mother was sick, she used to talk about a root she'd dug up as a girl. That would have been sometime back in the nineteen-twenties, I guess. The women used to take packhorses up into the mountains and dig up these roots. They were supposed to have great medicinal value. People used it like money. A little bit of it was worth a lot in trade."

"What was it?"

"She called it 'haask.' Don't know another name for it. Some kind of hairy root. She talked about scraping off the hairs before washing them and laying them out to dry."

Rose took another drag and tapped her cigarette into the burn-scarred ashtray. "When she was in the hospital, she kept asking for that darned root. Maybe I should have taken her to a healer." She looked up, her eyes full of doubt.

I had no answer for her. The open pack of Kools lay about eight inches from my hand. If they hadn't been mentholated, I would have snatched one up.

"At the end, she talked a lot about those trips," Rose went on, her voice back in a casual mode. "Said her mother made their tipi cover out of flour sacks. She said it kept the weather out and let the moonlight in. I'll tell you one thing, though, you wouldn't get me out there in no flour-sack tipi!'' She laughed a smoky laugh and stubbed out her butt.

Dolores came back in with Paul suited up a la Barney in fuzzy purple PJs. His black hair was wet and spiky, and he smelled of soap. She deposited him on his grandmother's lap and removed the ashtray from the table. "Stay for supper," she invited. "We were just going to heat up some soup."

"Can I have a rain check? Luke promised to take me out."

"Oh?" Dolores raised an eyebrow.

"Just doing his penance," I told her drily. "He stood me up for dinner last night."

"Men," Rose growled as she combed Paul's hair with her fingers. He lounged against her like a contented pasha.

"By the way," I said, "you got a dictionary in the house?" I told them about the mark Luke had found on Charlie Herron's jacket and drew it for them on a yellow Post-It pad. Dolores brought out *Webster's Ninth Collegiate*, still in its dust jacket. Its pages looked pristine, unthumbed. I looked up "rune." Along with the definition, the dictionary provided a chart of twiglike letters. There were thirty-one runes, two for the "g" sound and three for the "k" sound. None of them resembled the mark I had drawn. I turned to the dictionary's table of alphabets. The mark wasn't Hebrew, Arabic, Greek, Sanskrit, or Russian.

Rose picked up the pad and turned it around in her hand. "This was on a pocket?" she asked. Paul reached for it, and she passed it over his head to Dolores.

"That's what's weird," I said. "It was on the back, low down." I smacked my hip. "About here. It looked as if it had been stamped into the fleece."

"Maybe he got himself branded," Rose suggested.

"Branded?"

"With a branding iron." She made a thrust with her arm. "Zzzt," she hissed.

"Shhuh," Paul gurgled.

"Zzzt," she corrected. "Was it burned in?" She sounded hopeful. Clearly the idea of branding a California developer pleased her.

"Didn't look like it."

"Shhuh," Paul tried again.

"Zzzzzt!" Rose encouraged.

Paul laughed, delighted. Dolores ignored them. The puzzle intrigued her. "If it's somebody's brand, you could look it up. How big is it?"

"About that size," I told her with a nod at the pad. My drawing was about an inch in diameter.

"Too little," she decided.

"A mini-brand, then," Rose argued, reluctant to give up the notion. "I wonder who owned him."

The phone rang. Dolores picked it up. "It's for you," she said. I felt a constriction in my chest. Who else besides Luke would know to call me here? Was dinner off? But a woman's voice came on the line. To my surprise, it was Bernadette Walker. "How'd you know I was here?" I asked.

"I didn't," she said. "I called to find out where you were. We're in luck. Buster Littlepond's here on the reservation."

"What?"

"He's been here for the last week, working with our substance-abuse programs. He says he doesn't feel like talking to the law, but he's agreed to tell us what he knows about Roland. Be at my office at six," she ordered.

Evidently, I had a new teammate. A bossy one. "I have an appointment at seven," I informed her.

There was a silence at her end. I let it go on for a couple beats. Then I asked, "Where's your office?"

"In Pablo." She sounded surprised that I didn't know. "In the tribal center. Dolores will tell you where it is."

IF I HADN'T been looking for it, the tribal office building would have been easy to miss. It hunkered down behind the shoulder of Highway 93, a single-story complex with a helmetlike mansard roof whose cedar shingles came halfway down the thick walls. I sat in the empty parking lot and watched the western sky turn red over its roof. Red sky at night, sailor's delight. If the adage worked as well in the mountains as at sea, the clear weather would hold another day.

At six-fifteen, I drove around the building looking for Bernadette's Lincoln. At six-twenty-five, I was about to drive back to the motel for my dinner with Luke, when her headlights swept into the lot. She led me through a maze of deserted white corridors, jingling keys and flicking switches as she went, and in her office, we waited for Buster Littlepond.

Her desk and the two chairs in front of it had a Scandinavian look—blond wood, contemporary lines. She booted up a spreadsheet on her computer and dove in. I studied a framed Sam English poster on the wall. It advertised a 1990 conference for Native American children of alcoholics. The artist's elongated Indians had a wavy, insubstantial look, as if they had been blown through a pipe. A shaman in a horned headdress sat cross-legged in the center of the picture. Over his arm, a blue path flowed like a long silk scarf. Woven into the fabric of the path were constellations from an Indian past: buffalo, elk tracks, horse prints.

A line from the Irish singer Sinnead O'Connor's rap surfaced in my brain: "If there's gonna be healing, there's got to be remembering." Like Native Americans, the Irish had been dispossessed of lands and language. Was that the universal key to wholeness, then? Remembering? Is that what Eddie was doing at Lost Pipe Lake—re-creating his past? Had he found what he was looking for?

At six-thirty I used Bernadette's phone on the desk and called Luke. By a small miracle, he was in his room. It sounded like a party in the background.

"We're even," I told him. "I'm not going to be able to make our dinner date."

"Oh," he said, surprised. "Well, okay," he allowed cheerfully.

Too cheerfully? "I'm supposed to be meeting a guy called Buster Littlepond," I told him.

"What?" he said. In the background, a woman whooped. "Will you guys shut up for half a minute?" he complained. "Sorry," he said to me. "The troops have arrived."

I filled him in on the proposed meeting. "Only problem, he hasn't showed up."

"Where are you? Are you alone?" he quizzed. He sounded

like a concerned father on the end of the line. When I told him that Bernadette was playing chaperone, he was only partially mollified. "Guys like Littlepond—" he warned, then broke off. "Just go easy, Lee."

Suddenly I was aware of Bernadette, pretending not to listen. "See you later, then?" I asked.

"Count on it," he answered firmly. "See ya."

"'Bye. Wait! Luke?"

"Yeah?"

"Tell your pals to pack all their gear in pillow-size bundles so they'll fit in the panniers. It'll save time in the morning. They can use garbage bags if they don't have stuff sacks."

"Your wish is our command, fair lady," he declared gallantly.

MAYBE BUSTER LITTLEPOND had four flat tires. Maybe he was running on "Indian time"—that dreamy drift-along-with-your-inner-voice modus operandi that irritates the hell out of conceptual people like me who rely on Timex. Whatever the reason, he showed up an hour and ten minutes late. I felt the same hostility that invariably infects me in doctors' waiting rooms. Like doctors and God, Littlepond made no apology for arriving late.

He was intimidatingly big and ugly. Long leather-wrapped braids hung down his bulging front like a pair of greasy whips. His misshapen face, dark as an aged ham, was eroded by nameless excesses: pitted skin, broken capillaries fanning out from a spongy nose that once might have been proud as a raptor's beak. Nonetheless, beneath the slab of his brow, his dark eyes were lively. His good-humored presence flexed its way into each corner of the room. If Bernadette was a slow, steady burn, Buster Littlepond was a sparkler. If Bernadette had learned to manipulate her way behind the scene, Littlepond was up front. He projected an all-or-nothing "Once more into the breach, dear friends" kind of forcefulness that I imagined would be effective with drugged-out kids. With me—well, perhaps if he'd showed up on time, I'd have found him charming. As it was, his cockadoodledo left me chilly. I was content to let Bernadette do the talking and the smiling for us both.

The preliminaries (where was who and who was doing what)

were long, jovial, and tedious. I imagined myself sitting opposite Luke in the motel restaurant, his face in candlelight, the lake lapping in the dark on the other side of the window. I thought about how a rare filet would taste with a California cabernet and shifted in my Scandinavian chair. *This had, better be worth it,* I warned whatever deities were listening.

Finally Bernadette came around to Roland and his death. There was a moment of silence as they tested their footing. Then Bernadette asked, "How did Roland get involved in AIM?"

Littlepond nodded, as if he had expected the question. "He just showed up. The way people did back then. Like any movement, AIM was fluid at the edges. We had a lot of white kids dropping in and out."

"And Roland was one of them?"

Now the jolliness was gone. "He said he was one-quarter Cree."

Roland's bloodline hung stiffly between them, like a piece of frozen laundry. Littlepond moved on past it, his voice measured like a politician going on the record. "He latched onto me at a demonstration in Boston. Thanksgiving Day. Mayflower II, the media called it. That would have been in 1970. I'd brought a group of people east for it and Roland was hanging around flashing press credentials for some underground rag. Venable, he called himself then. I'm pretty sure that was it. Roland Venable. Next time I saw him was at Wounded Knee, and he was Redhawk. Said Crow Dog had given him the name at a sun dance." He met Bernadette's gaze. "Crow Dog never gave him no name."

"Hmm," Bernadette responded sympathetically.

"The guy was a joke."

"I heard he was your right-hand man."

"Roland was *nothing!*" Littlepond burst out angrily. "He was like a woman, worse than a woman," he amended with a glance at both of us. "I used to send him out for my coffee. He was a gofer. He never attended any important strategy meetings. We *used* him, man. We used him to get food and medicine into Wounded Knee, used him to feed the FBI a bunch of bullshit. He didn't give away nothing on us. Not even close!"

"You knew he was working for the FBI?" Bernadette asked.

"Didn't take no rocket scientist. He kept fucking up, couldn't keep his little game together. He had one set of lies for us and one set for the feds. He couldn't very well tell them all he did was keep us in beer. He had to justify his salary," Littlepond argued. Then he shrugged. "Right from the beginning, there was talk about him, people were suspicious."

"Because he dyed his hair?" I wondered.

He turned and looked at me in surprise, as if he'd forgotten I was there. Then he turned back to Bernadette. "Roland wouldn't come to sweats," he told her, as if that settled it. He stood up, towering over us in the neat white cubicle. "I've got to run," he announced. Bernadette, small and plump, came around from behind her desk. We shook hands all around. Everything was jolly again.

"By the way," Bernadette asked him as he stepped into the hallway, "any idea who the girl was?"

Littlepond stopped and frowned. "The girl?"

"The girl who killed Roland."

He shook his large head. "No," he said gravely. "Can't help you there."

"You've seen the picture of her?" Bernadette persisted.

"Oh, yeah. Hard to miss it."

I took a breath and jumped in. "I don't think she'd seen him before," I told Littlepond. "She came out of the woods asking for Roland Redhawk. She asked him, too, like she was double-checking. She marched over to him and said 'You're Roland Redhawk?' I thought she was some kind of wilderness cop. She sounded as if she were going to give him a ticket. Then she shot him. With two arrows."

Littlepond listened politely. No doubt he'd heard worse stories. "Makes you think someone hired her," I concluded lamely.

"Could be."

"There's a rumor going around that Bernadette's behind it." Suddenly I wanted him to jump in and rescue her. Maybe I was being childish. Maybe it was something he projected—the magnetism of a man who saves children.

Littlepond sized up Bernadette. "That right?" he asked, amused.

"Development's a pretty touchy issue around here," she said wryly. "Heard the planners up in Flathead County have started wearing bullet-proof vests. Some of the rugged individualists up there don't much care for their plan." She gave a cavalier little shrug. "If you can't stand the heat."

"Yeah." He gave her a comradely smile of approval. "Real good to see you again."

"Thanks for stopping by," Bernadette told him.

BERNADETTE SETTLED back behind her desk as if the night's work was still ahead. I was tired and hungry, too restless to sit down. "What was that about sweats?" I asked Bernadette. "Roland was worried his black hair would run?"

Behind her round glasses, her eyes were thoughtful. "They say you can't lie in a sweat ceremony, that the sweat lodge brings out the truth."

I paced the ten feet of carpet in front of her desk. "Something doesn't jibe," I complained. "Something's not right. Roland wasn't a complete dodo—not the way Littlepond made him out: *Worse than a woman.*"

She raised a humorous eyebrow. "Buster's old-fashioned."

"Charitably put. What I mean is, Roland didn't come across as a clown. At least, not to me. Underneath all the sucking up he did on our trip, there was this edge of intelligence."

Bernadette nodded. "You're right. Roland was no dummy." She took off her glasses and massaged the bridge of her nose. "He must have embarrassed Buster. From all I've heard, the big shots in AIM were pretty heavily into power games. Roland must have taken Buster down a couple of pegs."

"How do you mean?"

"If your gofer turns out to be a FBI plant, who's the dummy?" She replaced her glasses. "Well," she said briskly, "if nothing else, we got a name."

"Roland Venable."

"Venable," she repeated.

"Know any Venables?"

"Nope. Not a name from around here. But I'll ask around." She flicked on her computer. The screen glowed blue, a dismissal.

ELEVEN

I MADE IT BACK to the motel by eight-thirty and bumped into Luke in the parking lot. He and Webb Chapman were on their way out, a meeting with Search and Rescue. Hurriedly, I gave them Roland's 1970 nom de guerre. They both brightened. "Hot dog!" Luke exclaimed.

"Don't get too thrilled. It may be another alias."

"It's a lead," Webb said gratefully. "Do you know how many files the FBI has on Wounded Knee?"

"How many?"

"Three hundred and fifteen thousand. And some of them are hundreds of pages long. Can you believe it?"

"We got the GSR on Herron's jacket," Luke said. "It was negative."

"GSR? Sorry guys, you're going to have to spell it out. This time of night, my brain's got sand in all the cracks."

"I doubt that," Webb said gallantly.

"Gunshot residue," Luke said. "The lab found no powder around the entry wound. Which means your friend Roland Redhawk a.k.a. Venable wasn't struggling for the gun with Herron when it went off. If they'd been wrestling over it like Roland told you, there should have been powder on Herron's jacket. Herron was shot from a distance."

"Probably more than six feet," Webb said.

Despite all the suspicions I'd entertained about Roland, the news still shocked me. "But why?" I protested in a near-wail. "Why did Roland kill him?"

They shrugged my question away. "Most people don't need a big reason," Webb observed.

"Maybe we'll find something more when we get up there," Luke said. He didn't sound particularly hopeful. Then he perked up. "Have a look at this!" He latched onto my arm and walked me down the row of parked cars.

"We're running behind, ol' buddy," Webb warned.

"Won't be a minute." He stopped in front of a Mercedes. "Look."

I looked. A dark Mercedes sedan. The floodlights overhead washed away its color—it might have been burgundy or dark green, or blue black. Montana plates. The mud on the fenders was pale. No visible dents or scrapes. No ominous dark splashes or smears.

Webb joined us. He and Luke watched me with interest. "What?" I demanded.

"Keep looking," Luke urged.

My stomach growled. "Would you mind telling me what I'm supposed to be looking at?"

He reached out and touched the insignia on the hood. "This look familiar?"

Three spokes inside a circle. "The mark on the jacket," I said slowly. "Only upside down."

"You got it."

"It doesn't make sense," I objected.

"You got it," Webb echoed wearily.

I walked back with them to their car. For the second time that evening, I said to Luke, "See you later, then?"

"This shouldn't take too long," he said. "I'll stop by your room when we get back."

We both sounded perfectly casual. Webb wasn't fooled. He grinned knowingly at us. I went into the lobby puzzling over the satisfaction on his face. Was it a male smirk as in Welcome-to-the Cheating-Club, pardner? Or *(Go ahead, Squires, clutch at every passing straw)* did I detect a hint of relief in his grin? Did Webb disapprove of La Barb?

Talk about cheating hearts. The woman needed a transplant, not family counseling.

Yes, and now talk about casting the first stone. I pocketed my deadly little rock of judgment and stopped at the front desk to rent a VCR. When I gave the clerk my room number, he looked up. "Are you Lee Squires?"

"Yes?"

"Your friends have been looking for you," he said. "They said they'd be in the bar."

"Friends?"

"They said they were your friends." A man carrying a salesman's sample case walked up to the counter. "Checking in, sir?" asked the clerk.

THE BAR WAS Sunday-night slow, only a sprinkling of business travelers quietly sipping beer. Gwen Mears and Mary Ann Dellarobbia were the only women in the bar. They sat at a corner table with a bottle of bubbly in a bucket beside them. Both were wearing black tops with their jeans: Mary Ann's was a snug knit that made her heavy breasts look like water balloons; Gwen wore a velvety chenille tunic with a Renaissance look. She had unbraided her auburn hair and it fanned over her back like a crinkled cape. I noticed she also had changed the pearl in her nose to a ruby. Mary Ann, for her part, had moussed her short curls off her face and applied green wings of paint to her eyes. Sitting there dressed up, they projected a glossy, slightly sinister look, like a pair of witchy black birds flown in from a foreign city. I joined the coven. "What's the occasion?" I wondered.

"We're outta here," Mary Ann announced. She hefted the champagne bottle out of the bucket. "Have some. Hey, Tommy," she called to the bartender more loudly than necessary, "bring us another one of these fucking sherbet glasses, will ya?" The beer drinkers stared from their stools. Somehow I had the feeling we were not going to have to fend off any of them from our table.

"Thanks, but I think I'll stick to bourbon," I told the girls. I ordered a Jack Daniel's from "Tommy," an impassive-faced kid with circles under his eyes. "You got anything like peanuts?" I asked him.

"You want peanuts?"

"Please," I said meekly. I turned back to Gwen and Mary Ann. "So you're leaving?"

"Tomorrow morning," Gwen said.

"We're wasting our time hanging around this dump," Mary Ann said. She flicked the dinky bowl of her motel-issue champagne glass.

I smiled. "You were expecting a Baccarat flute?"

"With a hundred-dollar bottle of fizz?" she challenged. "Yeah."

My bourbon came and a bowl of peanuts. I signed the chit and we raised our glasses. "Mud in your eye," Mary Ann said.

"Salut," Gwen said. Then she added sarcastically, "To Lost Pipe Lake. You heard the cops won't let us have our film back?

"Yeah. Frustrating," I commiserated. "What are you going to do?"

"There's nothing we *can* do. The cops won't give an inch, and neither will your friend Dolores."

"Dolores? What has she got to do with it?"

Gwen snorted. "Look, we contracted with her and Pete to get footage up at the lake. We paid up front. She owes us."

I took a large swallow of bourbon. "What, you want your money back? It wasn't their fault that your film turned out to be evidence."

"It wouldn't be evidence if Pete hadn't been negligent," Gwen argued. "He never should have let Herron bring that gun along. There's no excuse for it. After all, Pete's the one who was supposed to be in charge. It was his show. Now two people are dead, and we've lost our best footage. At the very least, I think they have an obligation to get us back up there. After all, it's free advertising for them. You'd think they'd realize that we're doing them a big favor. A humongous favor, in fact. I mean, when this flick airs, we're talking national exposure."

"Forget it," Mary Ann snapped. "Fuck the llamas. We don't need them. We got enough angles to play with. What we're short on is *time*."

"Dolores doesn't seem to understand the word 'deadline,'" Gwen informed me. "I told her it didn't have to be Lost Pipe Lake, it could be any lake, but she said we had to wait till Pete got back."

"He's gone hunting," I said.

"Yeah, big macho deal," Mary Ann said. "He's gone hunting and the little woman doesn't know when he'll be back. Little woman, my ass. Like, forget it!"

Gwen closed her eyes and let out a resigned sigh. The ruby in her nose caught the light darkly, like a droplet of blood. She opened her eyes. "It's too bad," she said, leaning toward me over the table and lowering her voice. "It's this kind of thing that gives minority businesses a bad name. Felicity really should scratch them off her list."

They must have noticed a change in my face. "Hey," Mary Ann said, "it's got nothing to do with you. Your cooking was great. Seriously."

I drained my glass and put it down. "I think you two are the wrong people to be making a film about Indian country," I told them. I scooped up the bowl of peanuts and left.

BACK IN MY ROOM, the red light on the phone was blinking. During the usual irritating search for my half-frames, the VCR arrived. Even more irritatingly, I had no singles in my wallet. I tipped the bearer a five, found my magnifiers in my jacket pocket, and punched the message-retrieval buttons on the phone. My mother's recorded voice lilted into my ear. "Lee, dear," she said, "please call before you leave. It's important." She paused, then let out a quick sigh. "I also wanted to remind you about moonlight. Artemis reveals things by moonlight. She's not only goddess of the Hunt, she's goddess of the *Moon.*"

I let out a large groan and, with a quick jab to another button, wiped out my mother's lunacy—as it were. It was after nine-thirty. Eleven-thirty back home. An hour when other people's mothers were safely asleep in their beds. My mother, however, happened to be a night owl. She often worked until three or four in the morning. There was no question in my mind that she would be awake. The problem was that I did not feel up to another long-distance psyche-to-psyche with her. On the other hand, if I neglected to call her back, no doubt she'd try again—and if Luke showed up, it might be right smack in the middle of a strategic moment.

Furthermore, I must confess that underneath my impatience with her Delphic pronouncements, there was always the unnerving little suspicion that she might actually know what she was talking about. Of course, her patients had always regarded her as a guru, and during my growing up, she had taken a lot of interfamilial teasing for it. But after my father died six years ago, she had cut back her patient load to focus on teaching. Now, on the eve of turning seventy, her own throat-cutting colleagues talked about her as if she were a candidate for therapeutic sainthood. I punched in the saint's number.

She must have been at her desk. She picked up on the first ring. "Ah, Lee," she said, her voice happy and girlish. "Perfect timing! I was just about to take a break."

"Mom, I don't have long to talk," I warned ungraciously.

"Of course." Her tone became crisper. "I wanted to remind you about—"

"Moonlight?"

"Well, that too, but this afternoon I was checking a reference in Bulfinch's *The Age of Fable,* and my eye happened to fall on a passage about the Calydonian Boar." She paused significantly.

"The who?"

"The wild boar was one of the animals sacred to Artemis. As goddess of the Hunt, she nurtured all living things. At Ephesus, the image of her torso was covered with breasts. But she was also a hunter, a killer. In Sparta, one of her names was 'Butcher.'"

"Fancy that."

"When she was angry," my mother sailed on, "she unleashed a monstrous boar." I heard the rattle of pages. "Listen: 'Its eyes shone with blood and fire, its bristles stood like threatening spears'—" She stopped and turned a page. "Ah, here we are: 'The growing corn was trampled, the vines and olive trees laid waste, the flocks and herds were driven in wild confusion'—and so on. You see? The corn? The vine? The boar destroys *everything!*" The distress in her voice was genuine.

I took a big breath. "Mom?"

"Yes?"

"What are you getting at?"

She thought about it for a long moment. Then she said, "I suppose I'm worried that you are too naïve."

I laughed in surprise. "*Naïve?* Me?"

"No?" she said, inviting correction.

But I knew her too well to fall for it. I tossed the ball back to her. "First you worry that I'm too civilized. That I'm ignoring my 'inner wilderness.' I think that's how you put it. Now you're worried that the wilderness is too dangerous. That—what, my crops will be destroyed? My stand of academic corn, perhaps? The sweet, heady wine of my verse?'' The words rolled off my tongue as sharply as cheap bourbon. ''These are *your* worries, Mom, not mine. I'm worried about loading Pete's llamas so they don't break down on the trail. I'm worried did I buy enough potatoes and are my knees going to hold up on the trail and is my middle-weight sleeping bag going to be warm enough if it snows and why didn't I put a new coat of Sno-seal on my boots.'' I paused for breath. ''Shall I go on?''

There was a silence at the other end of the line. ''Perhaps I'm projecting,'' she said humbly.

Her concession disconcerted me, as if a grand master fencer had inexplicably lowered her guard. Suddenly she sounded old and frail. I felt a small stab of alarm. ''Mom, are you all right?''

''Of course,'' she scolded, back to her old self. ''I'm fine. Just be careful, darling.''

''Don't worry. When it comes to angry pigs, I've had more experience than you think.''

She laughed her charming laugh. ''I'm not sure I find that reassuring,'' she told me.

I hung up, then remembered moonlight. What had she wanted to say about moonlight? I pushed it out of the way, found the telephone directory in the drawer of the night table, and looked up Eddie's Auto Repair. After telling his story to Rose that afternoon, the question of what Eddie had found—if anything—at Lost Pipe Lake had been worming around in my frontal lobe. None of your business, I told myself. But curiosity kept wiggling. Quickly, I dialed his number, before reason intervened.

''Eddie, it's Lee.''

''Who?''

''Lee Squires—Pete's cook? I was along with you up at Lost Pipe Lake.''

''Oh, hey there,'' he greeted me, surprised.

I hadn't planned what I was going to say. It came out in a rush. ''Listen, Eddie, I'm sorry to bother you, but could you please tell me the end of your story?''

"Excuse me?"

I backtracked. "I can't get the story about your father out of my mind. I keep wondering if you found what you were looking for up at the lake."

In the background I could hear the noise of TV cops and robbers. "I can't say I was looking for anything in particular," he said. "But I reckon I got what I needed."

"That's good."

"Yeah," he agreed.

"Did you find your father's grave?" I wondered. "If you don't mind my asking."

"No. I don't mind. Fact is, I never looked for it. What with all the goings on, there wasn't much chance even if I'd had a mind to." A TV siren wailed in the background.

"I'm taking Luke Donner back up there," I told Eddie. "He's the guy who was out there to talk to Kevin? Maybe I could look for it," I offered.

"If you like," he said politely.

I found I did. "Do you mind?"

He chuckled. "Don't make no difference to me. It's just an old grave. Can't think there'd be much to see, even if you managed to find it."

"Where do you think it is?"

"Somewhere above where we camped, I reckon. My mother said they buried them on the east side of the lake after they crossed back onto the reservation." He stopped.

I waited.

"Huh," he said.

"Yes?"

"I'd forgotten all about that," he said, intrigued by a turn of memory. "My mother said that while they were digging the grave, Coyote appeared to them. In broad daylight. She said Coyote escorted them halfway down the mountain, then vanished."

"A coyote?"

"Well, she said 'Coyote.' According to Salish legend, the Creator sent Coyote and his brother Fox to rid the world of evils." He let out a resigned sigh. "It was probably just trying to draw them away from its den," he said.

I thanked him and promised to call him when I got back. Raging Boars and Savior Coyotes. I poured myself a bourbon and ran a bath. The water was hot enough to turn my skin bright pink, but the tub was about as luxurious as a short sheet. (House sitting other people's mansions had spoiled me: the master baths invariably boasted six-foot porcelain tubs, if not two-person tiled Jacuzzi pools.) I alternately sat and lay in the steamy water and reran my encounter with Gwen and Mary Ann. How much worse had I managed to make things for Dolores and Pete with my sweet adieu? Never mind the loss of "free" advertising in their eco-film. If any publicity is good publicity, thanks to media coverage during the past week, Mission Mountain Outfitters had enough exposure for a lifetime. I was concerned, however, that the girls would sabotage Felicity's goodwill. Had I screwed up a pipeline to the East Coast "carriage trade," as Felicity had put it? Had I screwed up my own chances for a working-class ticket to the Amazon?

I got out of the tub, pulled the plug on steaming jungles popping with parrots, and dried off. I put on a new pair of cotton underpants and an old button-down shirt in blue oxford cloth that I'd ironed back in Washington. Then I settled down with a short bourbon, my bowl of dry-roasted peanuts, and The Mouse. I pushed Play on the VCR. The tape opened with an old news clip of Walt himself. He sat at his drawing board in a striped suit and told how Mickey's birth back in 1925 had been a happy accident, a last-minute doodle for a newspaper comic strip. The doodle that roared. Now, back home, the forces of historic preservation were driving around with "Kill the Mouse" bumper stickers on their Volvos.

There was a knock at the door. I pushed Stop, peeped through the eyehole, and let Luke in. Even this late in his long day, he looked jaunty. His shirt was still crisp and so were the creases in his twill trousers. The shirt looked designer-expensive: grey-and-tan tattersall on cream—a subtle compliment to the charcoal weave of his jacket.

As for me, I'd left my top three buttons undone and squirted a blast of Eternity in the gap. I felt pretty fetching.

Not fetching enough. We started a kiss, then Luke pulled back and made a face. "Peanuts?"

"You prefer Crest? You got me in the middle of supper." I gestured to the night table.

"Peanuts and bourbon?"

"Something wrong with that?"

He looked at me as if I were being difficult. Then he said ruefully, "I've been thinking about you all day."

I felt as if a valve had opened in my heart. A gentle joy slowly flooded through me. "Funny you should mention it," I said. "Me too."

SOME INDETERMINATE amount of time later, Luke's clothes were hanging tidily in the closet. (I don't know why this disconcerted me, Did I expect him to fling them wildly on the floor? I suppose I did.) Luke himself was stretched lazily on the bed beside me, and Walt was back on the VCR spouting a genial history of his empire. I found it hard to keep my eyes on the screen. In the soft lamplight, Luke's skin glowed like pale honey, but the small taut hollows at breastbone and hipbones gave his body a hungry look. Across his chest, he had only a sprinkling of coppery hairs, but on his lower abdomen, a dark stripe tapered upward from the thatch in his groin. His nakedness provoked an odd, quasi-maternal impulse: like the mother of a newborn, I wanted to inventory his parts, to inspect the miraculous modeling of his genitals, to count his fingers, memorize his toes. I reversed my position on the bed, lying stomach down, head toward his feet and the television. The skin on his feet was paler than the rest of him. Beneath the white skin, a blue vein traversed his arch. Meanwhile, on the TV screen, Disney couples waltzed to the strains of "Some Day My Prince Will Come." Snow White and her prince. Cinderella and her prince. Beauty and her prince.

This we need. I hit Fast Forward. The Mouse appeared. In black-and-white. The cartoon was called *Steamboat Willie.* Mickey, a.k.a. Willie, was a deckhand on a riverboat. There was no story line, only a tenuously connected series of sight gags: the boat's phallic funnels pumping smoke; a cow's swollen udder squirting Mickey in the face; Mickey squeezing a ducklike horn in a rendition of "Turkey in the Straw." The only menace in the cartoon was the boat's captain, a bigger-than-burly cat whose front tooth slid open like a garage door to emit a black stream of tobacco juice.

The rest of the cartoons were all in color. All were variations on a theme of Little-Guy-Wins-Out. We rewound and watched *Steamboat Willie* a second time.

"Pretty dumb," Luke observed.

"No guns," I said. "You think maybe Kevin saw a different one?"

"He may not have meant any one in particular."

"You mean he was talking generically? A common dumbness? The shooting looked like slapstick?"

"I don't know, Lee."

"Some quality of movement?" I tried. "Actually," I reflected, "that early animation is pretty nifty."

"A lot smoother than the stuff they're showing today."

"You watch Saturday-morning cartoons with Jason?"

"When I can."

Home-front reality dropped between us like a lead-weighted curtain. I got out of bed and put my shirt back on. From my backpack, I fished out the pamphlet on bow making I'd bought at Roland's trading post. I perched on the side of the bed and told him about my visit with Charlene and Bernadette. He leafed through the pamphlet, then looked up at me questioningly.

"It occurred to me that your killer didn't make her bow up at Lost Pipe Lake."

"Yeah, that much was clear."

"It was?"

"You can see it pretty good when you slow the film down."

"Well," I corrected automatically.

"What?"

Thank you, Professor. I hurried on. "If she was carrying it, someone on the reservation might remember. Especially if she was hitchhiking with it. I just wondered if you'd thought of it."

"O ye of little faith."

"Yeah, well, genius strikes again."

"Hey." He reached up for me. His eyes were earnest. "Keep on wondering. I need all the help I can get."

TWELVE

WE LOADED UP Pete's van at 6:00 a.m., in the dark. There was ice on the windshield, and the black trash bags filled with gear crackled in the cold. As I weighed the bags with my hand scale, their contents shifted and slid and the thin plastic stretched dangerously around jutting corners and hard edges. In terms of loading the llamas, a couple of kitchen sinks would have been as manageable. "You leave anything behind?" I grumbled to the technicians.

"My rape kit," the woman said briskly. Her name was Jenny Lazlo. She was wearing a mauve-colored mountain parka and peach-colored makeup. Her brown hair was big and perfect: like a Louis XIV wig, each curl was firmly articulated. On her ring finger, she wore a tiny diamond set in a thick gold band. On her feet, she wore hiking boots, immaculate enough to be virginal but, on second glance, well broken in. She was the serologist in the team. "I do anything that oozes," she cracked.

The other half of the team was an older man in a grey jacket named George Wheatley. "Wheat," they called him. He was tall and stooping, as if his spine had permanently accommodated itself to the curve between lab stool and microscope. Beneath a navy blue watch cap, his eyes were mild and sad. Luke introduced him as "Latents."

"You going to fingerprint the trees?" I wondered.

In a baritone stronger than his eyes, he said, "Actually, my specialty is footwear."

What flashed into my sleep-deprived mind, was a picture of him kneeling at the feet of a woman wearing four-inch ruby red spikes and nothing else. "Footwear?" I echoed stupidly.

"Shoe prints."

"Ah, yes." The woman vanished. Now he was kneeling with Cinderella's glass slipper in his hand. *Maybe coffee will help,* I told myself. I hefted the last two plastic bundles into the van and signaled Luke who, notebook in hand, was conferring with Webb and a deputy. Luke took a sleeping bag from the trunk of his car and tossed it on top of the load. I added another four pounds to my calculations. "That's it?" I asked them. That was it. Close to three hundred pounds of it. Courtesy of Dolores's brother Louis, the kitchen, medicine/vet chest, food and llamas would meet us at the trailhead.

We piled in the van and I pulled out of the driveway. Luke sat in front with me. On the other side of the stick shift, I could feel him relaxing, relieved to be under way at last. Less than a minute later, I turned into a McDonald's drive-through. "Sorry," I apologized. "Driver needs a fix."

I ordered coffee. They ordered coffee and four Egg McMuffins, two for each of the men.

"Make it five," Jenny changed her mind. "Last Breakfast," she joked.

"Make it six," I called into the menu board.

WE DROVE TOWARD the Missions, cutting the satiny tastes of egg and cheese with scalding coffee. No one talked. Night began to lift. Against a dark grey sky, the mountains hulked up over the windshield, as if showing their power before settling down into daytime.

"She might still be up there," Luke said. His was voice conversational, nonchalant, but the silence in the van sharpened.

"That'd be fun," I said.

"Just a possibility."

"Now he tells us," Jenny said from the backseat.

"I met with the Search people last night," Luke told us. "They say if she'd been up there, either one of the K-9 teams or their helicopters would have picked her up. They've been playing with a heat-sensing toy developed in Vietnam. They claim it got every mule deer in the Missions. They're ninety-nine percent sure she's vacated the area."

Wheat spoke up. "But you're not?"

"Well, the sheriff's investigators ran into a piece of luck. They found a bus driver up in Kalispell who recognized the suspect's picture. The driver says he let her off by the side of the highway a couple miles north of Kicking Horse Reservoir. Thinks it was on a run about two weeks ago. He remembered because she asked to be let off in the middle of nowhere. He said she was carrying a bow over her shoulder and an army rucksack."

The news surprised me. Why hadn't he mentioned it last night? "When'd you hear this?" I asked.

"This morning while you were loading up. According to the driver's statement, he asked her if she was going hunting. He said he was just trying to be friendly."

"What else is new," Jenny said skeptically.

"Apparently she got prickly, told him off. Said she'd been hunting for as long as she could remember. He thought there was something odd about her. Couldn't put his finger on it." Luke consulted his notebook—a small pocket spiral. "'Disjointed' was the word the driver used. He wondered if she was on something. Last he saw of her was in his rearview mirror. She was ducking under a fence line on the east side of the highway."

We rattled across a bridge over a canal that irrigated potato fields and began a gradual climb into forest.

"None of the bus drivers interviewed recall seeing anyone of her description last week," he said thoughtfully. "Ditto airport personnel."

"Maybe she hitchhiked out," Jenny suggested.

"Maybe she destroyed the bow," I suggested. "Mission accomplished. She'd be harder to spot without it."

"Maybe," Luke said. He paused. "But we're assuming she's still armed." It was an instruction.

"Hang on," I told them. I downshifted and took a tight uphill turn. The van chugged. I gave it more gas. Gravel slipped under the rear tires. We bumped over a culvert, and a plastic bag of gear slid into Jenny's back. "Jeez," she complained.

Luke turned sideways in his seat, talking to all three of us. "Okay," he said, "I'm going to lay out what we've got. Jenny, I know you did the blood workup, but bear with me. We're all in this together. Believe me, the only way we're going get anywhere on this case is through teamwork. So feel free to jump in with questions. The only stupid question is the one you keep to yourself.'' He glanced at me. ''Lee, that means you, too,'' he added.

''Yessir.''

He gave me a half-smile, then flipped the pages in his notebook. The briefing was chronological, starting with Herron's death at our tents and ending with Roland's on the rocks. The evidence included Herron's jacket, autopsy and ballistic reports, the filmmakers' footage of the girl. There were no surprises. Herron had been shot twice in the chest with his own gun at a distance of over six feet. Both Herron and Roland had been drunk—blood tests run almost twenty-four hours after death showed measurable amounts of alcohol. What I hadn't heard before was the data on the arrow that the girl had left in Roland's left eye.

Luke read from his notes. ''No recoverable prints. Victim's blood matches blood on arrow. Traces of deer blood.''

I jumped in with a question. ''How old was the blood?''

Jenny said, ''Inconclusive. We don't have reliable tests for the age of blood.''

''So she might have been hunting deer anytime before she killed Roland—the day before, a year before?''

''Correct.''

''The ground searchers didn't turn up any sign of butchered game,'' Luke observed. ''No fire rings, no cans, no trash. She knows what she's doing in the woods.''

''A low-impact killer,'' Jenny quipped.

Luke waited, allowing room for another question, then went on. ''The shaft of the arrow is an Easton ACC, carbon-graphite-coated aluminum. A dozen of them'll set you back about ninety bucks—more than twice the cost of plain aluminum.''

''Fast, light, and sexy,'' Jenny said. ''A competition arrow.''

''What does that mean?'' Wheat asked.

''A lot people don't like to use them for hunting,'' she explained. ''It's not only the expense. If you happen to hit bone real hard, the carbon's likely to shatter, and you'll end up with tiny splinters in your meat.''

''Both shots were bull's-eyes,'' Luke said. ''She was no beginner.''

I saw the arrow angling into Roland's left eye socket. The gold rim of his shades made a lopsided circle around the shaft. Beneath a piece of dark plastic lens, blood trickled into his hairline. "She was twenty feet away—if that," I said grimly. "She could hardly miss."

"It's a whole lot easier to miss up close and personal than from a couple hundred yards away," Luke said. "Buck fever, hunters call it. You get too close, and your nerves can go to pieces on you."

"She shot at twenty feet?" Jenny said. "Under twenty *yards* and it's all between the ears."

"You bow-hunt?" Luke asked her.

"I go out with my husband. Weird. With a high-tech arrow like that, you'd think she'd have a compound bow, not a homemade job."

"Or the other way around," Luke said. "Why didn't she make her own arrows? Cedar shaft with a flint point, something traditional. But the point she used was a steel broadhead." He glanced at his notebook. "A Satellite, Titan 125. She could have bought it and the arrow anywhere in the country."

"You check the local vendors?" Wheat asked.

"Every sports store between Columbia Falls and Missoula. No one could make her." He flipped another page in his notebook. "Fletching. The fletching was feathers. *Owl* feathers."

"Illegal," Wheat pronounced.

"What do you mean?" I asked.

"It's illegal to use the feathers of birds of prey."

"Even if you pick them up off the ground?"

"Yep. Some woman artist was arrested not too long ago for using an eagle feather in a collage. Only the Indians have license to use them."

"So what do non-Indian archers use?" I wondered. "Plastic?"

"Or turkey feathers," Jenny said.

Luke folded up his notebook and slipped it back into his breast pocket. We jolted up a section of washboard. "Not as romantic as the pinions of a raptor," I observed. "Did you know that Benjamin Franklin favored the turkey as our national bird?"

No one was interested.

"They weren't *spotted*-owl feathers, by any chance?" Jenny asked.

"Great gray owl, they think," Luke said.

"Too bad. The sooner those spotted suckers are extinct, the better."

I felt my inclination to like her folding up.

Luke turned back to Wheat. "What's the great gray's range? Wheat's a birder," he explained to me, but it was a warning to Jenny as well.

"Mostly Canada. They go up to central Alaska. Here, we're pretty much at its southern breeding limit." He thought about it. "Well, they breed down into the Sierra Nevadas, too. Doesn't exactly pinpoint your prep." He turned to Jenny. "Not like a spotted owl would," he said levelly.

In the rearview mirror, I saw Jenny staring out the window. Wheat warmed to his subject. "Owl feathers are softer than other birds," he told us. "Even the primaries, which are relatively rigid, have a soft leading edge. It's the softness that gives them silent flight."

"But I remember a noise," I objected.

"Probably the bowstring," Jenny said, rejoining the conversation.

We rode the next mile in silence. Then Luke asked, "Wheat?"

"Here."

"If you were going to look for owl feathers up here, where would you look?"

Wheat leaned forward, spoke with authority. "The great gray likes to hunt out in the open. It'll scout from the treeline, fly out over a field, then carry its kill back to the woods. So I'd look for a nice big clearing and watch it at dusk. If you can follow the owl back to its tree, you might find feathers among its pellets underneath." He paused. "Mostly, the gray eats voles," he informed us. "Not like the great horned owl. That one'll eat just about anything. Mice, gophers, rabbits, skunks, cats."

Jenny stared at him. "House cats?"

His watch cap bobbed an affirmative. "House cats, geese, herons, insects, scorpions, even," he enthused.

Jenny looked back out the window.

Luke gave me a wink.

DELORES'S BROTHER Louis was waiting for us at the end of the road with an open horse trailer full of llamas. As if straining for branches just out of reach, they stretched their necks up over the side racks and peered at us sideways with their round, dark eyes, shiny as marbles. I was glad to see them. My mother's mythic boar was lurking around the edges of my consciousness. (Had I dreamed, during what sleep I had back in the motel with Luke, about little piggy eyes burning with blood and fire?) The llamas, with their camellike heads, rabbity ears, and dainty, deerlike feet, may have looked like chimerical composites, but they were reassuringly solid. They were beasts of burden. Their raggedy wool coats smelled of straw and dust. They were aloof, nimble, and a lot more forgiving than horses and mules in the same circumstances. Despite inexpert cinching and trial-and-error loading, we didn't have to worry about getting kicked or stomped.

LOUIS, A BRIGHT and bubbly young man who was missing the top of one ear, served as the voice of experience. Under his cheery direction, everyone pitched in. By the time the sun floated up over the mountain above us, all the lab gear had been distributed and secured in the panniers. I passed out candy bars and bags of gorp. "Lunch is as-you-walk," I told Jenny and Wheat. "The boss man says no time for picnics."

"Anyone need a water bottle?" Louis asked. "If you want to tank up, there's a couple of jugs in the front of the truck. What about tents? How many do you want to take?"

"I brought my own," Jenny said.

"Give us two," Luke said. "Lee and I will take one. Wheat, you can have the other."

This surprised me. For propriety's sake, I had expected that Luke would share with Wheat. But neither Wheat nor Jenny raised an eyebrow at the arrangement. How well did they know Luke? Surely they knew he was married. Was Luke relying on some professional code of discretion? I found it hard to believe that cops gossiped less than any other group of human beings.

We secured the tents and sleeping bags on top of the panniers, then clipped rain covers over the entire load. As promised, Dolores had sent along a cast-iron Dutch oven. Louis slipped it into one of Fluffy's panniers and balanced the other with a small cooler. "Compliments of Dolores," he said. He gave me a conspiratorial wink. "In a case of emergency."

"What is it?"

"Rocky Mountain Kool-Aid."

"Any kin to Rocky Mountain oysters?"

"All the better to wash 'em down with."

"Ready?" Luke said impatiently.

"You're all set," Louis said. We shook hands and moved out—a parade of seven llamas, two forensic scientists, and one homicide investigator led by a weak-kneed cook. I missed Pete. The forest seemed ominously dark and dense. *What if I get us lost?* I worried.

A fluty little voice mocked: Just follow the yellow brick road, dear, then hang a left at the second star and go straight on till morning.

THIRTEEN

THE LANDMARKS were as elusive as Oz: the trail crossed Angus Creek farther up than I remembered; the place where Pete had cleared the deadfall off the trail turned out to be below—not above—the turnoff to the campsite Eddie that had found for us on the way down. But we didn't end up in Never-Never Land. Even without signs of previous traffic—our own and the march of officialdom—the way would have been readable. Following Pete up the side of the mountain, the path may have *felt* as steep as a goat track, but after listening to Eddie's story, I saw that, in fact, it was an old road. Its original breadth was obscured by dense shoulder-high thickets, and crisscrossing game trails had eroded its switchbacks, but generations of Salish hunters with horses and travois had once moved back and forth on it over the Missions.

Of course, we were all huffing and puffing. Unexpectedly, Luke more than the rest of us—too much paper-pumping, he quipped. There was an edge to his joking. Clearly, the realization that he didn't have enough steam to take the mountain in a single bound bothered him. It rankled that he was sweating more than Wheat the Wan Birder and Jenny, whose hair remained perfect.

"You're in good shape," I said to Jenny during one break.

"My husband and I like to still-hunt."

"Still-hunt?"

"That's where you track your game instead of sitting in a blind and waiting for it to come to you. We'll cover a lot of ground in a day."

We made good time. Just after two o'clock in the afternoon, we climbed out of the woods into the meadow above Lost Pipe Lake. Again, there was the unreal sense of having stepped into Eden—an endorphin high, perhaps. But this time around, the prospect of meadow and sky wasn't a shimmering *paradiso*. Grey clouds cast large shadows. The late asters were gone. A week of frosts had turned the ground cover red—mahogany red, crimson splashes of flame. It was as if during our absence, the blood of killings, old and new, had seeped out of the ground and was manifest in the grasses and shrubs. If this was paradise, it was Paradise Lost, that "narrow room" filled with "Natures whole wealth." Satan had flapped over its high wall and settled on the Tree of Life like a "Cormorant devising Death."

We crossed the ruddy ("rosy-hued," Milton might have said) meadow to the far side where the terrain dropped sharply down to Lost Pipe Lake. We stood there surveying the scene while the llamas chewed their cuds. In the slanting light, the lake looked jade green. I pointed out the relevant sites: our former kitchen, directly beneath us and hidden by the tops of pines; our old tent site, a narrow strip of grass and rocks on the far side of the lake's "stem"; further up, the spill of boulders, still shrouded in plastic sheeting, where Roland had died; the girl's escape route into the snag-spiked forest.

"Okay, listen up," Luke said in his take-charge mode. "Here's the drill. We unload here, suit up, and get to work. We'll do a walk-through, then I'll make assignments. Lee, you can make camp up here. I don't want you down there at all. Same goes for the llamas. We've got enough contamination as it is."

"We're going to need water," I told him.

"Yeah," he agreed. He pondered the problem. "Can you get it out of the creek?"

The spill of water out of the lake's narrow end was the beginning of Angus Creek. It tumbled sharply down the fall line over a bed of rocks and rotting logs, then looped back around through the woods to parallel the trail. We needed cooking and washing water. The llamas needed drinking water. But unless I was willing to risk breaking either one of my own or a llama's limb scrambling over wet rocks, the nearest safe access to creek water was almost a mile back down the trail. A mile down. A mile up. *Shit,* I thought. "Sure," I said. (Clearly, my Inner Bitch was out to lunch somewhere.)

Luke caught my hesitation. The man knew how to listen—no question about that. "Tell you what," he said. "Why don't you wait till we see what we've got?" He glanced over his shoulder at Carbon and Ringo. "Unless these guys need a drink now."

"They can wait," I told him.

He eyed the ground at our feet. "This is pretty level. We'll camp right here," he announced. "Better out in the open, where we can see what's coming. Set the tents up close together," he ordered. He sounded grim and manly enough for the last scene in an Alamo movie.

"Circle the wagons, huh?"

He didn't lighten up. "Let's get a move on," he instructed us sternly.

"I'll set up my own tent, thank you," Jenny informed him. "No offense," she said to me. "But if I end up with a rock under my ass, it's gonna be a rock of my own choosing."

"Fine with me." I looked at Wheat. "What about you?"

"Whatever," he said, bowing out of it.

I unsaddled the "boys" and found their picket stakes while Luke and his team sorted out their plastic bins and toolboxes, aluminum camera cases, and cardboard cartons. The llamas had packed in a movable hardware store. There were battery-powered floodlights, tripods and tape measures; Ziploc bags full of pens and markers, shoeboxes full of tape, big file boxes full of forms, little file boxes full of index cards. There were screwdrivers and hacksaws and tubes of glue and cans of spray paint. There were pill bottles, Dixie cups, coin envelopes, cellophane envelopes, brown paper bags, clear plastic bags, and a large wheel of yellow evidence tape that declared "Montana State Crime Lab" every six inches. The crime team zipped themselves into orange coveralls. The orange suits looked out of place, flags from another world. Luke and his two teammates might have just hopped off a D.C. snowplow—or clanked out of a caged van. "Back in your nation's capital," I remarked, "it's the prisoners who wear orange, not the cops."

"My navy blue one's in the wash," Jenny said. She looked down at the knee-high sea of gear. "You want us to carry this down now?" she asked Luke.

"It can wait," Luke said. The bunched tips of his latex gloves protruded from a side pocket like an obscene flower. He retrieved a mini cassette recorder from his pack, flicked it on, and intoned the date, time of day, case number, and investigating officers.

"Weather, partially cloudy, light wind out of northwest quarter—" He stopped, clicked off the machine. "Air temp?" he called over to Wheat.

Wheat rumbled through a container and pulled out a thermometer. "Sixty-three degrees, Fahrenheit," he called back.

"Sixty-three degrees Fahrenheit," Luke repeated into the recorder.

I WAS TOO BUSY with my own work to watch them at theirs. My kitchen fly was cut from recycled parachute nylon: a large, brightly striped rectangle that Pete had salvaged from a sky diver. Usually we simply stretched it out between a convenient pair of trees. Setting it up in open meadow meant hunting up some pole-size saplings, chopping them down, and rigging up a makeshift frame—definitely higher impact than camping in the trees but it wasn't the eco-police I was aiming to please. The llamas folded up their legs, sank down into whortleberry and bear grass, and watched me come and go. Seven heads on long necks swiveled noiselessly above the meadow like synchronized periscopes. When the investigation team came back up from the lake at four o'clock, two tents and the kitchen fly were up, Dolores's elk stroganoff was defrosting on a "countertop" stump I'd rolled out of the woods, and a pot of coffee was waiting on the propane stove. I passed around a box of gingersnaps with the coffee—plain old store-bought gingersnaps. But high up in an alpine meadow on an autumn afternoon, the combo of ginger, molasses, and coffee had an ambrosial tang. We stood in a semicircle passing the box back and forth, drinking coffee out of black enamelware cups. Within five minutes, the cookies were gone—a two-day supply, I figured.

"I'd better get my tent set up." Jenny drained her cup, then scanned the kitchen. "Where's your sink?"

I pointed to a red plastic basin. "What about water?" I reminded Luke. "I used the last of what we carried up here for the coffee. If you want me to get it out of the creek, I'd better get cracking. It's a bit of a hike."

"Right," he said. His eyes were preoccupied, but his jaw had relaxed out of its military set. "You can use lake water if you'd rather. Just stay on this side."

Wheat put his empty cup in the basin. "Good coffee," he complimented me. Then he took off his steel-rimmed glasses and blinked. "In your statement?" he asked.

"Yes?"

"You said the girl was wearing sneakers."

"Right. Red low-tops. They were pretty shot. They looked like something out of a Goodwill bin."

"An old-style tennis shoe?"

"Yeah, like Keds."

His round, genial face wore a frown. He put his glasses back on and consulted a notebook. Then he looked down at my boots. "You were wearing those?"

"Yes. Mary Ann was wearing Tevas with socks, and Gwen was wearing lightweight boots, the new nylon kind. Pete's boots were heavy-duty leather."

"Timberlines," Wheat supplied. "And Kevin Herron was wearing Nikes."

I stared at him. "Kevin? Kevin wasn't anywhere near Roland. At least not after breakfast. After the shooting, Felicity and Eddie kept him with the llamas. Pete was the only one over there with us—until the cavalry arrived." I let out a blast of exasperation. "I've only gone over this maybe three dozen times."

Luke was listening with interest. "What is it?" he asked Wheat.

"The only athletic-shoe prints I saw were the boy's Nikes. And those I did see were in the vicinity of the campsite, not at the site where Redhawk was shot."

Luke raised his eyebrows. "No sneaker prints under the plastic?"

"None that I could see. I haven't identified all the boot prints. That's going to take some doing, what with all the traffic. There's one that looks like it might be interesting. A boot toe. But no old tennis-shoe prints."

"She was wearing sneakers," I protested. "She was wearing red sneakers, tennis shoes, whatever you call them. One of them—the right one—was tied with brown shoelaces."

Wheat looked at Luke.

"It had a fat drop of blood on it," I insisted. "From the arrow she'd yanked out of Roland's chest. There was a big drop of blood on the toe. I remember, because it looked so dark on the red canvas." I pulled back the image. "It was on her right foot. I can *see* it!"

Wheat said to Luke, "What about the film? You got her on tape. Are her feet in it?"

Luke perked up. "Wheat, you just earned your keep. I'll get Webb to check it out."

I felt a chill of panic. "Wait a sec," I said. "I don't get it. She didn't fly in and out. How come there are no sneaker prints? God Almighty, I *saw* her sneakers!"

Their eyes were sympathetic. The afternoon wind lifted wisps of Wheat's pale hair. Luke's hair, dark auburn, didn't ruffle. Though it was definitely receding, the body of it was still as thick as a teenager's. (To my albeit-besotted eye, Luke's prematurely balding brow gave him an aura of nobility; I was reminded of a bust of Caesar.) "I saw sneakers," I repeated to the noble brow. "You think I was hallucinating?"

"Call it your poetic imagination at work." He wasn't being glib. His manner was earnest, considerate. "You were in a state of shock. In circumstances like that, eyewitnesses often give conflicting accounts. That's why we collect physical evidence. That's why we're up here doing a reconstruction." He turned to Wheat. "I'll see if I can raise Webb."

LUKE EXCAVATED his phone and walked away from camp, out into the meadow, to make his call. Jenny and Wheat and I repacked the lab hardware in panniers, resaddled and reloaded the llamas, and led them down to our old kitchen site in the pines at the edge of the lake. Jenny and Wheat organized their equipment into a supply depot while I filled our water jugs. Then I led the llamas to the water. They stepped daintily around mossy rocks, stirring up underwater puffs of silt. One or two ventured a few polite sips. Jake just stood there, nose up, snooty as an English butler. "Suck it up, pal," I told him. "Cool, muddy water. Yum."

I checked out huckleberry bushes at the water's edge. Birds

and animals had scarfed up all the ripe berries. The few remaining were lavender red and left sharp spots of sourness on the tongue. I thought about red sneakers. I wasn't quite able to concede to Wheat's expertise. It was not that I took particular pride in my memory (all those suddenly evaporating names, those disappearing keys and glasses). But the notion that I had manufactured a false memory shocked me. If, in fact, the killer had not been wearing sneakers, what mechanism of the mind had betrayed me? Perhaps my memory had, quite literally, taken poetic license. In her autobiography, Doris Lessing writes that memory is a careless, lazy organ. We make up our own pasts, she notes, from old photographs, from parental stories that begin "When you were a baby..." But what had triggered the fiction of bag-lady red sneakers? What "old photograph" had my memory used for its lie? Or was the deception entirely meaningless, a stress-induced pastiche of random firings in the brain?

I picked enough berries to cover the palm of my hand and offered them to Wheat and Jenny. Wheat looked at me with sad eyes. "This is not a bribe," I informed him.

"I'm not supposed to eat berries."

"Please don't tell us why," Jenny said. "Here," she said to me. I funneled the trickle of berries into her hand. She tossed them into her mouth all at once, then screwed up her face. "Wow, that really puckers you up." She turned to Wheat. "I'm ready, babe!" She made loud, lewd smacks in his direction. Wheat allowed himself a mature smile.

"Wheat?" I asked.

"Yes?"

"You're sure about the sneakers?"

"Yes," he said.

Luke came trotting down the path. He had reached Webb on the cellular phone, loud and clear. Webb would have a look at the film. Luke would check back after supper. He caught his breath and noticed the lineup of boxes and bins and bags. "Great," he approved. "We've still got an hour of daylight. Let's get back over there."

I herded the llamas back up to the meadow, pumped our drinking water through Pete's filter, and chopped up a pair of green apples and half my cabbage for a slaw. I made a dressing of peanut oil and balsamic vinegar, then zinged it up with soy sauce, brown sugar, and a healthy shake of cayenne. Maybe my supper was going to *look* as bland as a hospital meal—beige stroganoff, tan rice, beige slaw—but it didn't have to *taste* beige.

They hiked back up from the lake in the dusk. A pinkish light caught the tops of clouds and deepened the meadow to purple. Luke was in an expansive mood. They had completed mapping and "triangulation" of the site where Roland had been killed. They could start collecting blood and boot prints first thing in the morning.

"How do you collect boot prints?" I asked.

"First we photograph them. Then we cast them," Wheat said.

"In plaster?"

"With dental stone. It's lighter and stronger than plaster of paris and you get finer detail. Then we identify them."

"How? You memorize all the makes?"

He smiled. "I know a few. There are tens of thousands of athletic-shoe styles. A lot of them are referenced in the FBI's footwear collection. Most manufacturers submit their designs every year—but they'll hold back new lines of athletic shoes. The competition's pretty fierce in that area. Athletic shoes and resoles. Those are tricky ones." He zipped himself out of his orange suit, found his binoculars in his pack, and ambled out of camp to scan the evening sky for owls.

Luke ducked under the kitchen fly to fill his water bottle and emerged with the last-minute cooler Dolores had sent with her brother Louis. I'd forgotten about it. "Look what I found." Luke was beaming. He held up a beaded six-pack of Coors. "Want one?" he asked me. "Or you gonna keep sucking on that flask of yours?"

"Watch yourself, boy. You had a pull or two on it yourself last night."

Jenny drawled, "Well, while you two are making up your minds, pass me one."

Luke gave her a beer, then cracked one open for himself. I decided to wait. Jenny asked for hot water to wash up. I heated up a pot on the propane stove, and she carried it off with her beer for private preprandial ablutions. Luke put his arms around me and gave me a deep, beery kiss.

We came up for air. "Was that a moan, ma'am?"

"Naw," I said. "Just the earth moving."

I NEED NOT HAVE worried about the paleness of dinner. It was too dark to see it by the time I dished it up. We sat cross-legged on a ground cloth around a lantern, our plates eclipsed by the shadows of our heads. A curious fact of camp cuisine: taste tends to evaporate from food one can't see. Despite the perks in my salad dressing, despite the rich complexities of Pete's elk, what came through in the dark was mainly texture and temperature: the cool crunch of the slaw, the hot creaminess of the stew, the chewy grains of rice.

I had not gotten around to building a campfire and the night air was chilly enough for wool hats, but the food didn't last long enough to get cold. Making like Cookie Monster that afternoon hadn't spoiled anyone's appetite. "What's for dessert?" Luke asked after his third helping of stroganoff.

"Finish up the slaw," I suggested.

"For dessert?"

"It's not green. It won't kill you."

"You guys eat like you got two backsides," Jenny scolded.

I put on another pot of coffee and passed around a jumbo-size Hershey's chocolate-with-almonds bar.

Luke went off to phone Webb again. Wheat and Jenny helped me wash the dishes. Eco-purists scrub dishes with pine cones. We used nylon scrubbers and biodegradable soap. Eco-extremists advocate recycling the dirty water by filtering and drinking it. We had more sense. We dug a sump hole and filtered the dishwater into Mother Earth.

We carried the food boxes over to the woods and roped them up into the trees. The beer we left on the ground in its cooler. I found my flask and, for the labors of the day, awarded myself a healthy slug in my tin cup. I didn't add water. Like old-time cowboys say: Never dilute good whiskey with water unless you're out of good whiskey.

Luke came back from his talk with Webb with more info about

Roland. There was nothing wrong with Buster Littlepond's memory. Roland had, in fact, been Venable before taking on the name "Redhawk." He had grown up in Chicago, where his father ran a neighborhood grocery store and his mother worked night shifts as an aide in a nursing home. Both parents were second-generation Polish—the original family name had *z*'s and *c*'s and *w*'s crashing up against each other, cushioned only by occasional *y*'s. Venable was an adaptation for the New World.

There were five children in the family. Roland was the oldest boy. His youth was what social workers call "troubled." He repeatedly had been expelled from parochial school: fighting, possession of marijuana, possession of a knife, drunk in class. At fourteen he dropped out of school, was picked up on a robbery charge, and spent six months in a juvenile "home." At eighteen, he did time for holding up a liquor store. In jail, he snitched on inmates. He got out on parole, hooked up with the American Indian Movement in Minneapolis, and shortly thereafter was recruited by the FBI as an informer.

"He used to go around to the churches raising money for the Indians," Luke told us. "But the money never made it into the AIM treasury. No one knows how much he got away with. Webb says he boasted to the FBI that he 'diverted' over a hundred thou out of the movement."

"Whew," Jenny commented. "I'm surprised AIM didn't come after his scalp."

"Maybe they did," Wheat said.

In the darkness, you could almost hear the wheels in our brains turning. "You mean the girl?" I asked out loud. "You think AIM sent her?"

Wheat didn't answer. I scrolled back to my meeting with Buster Littlepond. He had seemed amused when I blurted out the rumor that Bernadette had ordered Roland's death. Had Littlepond himself ordered it?

"Why wait twenty-odd years?" I objected. "They could have found Roland. He didn't change his name again. He wasn't exactly in hiding all that time."

Luke acknowledged my point with a small grunt. "From what I understand," he said slowly, "like a lot of radical groups, the

AIM organizers were pretty sloppy about money. Petty cash disappeared all the time. It would have been easy enough for Redhawk to milk the movement. But my feeling is this isn't about money. For all practical purposes, AIM's defunct. Killing off Redhawk now isn't going to bring back whatever AIM money he stole back then. As it is now, no one stands to benefit financially from his death. He and his wife don't own anything. After the death of their last child, they turned their trading post and their museum over to the Flathead tribes. Ditto their home."

"You think he used AIM money to set up his business?"

"It's possible."

"Actually," I mused aloud, "he came a long way: delinquent to philanthropist."

Jenny said, "Hey, all he needed was a little hundred-thousand-dollar boost."

"What about the movie of the girl?" Wheat asked. "Did Webb have a look at the tape?"

"Oh yeah. He says you can see her feet for a second or two before Mary Ann zoomed into her face. Looks like boots—or some kind of high-top. Dark, maybe black—soles and uppers same color. There's no detail. She was running and the focus is blurred." Luke yawned. "Excuse me." He turned to me. "I asked him if she could have been wearing red sneakers. He said, 'No way.' " Luke yawned again. "Sorry folks, I've got to turn in. See you in the morning."

It was only eight o'clock. I sat up maybe half an hour longer with Jenny and Wheat. Jenny had left a baby girl at home with her husband, an out-of-work logger. The baby's name was Dawn.

"How old is she?" I asked.

"Two-and-a-half," Jenny said proudly. "And into *everything*. She's a regular pistol!"

I remembered my daughter, Rachel, at that age, round and pink and laughing.

"You got kids?" Jenny asked me.

It was always a dilemma: to "share" or not to "share" Rachel's death with passing strangers. For a couple of years afterward, I told the story of her cancer compulsively. The discomfort on people's faces had been oddly satisfying. Now, however, I needed to be fairly drunk before it came out. Maybe that was progress. "No kids," I told Jenny. "One ex-spouse."

"What about you, Wheat?" Jenny persisted.

"My wife and I have two sons."

"That's nice," she said brightly, making the effort. "How old are they?"

"Old enough to know better," he said curtly. The disapproval in his voice shut us up. I felt a squirt of old anger: *Your sons are alive!* I wanted to cry out. Overhead, rents in the clouds revealed cold patches of stars. Without a campfire to cast a circle around us, the night seemed limitless. It reached out behind our backs, swallowed up the mountains, and kept on going.

FOURTEEN

I WOKE UP sweating in the prison of my mummy bag. I worked my arm up, pulled down the zipper, and let in an blast of icy air. The inside of the tent was suffused with a pale light that erased all color—the silky lumps of our sleeping bags were charcoal, the wall of the tent was oyster grey. I worked my arm up out of the bag and squinted at my watch. Ten past midnight. The chiaroscuro was moonlight, not morning. I debated the pros and cons of getting up to pee and drowsed off. The rip of a nylon zipper woke me again. It wasn't Luke—he lay as still as a stone. It was Jenny next door. The moon was still up and I could see her silhouetted on the side of our tent as she stood up. She shivered, drew her jacket around her, and bustled off. A few minutes later, she hurried back, passing closer this time. Her shadow was sharper than before. Her step was jerky, a walk-hop, as if she were barefoot and picking her way between clumps of the icy grass.

Then it hit me.

Sort of like a cartoon. An old one in black-and-white.

Forget the Mouse. Kevin had been describing silhouettes! Shadows moving across the backlit screen of his tent. What he had seen was a shadow play featuring the death of his father. The realization felt less like a flash in the brain than a punch in the solar plexus. It took the breath out of me in one loud gasp. Luke didn't stir. I rolled over a quarter-turn and shook him awake. "What's the matter?" he said quietly, his voice surprisingly clear of sleep.

I explained in whispers, then unzipped my bag, unzipped the tent, and crawled outside in Polypro underwear and frozen boots to demonstrate.

"Move closer," Luke said from inside the tent.

I took a step closer.

"Closer."

I took another step.

"Damn," Luke muttered appreciatively.

A complaint from Jenny pierced the moonlit wall of her tent: "Whatever game you two are playing, would you mind wrapping it up? Some of us around here have to work in the morning."

I clumped off to relieve my bladder, then crawled back into the tent, back into the slick coolness of my bag. Luke rolled over against me. "Kevin must have seen Roland outside his tent," he murmured into my ear. "Roland woke the boy up getting the gun, then shot Charlie from beside the tent. Unzip," he whispered.

"There's not enough room," I whispered back.

"Open up. In the name of the law." His hand worked its way into my bag, tugged at my waistband.

I giggled. "You don't have a warrant."

"Shh," he said.

I unzipped. "This is going to be tricky," I warned.

"Mmm," he agreed and with a raucous rustling of dark nylon we wrestled our knees and elbows into a single cocoon.

I WAS THE FIRST ONE up in the morning. Some time before dawn, a silent snow had fallen, no more than a couple inches. Like a threadbare blanket, it lay raggedly over the meadow, red shrubs and ocher grasses poking through. Small frozen lumps of it clung to the llamas' raggedy backs—the way little ice balls cling to woolen mittens. I moved the llama's picket line to a fresh grazing area and scattered their piles of droppings. (As it happens, kicking shit is a more satisfying occupation than the colloquialism suggests.) Then I went down to the lake to wash. The sun had not yet risen, but pale golden clouds were perfectly reflected in the dark, glassy water. The lake looked magical. It was easy to imagine an arm clothed in white samite slowly breaking the surface to reclaim the sword Excalibur after the fall of Camelot. "For now I see that true old times are dead," the bold Sir Bedivere had mourned, "When every morning brought a noble chance / And every chance brought out a noble knight."

But I wasn't feeling mournful. Perhaps it was the clean sharpness of the air. Or maybe the way Luke had held me in the night, as if I were precious to him.

Precious till the party's over. You know the ground rules: A good time is had by all; no sniveling when he leaves you at your door.

Still, squatting in a patch of snow-dusted elk sedge, splashing myself with icy water, the future seemed remote. Lost Pipe Lake had become new and secret again, uncharted country. If a mystic arm seemed possible, it was also easy to believe that noble chances hadn't gone down the tubes with King Arthur.

I picked enough huckleberries for breakfast pancakes, refilled our water buckets, and lugged them back up to camp. Although old-fashioned campfires are frowned upon by even temperate greenies (the fire sterilizes the soil below it, leaving a scar that discourages plant growth), if I was going to bake anything in my Dutch oven, I needed coals. We might as well enjoy the blaze at breakfast. I dug an "ecologically correct" fire pit, reserving the wide circle of sod and top soil for later replacement, then went off to find wood and retrieve our food supply from the trees.

As I lowered the food boxes onto the ground, I noticed that our beer cooler had been moved. It was several feet away from where I had left it under the tree. It was also open. I looked inside. Instead of four beers and a six-pack, there were now two beers and a six-pack. Had Wheat raided the beer box in the middle of the night? Or had he and Jenny each enjoyed a brew after I had gone to bed? Either way, no problem. So why did I feel annoyed? Was it because they had excluded me from their party? Or was I turning into a kitchen tyrant—the sort of cook who dishes out the goodies happily, but sulks when someone helps himself? When I was growing up, my best friend's mother had employed such a cook. Her name was Linda. She was as large and black as Aunt Jemima and (given the stereotype) disappointingly fierce. The family was afraid to enter "her" kitchen.

I inspected the ground around "my" beer cooler for telltale footprints. The snow was patchy under the trees, and I had already trampled away most of it in the process of lowering our pantry boxes from their nightly perch. Moreover, the carpet of wet pine needles resisted impressions. My respect for Wheat's ability went up several notches: "reading" even my own scuff marks was like trying to decipher sea-washed remnants of a message written in the sand. I found a clean patch of snow, stepped in it, and studied the mark left by my boot. The vinyl "cleats" were triangular. They lined up to make a row of four diamonds. Diamonds on the soles of my shoes. *Honey, take me dancin'.* I gave the ground around the cooler another look, admired a few of my diamonds, then knelt down and started scraping up pine-needle-threaded snow and packing it around the beer. On previous wilderness trips I'd cooked for, my clients would have sold their BMWs—never mind their souls—for a cold one at high noon.

I skimmed up the snow, widening my circle, and my eye caught a boot print that stopped the sweep of my arm. The pattern, though blurred, was composed of chevrons, not diamonds. Aha! A clue! I stood up feeling as clever as Holmes himself. I put my foot next to it and compared the two prints. It was virtually the same size as my own. Jenny must have been the culprit. Though I would have said her feet were smaller than mine, Wheat and Luke's were unmistakably bigger. Moreover, since the print had been made in snow, she had been to the cooler sometime after our respective midnight trips to the bushes. Sometime after the snow, had she downed a couple beers alone in her tent?

The way you down a nightcap alone?

Of course, she could have gotten up to pee a second time, after the snow, and left the print walking past the cooler. I moved back to the prebedtime beer-party explanation. That meant Jenny had had two beers, Luke one, and Wheat one.

Dangerous sign, Squires, counting other people's drops of alcohol.

Resolutely, I pushed the matter back into a dark closet in my mind and turned to visions of a crackling campfire, steaming coffee, and huckleberry pancakes. I would have to make two batches, one without berries for Wheat.

AT BREAKFAST, Luke was upbeat and brimming with energy. He was chafing at the bit to get down to the lake and test out our midnight hypothesis. He hoped to find the casings from Charlie Herron's gun and was willing to bet any takers they'd turn up near the site of Kevin's tent. Wheat and Jenny were bemused, like indulgent parents watching their child on Christmas morning.

"Kids tell the truth," he insisted. "We just don't listen."

Wheat, who had cut his stack of pancakes into tidy towers, swallowed a maple-soaked mouthful. It didn't sweeten him up. "Not all kids," he observed grimly.

"What?" Luke said.

"Some of them lie."

We sipped our coffee. Jenny helped herself to another berry-studded pancake. "This is the life," she said. "Catered crime scenes. Maybe you ought to go into business. Get rich quick."

"I don't think the body count's high enough. Now, D.C., it might work."

"Or L.A.," Jenny said. "Wheat's from L.A."

"Stay in Montana," Luke said, and my heart did a quick little rhumba. "If the homicides keep up like the last couple months, we can keep you busy."

Wheat loaded another tower on his fork, then paused in midair. "Crime scenes are pretty stressful," he warned me. "Not like this. You won't feel much like picnicking when you have to work around someone's dead body." Emphatically, he shoveled his forkful of pancakes into his mouth.

"She was there, Wheat," Luke reminded him. "Up-close-and-personal."

He swallowed his mouthful, then reiterated solemnly, as much to himself as to me, "There's a lot of stress in this line of work. It takes a toll."

"Where's my violin," Jenny said. "The little bitty one."

Luke wouldn't drop the ball. "You could specialize in reconstructions. 'Gourmet Reconstructions,' " he announced with a flourish.

I winced. "Sounds like something for the optional-surgery crowd. Lee's Liposuction Lunches."

"Nip-and-Tuck Catering," Jenny chimed in.

"Now *that* might fly in L.A.," I approved.

"You gonna run off and cater to a bunch of old movie stars?" Luke complained. "What about us poor hardworking cops?"

I raised an eyebrow. "Eat doughnuts."

THE TEAM SPENT the morning working down at the lake. For my part, I spent a lazy hour scrounging for more berries in the woods and picked a scant cup—not enough for a pie or cobbler, even if I counted Wheat out. I decided to atone for last night's lack of dessert with a chocolate cake. A Montana rancher friend had given me the recipe; the family's cook used to use it on cattle drives back in the fifties. It's an eggless cake which scores points with the cholesterol-challenged crowd, and because there's cocoa powder in it, I tell guests it's called Stir-Crazy Chocolate Cake. But privately, I think of it as the Three-Holer because you make three wells in the dry ingredients. Into one, you pour oil. Into another, you pour vanilla. Into the third, you pour vinegar. Then you pour two cups of cold coffee over the whole thing and stir with a fork.

By the time the campfire had died down enough for baking, I had mixed it up in the Dutch oven and sprinkled cinnamon and sugar on top. I put the lid on, set it in the fire pit, and arranged a judicious pile of coals on the lid.

That was dessert. I did the rest of lunch on the propane stove: a chowder made with trout from Pete's freezer. There was enough of the trout's delicate meat to call the dish a stew. Garnished with butter and crumbled bacon, dished out in Pete's speckled black enamelware bowls, our lunch looked like a foodie's "roughing-it" fantasy. We spooned it down with piles of saltines—but no beer. They opted for coffee. The mystery of the missing Coors would have to wait. I wasn't about to open an inquiry. As for the cake, it came out a bit dry at the edges, but earned me its usual share of points.

Luke was more subdued than he had been at breakfast. He had used tribal-police sketches and Felicity's panoramic shots to locate our old tent sites and the spot between them where Charlie's body had lain under the blue tarp. After mapping and measuring, he had laid out a grid where Kevin's tent had been, and started sifting, inch by square inch, for ejected casings. So far, he had nothing to show for his pains.

They went back to work right after lunch. I cleaned up and started a venison chili for supper. Luke had left Felicity's photos sitting on the top of one of the food boxes. I shuffled through them (it seemed a hundred years since she'd taken them, not just last week), then, out of curiosity, took them over to the edge of the meadow to match them against the scene below. Now, of course, there was no line of tents at the edge of the lake: the only spots of synthetic color were the orange suits moving back and forth. Moreover, as is often the case among amateur photographers (I speak from experience here), Felicity's snaps were considerably less dramatic than the actual scene: under the glossy finish of the panoramas, the intense blue of the sky was bleached out, the mountains looked pale and insubstantial, and grey snags staggered messily through the black-and-gold stands of pine and larch.

I looked up from the photograph. I would not have said there were so many dead trees, but there they were before me, littering the forest like piles of pick-up sticks. Had some kind of disease killed them? Whatever the cause, my eye had ignored the effect. What had registered, what I had "chosen" to see was the live trees and the blurred line of their reflection in the lake. Evidently, my eye was as "creative" as my memory. And somehow, working together, they had produced a nonexistent pair of red sneakers.

For the first time in a long time, I wanted reassurance from my mother. More often than not, I found her pronouncements irritating, if not ridiculous. But she could also be spookily on target. "Artemis sees things by moonlight," she had informed me. And, in fact, it was by moonlight that I had "seen" the meaning of Kevin's cartoon. I had to wonder what my mother would say about "Artemis" in red sneakers. I wanted to feel her cool, psychological hand on my brow, to hear her say, "You're all right," in the lightly humorous tone she used when doctoring her own children.

I reshuffled the photographs: several of llamas, a slightly tilted one of Pete, Charlie Herron shockingly alive and virile-looking. He posed ("swaggered" would not be unfair) against a backdrop of mountains. The view matched the one in front of me. Felicity must have taken it from the meadow the evening we arrived just before Charlie and Roland jogged off to jump in the lake. I studied the peaks and ridges in the picture, then glanced up at the reality. Despite last night's snowfall, the mountainside beyond the lake had less snow than it had the week before. The melt pattern

ʼas distinctive. Strips of bare rock fanned out on the slope like ıe splayed fingers on a petrogylph of a giant hand. I counted ve fingers. The one on the far left was slightly shorter than the thers—a kind of elongated thumb. I squinted, looked away, ›oked back. Now that I'd seen the "hand," it wouldn't go away.

Later that afternoon, I doused the fire with soil and hiked over › the hand. Once down from the meadow, the snowfield was idden by the treetops, and I managed to find the place as much y luck as by dead reckoning. All the topo map showed was a ıcreasing density of little elevation lines as the terrain and a trail f hyphens climbed up to a pass that crossed the reservation oundary into national forest land. It was down along this trail ıat Eddie's mother and the women in the party had fled with the odies of their men. And somewhere off the trail, perhaps near a ›yote den, the women had buried their dead in a communal rave. It could have been anywhere in the forest above Lost Pipe ake. But lacking concrete directions it's easy to latch onto mens, to follow "fingers" pointing the way.

I was not entirely sure why I wanted to find the grave. Certainly wasn't prompted by any archaeological sort of curiosity. Eddie's ory was linked in my mind to Kevin's loss—and, in some way, the loss of my daughter. I think now I was looking for a place f power, a way to bring the deaths of two strangers "to closure." ventually, Luke might come up with some answers, but I'd be ıck in Washington by then. Answers, I've noticed, tend to take nger than endings. They drift in piecemeal over the years, ıanging as we change, not always satisfying. I wanted an ending. raves can be helpful in that regard.

Below the "hand" in the snowfield, I found a wide clearing ughly semicircular in shape. Perhaps once, long ago, an ava-nche had scoured away the trees; grey rocks studded the thin il, and a jumble of dark, lichen-spotted boulders formed a nat-al retaining wall on the slope below the snow. A few alpine ruces, listing to leeward and narrow as bottle brushes, grew out cracks between the boulders. Clumps of chewed-up bear grass ıd juniper grew on the floor of the shelf.

The place was accessible from the trail: no ravine or gully

intervened. But digging a grave here would have been slow work even with picks. The women had been fearful, in a hurry to reac home. Would the party not have chosen easier ground—say, th soft loam under an old stand of pines? I hunted around for sunke ground or the remains of a burial cairn and found nothing. No did I find any old tipi rings or fire circles.

Vaguely disappointed, I climbed the wall of boulders for a loo at the "fingers." Up close, they seemed less portentous: paralle paths of bare rock that dead-ended about twenty feet up the slope The snow was about three feet deep on either side of the melte channels, but the "shoulders" had a scooped look, like the pat of a giant spoon. What had caused the strips to melt? I followe one of the paths up to its abrupt end. There was no spring seepin out of the rock. In fact, the exposed rocks were dry; my boot made wet diamonds on them.

Had bears slid down the slope, creating snow chutes? Was looking at evidence of animal play? The rock beneath the sno was dark. Snow compacted against it would be likely to melt i the sun. I felt a momentary surge of excitement. Had I discovere a grizzly playground? But there were no scuffed areas at the to of the "slides," no holes broken through the snow's crust, n paw prints.

I looked back across Lost Pipe Lake. I couldn't see our ten up in the meadow, but my red-and-white striped kitchen fly stoo out in the distance like a toy circus tent. And then, as I stoo there surveying the scenery, something shifted. It was as if telescope had been inverted. Now, instead of being the gazer, had the creepy feeling that someone was watching me. Had Luk followed me?

You wish. When the man was working, I didn't exist.

But the feeling persisted. The clearing seemed unnaturally stil Perhaps I had invaded some animal's turf. Was there a den hidde in the jumble of boulders? Slowly, nonchalantly, I climbed dow crossed the clearing, and sat down at its edge, my back again the trunk of a pine tree big enough to climb in an emergency.

If bears hadn't made the fingers, perhaps smaller animals ha The crust on the old snow might not give way under the weig of a coyote. Coyotes were more likely (if less romantic) tha wolves. Maybe coyotes had burrowed *up* the slopes, chasing field mice under the snow.

Come on out, I telegraphed mentally. *I won't hurt you.*

Nothing moved. For almost an hour, I sat there listening to my own breathing, my spine against the firm column of the tree. Coyote did not appear. Finding the old grave no longer seemed important. By the time I got up to go, the tension in my neck and shoulders had evaporated. I felt as if I had just taken a long swim.

WHILE I'D BEEN puzzling over five fingers, Luke had been puzzling over the five shots Roland had fired at Charlie Herron. That night, Pete and I and the company around the campfire had heard two shots, then three more. Two of the five slugs had been found in Charlie. But Luke had still not found any casings by Kevin's tent. Jenny and Wheat, who had completed their collecting, joined the hunt. When I took the llamas down to the lake to drink, I carried down a pot of hot coffee, but they didn't break. They sipped at it while they raked and screened an expanding grid of dirt. When the light went, they came up for supper, disgruntled and hungry.

I broke out the beer. They each took one without comment. *(Five left, and still counting.)* We ate hot corn bread and venison chili around the campfire. For a salad, I'd revived the iceberg with fresh snow collected from the cirque. I cut the head in wedges and mixed up a dressing of blue cheese, sour cream, mayonnaise, and lemon juice. Wheat passed on the dressing. Blue cheese didn't agree with him, he said. Nor, evidently, did beans. He'd picked them out of my chili and arranged them in forlorn little piles, evenly spaced around the side of his plate.

Luke ate for two, but he might have been packing in sawdust for all the delight he took in my efforts. Would my heart have quickened had he exclaimed, "How clever of you to dump a jar of salsa in your chili!" Or: "What a marvelous touch you have with a plastic lemon!" Maybe. Maybe I would have sworn undying love right there on the spot.

As it was, the detective was fixated on shell casings. "We'll find them tomorrow," he said. In the flickering firelight, his jaw had a stubborn set.

Wheat and Jenny exchanged looks. "Maybe Redhawk picked them up," Wheat suggested mildly.

"He didn't have time to hunt around for them in the dark. Eddie and Pete were on the scene almost immediately. Those empties are there," Luke insisted. "We just have to find them."

Wheat didn't reply.

"It wasn't all that dark," Jenny said. "The moon was three-quarters—bright enough to make silhouettes on the boy's tent. The brass would have glinted. He could have scooped them up."

Luke shook his head. "Not in the heat of the moment. Not as drunk as the guy was."

"He made two heart shots. That's more than lucky. If he wasn't too drunk to shoot straight, he wasn't too drunk to pick up the brass," Jenny argued.

"Then they should have turned up in his pockets," Luke snapped.

Jenny raised an eyebrow. She let out a breath. "You're the boss," she said coolly.

A polite pall fell over the team. Luke picked up a beer from the cooler and went off to chat yet another time with Webb—they'd been in almost-constant contact throughout the day. Wheat and Jenny cracked opened new beers and sipped them in silence by the fire. I started in on the dishes. Luke came back, volunteered to help. I gave him the least-wet dish towel. He plucked a plate from the rinse basin and gave it a brisk rub.

"I was thinking," I said. "After Charlie was dead?"

"Yeah?"

"It wasn't like Pete and I watched Roland every second. Pete had the gun, and Roland wasn't going anywhere. Pete and I both slept on and off till morning. Roland could have found the shells while we were snoozing. He could have gotten rid of them, tossed them somewhere later."

Luke kept polishing the plate. I could feel Wheat and Jenny listening. "It's a possibility," I insisted.

Luke gave a noncommittal little grunt and took another plate. We finished cleaning up, stowed the food back in the trees, then joined Wheat and Jenny at the fire.

Jenny promptly drained her beer and stood up, making it clea ıat while she had to work with Luke she didn't have to sit around campfire with him. "Excuse me," she announced primly. She trolled off in the direction of her tent, but in the next moment, ipped and fell. "Shit!" she exploded, rolling into a ball and ugging her left knee.

"You all right?" I asked.

"Yes, I'm all right!" she echoed angrily. "I only almost killed ıyself tripping over the fucking tent peg!"

Luke and Wheat moved to help her up. "Leave me alone, oddamnit," she told them, her voice calmer. Sullenly, she stood p, ostentatiously tested her knee, then limped to her tent and pped herself inside.

Luke threw another log on the fire, then went off to hunt up ome stones to mark the tent pegs. I took a beer from the cooler. *One to go.)* I'd been waiting all day for a taste of one, but it dn't taste as cold and wonderful as I'd hoped. I glanced around r Luke. He was kneeling by the offending tent peg, not moving. Luke?" I asked.

He didn't answer.

"What are you doing?"

He came back to the fire with a funny look on his face. "What it?" I asked.

He smiled slowly. The smile grew into a wide Cheshire-cat in. "I've got it," he announced triumphantly. He closed his es. "Thank you, Jesus," he intoned in the cadence of an evanlical preacher. He opened his eyes and grinned some more.

"You gonna share it with us?" Wheat asked.

"The mark on Herron's jacket. I knew I'd seen it before!" he owed. "It's the top of a tent stake! Look." He pulled out his tebook, drew a rectangle on a clean page. "Here's the tent." ıen he drew three little x's along each side of the rectangle. Here are the stakes. Herron was shot in the chest. He fell backard and landed on one of stakes to his own tent. The impact t a mark on the hip of his jacket. I was wrong. Kevin didn't e *Roland* silhouetted outside his tent, he saw his *dad.* Kevin oke up and saw his dad standing next to the tent. He hears the ots and sees Herron fall backward onto the ground. Given the gative GSR on the jacket, we know Roland was standing at least ten feet away—maybe more. We need to push out our grid We've been looking in the wrong place!''

''But Herron's body wasn't near their tent,'' I objected. ''I was over by the lantern where they'd been sitting.

''Roland dragged him back there,'' Luke said. ''He wanted t make it look like a fight. Which means he *definitely* didn't hav time to pick up the brass. What about Herron's tent—did yo notice any bullet holes?'' he asked me.

I thought back to the morning after Charlie Herron's death. had crawled inside his tent to pull out Kevin's sleeping bag. Late after the officials had given us the go-ahead, I had struck the ten folded it up and given it to Pete to pack on the llamas. ''I don' remember any holes,'' I told Luke. ''If they'd been there, I thin I'd have noticed.''

''Good girl,'' Luke approved as if I'd given the right answe ''Now, hand over that last beer—I deserve it!''

So he'd been counting, too.

FIFTEEN

THE NEXT MORNING was cold and clear, the grass in the meadow brittle with frost, the llamas' breaths visible, like puffs of exhaust from idling cars. I moved them to fresh ground and Luke went off with his cell-phone to renew contact with the buzzing hive of law enforcement below. He came back with a message for Jenny. "Your husband called in and said to tell you that your daughter's antibiotic is working," he told her.

She let out a sarcastic little grunt. "It oughta work, what I had to pay for it."

He held out the phone. "You wanta give him a call?"

She waved it away. "Nah, they're okay." But beneath her toughness, there was relief.

"Your daughter's sick?" I asked.

"It's nothing. Just a cold." She snorted in exasperation. "Happens every time. I pack a bag, she starts running a fever. Her timing's incredible!"

Luke refilled his coffee cup, blew across it. "As soon as we locate those empties, we'll pull out," he said. "With a little luck, you'll be home tonight."

The breakfast bacon snapped and popped in my pan. I picked up a fork and started turning the slices. "I wouldn't want to leave much later than noon," I said. "And we'll need a couple hours to pack up all the gear."

Luke glanced at his watch. "That doesn't leave a lot of the morning."

"It's not a problem," Jenny insisted.

BY ELEVEN-THIRTY, it was clear that we would be at Lost Pipe Lake for another night. Luke had found two of the casings and was determined to find the others. "Do you have enough food?" he asked. "Plenty, if you can handle veggie cuisine," I told him.

For lunch, I made a pot of leek and potato soup (a packet of instant mashed potatoes worked surprisingly well) and set out the last of the sandwich meats. Luke stacked up an inch of buffalo salami on rye, squirted on a precise spiral of Dijon mustard, and carefully aligned the top. He ate it with satisfaction, wiped his hands on a paper towel—I'd packed a roll of them for napkins—then showed me the sketch he'd made that morning. The two empties they'd found indicated that, in fact, two shots had been fired close to Herron's tent. Luke's finger indicated a side tent peg. "For Kevin to see a clear silhouette, Herron must have been standing beside the tent, not out front. The casings were here." He tapped two small x's at the front of the tent, then traced an invisible circle off its southwest corner. "Redhawk was probably standing somewhere in here. I think he shot twice, dragged Herron back to where they'd been sitting by the edge of the lake, and fired three more shots. We'll know more when we find the other casings. But it doesn't look like a mitigated homicide."

"Mitigated—what's that?"

"In Montana we have two categories of homicide," he explained, downshifting into his Teacher-of-Rookies mode. "Deliberate and mitigated. If you kill someone in self-defense, like Redhawk claimed, that's mitigated." He looked to see if I'd gotten it. I nodded, and he accelerated back to speed. "The two of them may have had words, but I'm guessing Herron walked away from it, went back toward his tent. Redhawk came after him and shot him. I doubt Herron knew he had the gun. If Redhawk had pulled Herron's own gun on him, he would have been furious. From everything I hear about the guy, he was confrontational. I can't see him beating a retreat toward his tent—not with Kevin in it. If he'd thought they were in danger, he would have put up a fight."

"You're saying Roland stole Charlie's gun and killed him in cold blood?"

"I'm saying that so far, there's no evidence to support Roland's claim of self-defense. There's nothing to indicate a struggle, nothing to indicate that Herron ever had possession of the gun."

My mind scrolled back through my conversations with Bernadette. "You could say Roland was one of my runners," she had informed me when we met at the Redhawks' trading post. "The rest is just a lot of noise." Clearly, her visit to Charlene had been an exercise in political damage control. During our self-guided tour of Roland's beadwork collection, she had taken pains to distance herself from "her runner." Roland, she had suggested, was not a "real" Indian. She had raised old dirt about his dyed hair at Wounded Knee. Later, she brought in Buster Littlepond to confirm the rumor that Roland had been an FBI spy.

Of course Roland's traitorous past didn't clear Bernadette of suspicion. But if she actually had hired Roland, wouldn't he have packed his own gun? Roland may have killed in cold blood, but the lack of his own weapon indicated a lack of advance planning.

On the other hand, Roland's own death appeared to have been planned sometime before our excursion. His killer had arrived on the reservation by bus, had looked for him at his trading post, and then had followed us up to Lost Pipe Lake with her bow. Her aim, according to Jenny, had been extraordinarily steady. Moreover, she knew what she was doing in the woods: she had escaped into the wilderness, managing to evade hundreds of searchers, dogs, and choppers equipped with infrared devices. What had drawn her to Roland? Did the long arc of her violence intersect the shorter line of Charlie Herron's murder? I felt as if I were trying to solve a geometry problem on an exam I hadn't studied for.

AFTER LUNCH, the team went back to their excavations. I replenished our supplies of water and firewood, filled my water bottle and zipped it into my backpack, along with my topo map and the steno pad I was using as a "daybook." As an afterthought, I tossed in the plastic refrigerator container that held the last wedge of yesterday's Stir-Crazy cake. I checked the llamas' pickets, then left them chewing cud in the meadow. I hiked down around the lake, giving Luke's operation a wide berth, and picked up the old track on the other side.

Yesterday's "hand" still beckoned—though now, due to more melting, the "thumb" had elongated so that the exposed stripes of rock resembled a sunburst more than a hand. The images tugged at me: an accidental sun, an open hand. I felt the prickling of resonance, the possibility of a poem. Like live notes from a piano floating out a window above a busy city street, the tune was unrecognizable, but evocative. I wanted to go back to my tree with paper and pencil and listen. Perhaps this time, I'd come away with some small gift. If nothing else, an afternoon of scribbling would provide a reassuring distraction from the frustrating geometry of the killings.

This time I found the shelf without difficulty. I slipped my pack off my shoulders, took a long drink of water, then left the pack by a boulder and climbed up for another look at the mysterious troughs in the snow. Along their sides, the snow had receded farther, leaving brittle edges of ice cantilevered over the rocky paths. The "thumb" path had definitely grown longer overnight. The uppermost rocks were still outlined with thin rims of snow; their exposed surfaces glinted wetly in the sunlight. I squinted in the brightness. My own shadow on the snow was sharp as winter. I was struck again by the stillness of the place. Back at home, the woods of Rock Creek Park rustled and whispered like a leafy sea. But here, high in the Missions, there were no deciduous leaves to catch the wind, no racket of squirrels and crows. I was not used to silence, I realized. I kept waiting to catch a distant drift of highway traffic, or the rise and fall of voices from the lake, or even the witchy shriek of a red-tailed hawk. But there was only rocks and bright air. Perhaps it was this high stillness, this absence of background noise, that encouraged a feeling of trespass. After my hour there yesterday, the details of the place—the textures of rock, the browning stalks of ferns—had become familiar; nonetheless, I still felt like an intruder who, having stumbled into a room, stops all conversation.

As yesterday, however, I found no animal's tracks, no scat—only my own footprints, old and new, stamped in the snow at the base of my "hand." Then, in a rim of shadow cast by a boulder, another print caught my eye. For several long moments, I stared at it blankly, not able to comprehend what I was seeing. I was looking at a boot print. A full boot print, close to the size of my own. It was studded with chevrons. It looked remarkably like the print I had found by our beer cooler that morning.

I squatted down beside it and measured its length using the span of my hand. My reach, I knew, was eight-and-a-half inches. The print was a good inch longer. I browsed around for more and found none. I retrieved my steno book from my pack and sketched the pattern of chevrons. I felt as if I were moving very slowly. I slipped the notebook back in my pack. My mouth felt dry. I unscrewed the lid of my water bottle and took a couple swallows. Then I remembered my cake.

I took out the container and considered it as if seeing it for the first time. It was an old one, the scarred plastic opaque, the color the old snow. The lid fit tightly enough to be "childproof." I pried it off and looked at the chocolate cake. The crumbs on the outside were dry, but its sugar-crusted top still yielded softly under my forefinger. I sucked back my own saliva, resealed the cake, and carried the box out to the middle of the clearing. I set it down on a flat rock. The gesture felt vaguely familiar. As a child, had I left offerings on rocks for "the fairies"? I had no actual memory of doing so. Perhaps it was something from a storybook, part of a tale my mother had read to me—or I had read to Rachel. I slipped my pack back on and without looking back (somehow that seemed important) hiked out to the trail.

If the discovery of chevrons in the snow pitched me into slo-mo, by the time I reached camp I was spinning on fast-forward. I didn't spot any orange suits at the lake, and when I ran up to the meadow, the llamas, eyes wide and alert, quickly rocked to their feet and clustered together. I found Jenny and Wheat under the kitchen fly. Wheat had his glasses on and was bent over my propane stove, reading its metal instruction plaque. (Wheat may be the only male I've ever met who stopped to read instructions.) Jenny was fiddling with the knobs.

"Oh, there you are," she said. "How do you get this damn thing going?"

"What are you doing?" It came out shrilly, an accusation. Wheat straightened up, peered at me over his glasses.

"I wanted a cup of coffee," Jenny retorted. "What the hell's eating you?"

I reached over and turned all the knobs to off. "You're going to let out all our propane. Where's Luke?"

She shrugged. "He had a date with the toilet paper. We're done. All we have to do is load up. We got the gear all together down at the lake. Luke thought if we got it up here tonight, we could get an early start tomorrow."

"Did you take two beers out of the cooler night before last?"

"What?"

"I said, did you take two beers out of the cooler the first night we were up here?"

"What are you talking about? I drank one beer. You gave it to me."

"That's all you had?"

"Jesus. I had one last night, too. So did Wheat and Luke. What *is* your problem?"

I pulled my pad out of my pack and flipped it open to my sketch of the boot print and shoved it at her. "Is this your boot?"

She looked at it. "No."

Wheat peered over her shoulder, then snatched the notebook away. "Where did you see this?" he demanded.

I told them.

They became still, their faces as grave as doctors considering the symptoms of bad news. "That's it, isn't it?" Jenny said to Wheat.

"Looks like it."

Jenny met my gaze and announced flatly, "She's here."

SIXTEEN

DOWN AT THE LAKE, the team's gear was neatly stowed, waiting for the llamas. The only things still unpacked were Wheat's casts. There were two of them, a left and a right, air-drying on a rack suspended between two plastic equipment boxes. Somehow, I had imagined a whole shoe shop of casts, mine and Gwen and Mary Ann's included. "Only two?" I asked Wheat.

"She's only got two feet." He picked up one of the lozenges of dental stone, carefully keeping his fingers on the edges. The back of the cast was clean. There was a crude "W" and a ragged line of numbers scratched into the white surface. The lifted side, however, was dirty—dried mud and bits of leaves had come up along with the impression—and though the chevrons weren't crisp, the pattern was readable. I held up my sketch next to the cast. Luke and Jenny pressed closer for a look.

"I'd say you gotta match there, honeybunch," Jenny drawled.

"Looks like it," Luke agreed.

Wheat turned the impression to catch more light. He took a ballpoint from the pocket of his orange suit and drew ellipses in the air over the ball of the foot. "A lot of wear here, forward on the ball of the foot," he said to Luke. "Heel's like new." He replaced the cast on the rack, picked up the other one, and examined it. "This one, the wear's more what you'd expect."

Luke looked at me.

"I told you she had a limp. I noticed it when we first saw her. I thought maybe she'd hurt her ankle on the way up. But it didn't slow her down on the getaway. She was moving. She sort of lurched from rock to rock—you saw it on the film."

Wheat said, "If the boots are hers, it's not a new injury."

"What do you mean, if the boots are hers? She was wearing them, wasn't she?"

"We can prove these were the boots at the scene. But we can't prove the wear on them is hers. She might have picked them up secondhand.''

The four of us gazed out across the lake, grappling with the idea of the killer's presence. I half-expected to see storm clouds looming dramatically on the jagged horizon, but nature wasn't acting on cue. The afternoon sky was benign. On the surface of the lake, thin blue ripples winked small coins of pale gold light. The rocks below the cirque where Roland had died were now in deep shadow, but farther along to the right, above the black tops of the pines, the snowfield where I'd found the killer's boot print gleamed like fresh cream. By a trick of perspective, the ''hand'' was invisible from where we stood on the lake's shore, but as the crow flies (or the injured deer bounds) it couldn't have been much more than a mile away.

''She's been here the whole time,'' Luke stated, as if he knew it for a fact. ''She never left. The goddamn choppers flew right over her. She must have found a cave somewhere up there.''

''Or an old den.'' I was thinking of Eddie's coyote. ''But you'd have thought they would have noticed the marks in the snow.''

''Not if she just skimmed off the top. It could have taken a while to melt down to rock. She must have run out of water. It was too risky to get it out of the lake, so she started scooping up snow.''

''She risked coming up to our camp, snitching our beer,'' Jenny pointed out.

''She was hungry,'' Luke decided. ''She would have been afraid to hunt, afraid of being caught out in the open.''

''She didn't take any food,'' Jenny objected.

''The cooler was easy access. Lee had our food boxes hanging in the trees,'' Luke reminded her.

''If she'd started messing around with them, we'd have heard it. The llamas would have made a noise about it,'' I pointed out.

''Only two beers missing?'' Jenny asked me.

''Yeah,'' I said.

''Wonder why she didn't take it all.''

''Maybe she hoped we wouldn't notice,'' Wheat said.

''We didn't,'' Jenny said.

"*I* noticed," I confessed. "I thought you guys had had a private party."

Like a butler on *Masterpiece Theater,* Wheat's thin mouth tightened in a fleeting twitch of distaste. Jenny let out a heavy sigh and turned to Luke. "What now, boss man?" She looked tired. Her lipstick had worn off and her hair, after three days, had deflated. She had pulled it back off her face with a turquoise bandanna that, in an incongruous way, complimented her orange jumpsuit. Despite the bright colors, she looked older, more severe.

Luke, on the other hand, looked about nineteen. His lean face was smooth, his hazel eyes slightly abstracted. Like a high-school athlete waiting for the starter's gun, his body shifted slightly from side to side, as if weighing strategies on the balls of his feet.

"There's one more thing," I told them. "I left her some food."

Jenny and Wheat stared. Luke looked interested. I went on. "I had some leftover cake in my pack. I left it out on a rock below the hand."

Luke said thoughtfully, "Where any animal could take it."

"Yeah. But it's in a refrigerator box. Besides, I had the feeling she was watching me. I think her hideout's somewhere in those boulders."

Luke's face remained noncommittal. We waited. "Okay," he said cheerfully. "Let's get the llamas down here. I want to get all this crime scene gear back up in camp where we can keep an eye on it."

AN HOUR LATER, Luke and I were back in the meadow, unloading equipment boxes from the llamas and arguing about my role in what was going to happen next. Wheat and Jennie had withdrawn tactfully to the kitchen fly.

"She isn't your average killer, Lee," Luke declared with some heat as he unloaded Oreo, a chocolate-colored llama with a white stripe running from his chin, down his neck, to his belly. "Roland, whatever his problem with Herron, was more typical. Alcohol and a firearm involved, he knew his victim, he had a record." A weary contempt crept into his voice. "I know those jerks like the back of my hand. The only thing that sets Roland apart is his age. Most of them are younger, flying on their own testosterone. But this girl's off the charts. She's smart, she's skilled, she's careful.'' He stopped and looked at me. ''Have you ever dealt with a psychopath?''

''Not that I know of.''

''Well, I have. I'm telling you, he was one of the most charming guys I've ever met, and he had absolutely no remorse, no feeling for his fellow human beings.'' Relieved of his load, but not his packsaddle, Oreo sidestepped impatiently. ''Whoa, boy,'' Luke ordered.

I stepped out of their way. ''What did this charmer of yours do?''

''Raped and killed a sixty-year-old grandmother. We found her breasts in a suitcase under his bed.'' He watched me closely. I kept my face blank. He went on, ''Like Jenny said, this girl's got ice water between the ears. She won't hesitate to kill again.''

''Right,'' I agreed. ''You get your troops up there with bullhorns and tear gas, and she'll kill someone else. She's invisible. And she's still got at least one arrow.''

''What makes you think she won't use it on a stranger bearing goodies?''

''Because she's starving. Because she won't kill the golden goose till she takes all the goodies. Because a goose is less threatening than a bunch of cowboys.''

He didn't answer. Distractedly, he turned to Oreo's saddle and released the front cinch.

''Luke, psycho or just plain screwed up, she's going to act in her own best interest. She's hungry. She's up against a wall—literally. Anyone who turned on a TV during a hostage situation knows that rule number one is get them talking.''

''That is exactly what I'm trying to avoid—a hostage situation. Do you want to be a hostage?''

''Of course not,'' I told him. ''But you've done this before. You told me you've talked people in. How many times have you talked someone in?''

''I don't keep count,'' he said crossly.

''You could coach me, Luke. She's already seen me, I know she has. She's much more likely to talk to me than a stranger.''

He didn't answer. Instead he turned his attention to Oreo, who was getting restless at the delay in being unsaddled. The dangling front cinch knocked against his legs. He rumbled in protest and skittered out of Luke's reach. The saddle, still held in place by its rear cinch, slipped down under his belly. As Luke, halter rope in his left hand, worked to free it with his right, Oreo's ears went back and his rumbling became louder. I saw an ominous lump sliding up and down beneath the white shag of his long throat. "Luke," I warned.

"Got it," he said. But it was too late. Oreo took aim at his tormentor and loosed a foul-smelling spray. Luke staggered back, taking the freed saddle with him, and Oreo trotted off trailing his halter rope, his mouth open, as if gagging on the reek of his own weapon.

Luke's face was scrunched up as tight as a green walnut. Oreo had gotten him on the side of his face, and greenish gunk dripped from his ear, an eyebrow, and his chin. He wiped his face on the sleeve of his orange jumpsuit. "Hoo-ah!" he gasped.

The stuff smelled as putrid as last week's innards. "God Almighty!" Luke sputtered. I went after Oreo and came back with his halter rope. Luke, using both sleeves and a bandanna, was still smearing and wiping.

I tried to straighten my face. "You okay?"

"You think this is funny?" he demanded.

I pressed my hand over my nose and mouth.

"It's not funny!"

"No," I said through my fingers, trying unsuccessfully to squelch the giggles. With a methodical dignity, Luke unzipped, stepped out of his orange suit, balled it up.

"It's in your hair, too." I cleared my throat. "You need some hot water."

We walked back to the kitchen fly, Luke holding the stinking orange ball of his coveralls at arm's length. "Why didn't you warn me?" he complained.

"I didn't notice until too late. I was in the middle of this argument with a cop."

He stopped walking. His focus latched back onto the case. "Listen," he said. "I don't want you to think I don't appreciate your willingness to help out."

Was he turning me down? I took a breath and hazarded, "Are you sure you aren't letting your personal feelings for me get in the way?"

His eyes widened for a second, then narrowed. "Personal feelings?" As if I had accused him of graft.

"Jesus Christ!" I exploded. Over at the kitchen fly, Jenny's and Wheat's heads turned. I lowered my voice. "Look, chum, I'm not asking for your heart on a silver platter. I'm simply volunteering for a job." *Lie number one.*

"You're not on the payroll."

"So? I get hurt, you don't have to worry about disability. Look, I don't have to be a cop to go back and see if the box is still there."

He thought about it. "And if it isn't?"

"I'll leave something else and come back down." *Lie number two.* I stepped back, giving him space. He stared at the reeking ball of coveralls in his hand. "Run it by Webb, why don't you?" I suggested. Webb, I was willing to bet, would be more enthusiastic.

LUKE CLEANED UP, then sat with his radio for close to an hour. I took a pull or two on my flask, but it didn't help—nor did the disapproving eyes of Wheat and Jenny. I took one of our plastic basins, mixed up a paste of whole-wheat flour, salt, and water. Then, kneeling over it, I started kneading working what was essentially Play-Doh into bread dough. A veggie curry was on my menu for supper and I wanted flatbreads to go with it—one of my English Comp students, a kid back from an exchange program in Nepal, had written a "process" essay on making chapatis. His *aamaa* his Katmandu "mother"—had made them for him every morning for breakfast on a little propane camp stove. He described the process skillfully enough to tempt me to try it, and my results earned him an "A." (I can't tell you how many students fail this "how-to" writing exercise. Essays entitled "How to Make a Peanut-Butter-and-Jelly Sandwich" invariably open with the sentence: "Put the peanut butter on the bread." Once I brought Skippy's to class and slapped the jar onto a slice of bread.)

But back to my chapatis. After ten minutes of hard kneading, the dough was textbook "soft and elastic." Moreover, through the double miracle of bread making, the edge of my anxiety had softened as well. When Luke came back from his phoning, my arms were pumped up, but I was no longer boiling for a fight. *It's his job, Squires, not yours,* I reminded myself as I admired my ball of dough. It was as resilient and warm as a baby's bare tummy.

"Okay, listen up," Luke said. As if we weren't. Arms folded across his chest, he considered me, as if looking over a dubious rookie. "Lee," he said severely. "Are you sure you want to do this?"

"Yes." I tore off a sheet of plastic wrap and bundled up my dough. "I'm sure." No applause. "What, you want me to sign a release?"

"That won't be necessary." He let out a small sigh of resignation. "Okay, you're on."

I felt a wave of energy course up through my body. I grinned at him.

"We're going to do this my way," he warned.

"Natch."

"I mean it, Lee. You're not going up there alone. We're going in there together. Hang on." He held up a hand to stay my objection. "I'll stay behind you, out of sight. We want to keep this as nonthreatening as we can. You go in, drop the bait, and get right out."

My mind was racing. "Then what?"

"We come back down here. If it looks like she's really up there, tomorrow we'll set up a perimeter, go in with Webb, and see if you can make contact. Jenny, you and Wheat are out of here. First light tomorrow, you head home. You're okay on your own?"

"Hey, it's downhill all the way to the shower," said Jenny.

"What about our gear?" Wheat asked.

"I talked to Dolores. Her brother, or Pete—if he's back—will come in with Webb and take out your stuff. You should have it in Missoula by the next morning." He turned to me. "Any questions?"

I had a couple of hundred, but I couldn't think of one.

Luke glanced at his watch. "Okay, let's get moving. We don't want to walk in there in the dark. We want her to see you if she's there."

"What about the goodie? What do you want to give her?"

He thought about it. "How about leaving out a toothbrush for her? A toothbrush and some toothpaste?"

"A toothbrush and toothpaste?"

He shrugged. "I've seen it work. Shows you're tuned into their needs, that you want to treat them like a human being."

"If someone gave me a toothbrush when I was starving, I'd think it was a sick joke."

Luke looked interested. "Besides," I went on, "for all we know, she brought her own along with her."

"The bus driver said she was carrying a pack," he conceded. "Okay," he decided. "We'll go with food. But nothing substantial. Just a taste, get her up for more."

"An *amuse-gueule.*"

"A what?"

"An appetizer."

Luke frowned. "Like cheese? Let's wait on the salt," he ordered. "If the cake's gone, we'll try another sweet."

LUKE SLIPPED ON his Smith & Wesson, and Jenny and I hastily rummaged through my pantry for a something small and sweet. Jenny seized a Ziploc bag of cookies. "What are these?"

"White-chocolate-chunk-and macadamia-nut cookies. Dolores's mom made them."

"You've been sitting on them all this time?" she demanded. She opened up the bag and took a large bite out of one. "Ummumm," she approved, her mouth full.

"I don't know about the macadamia nuts."

"Right. Hold on to these mothers. God, you can taste the butter!"

"Think comfort food," I told her. "What did you like as a kid?"

"Marmalade," Luke said.

"Marmalade?" I remembered my childhood dislike of the shreds of rind.

"What's wrong with that?"

"Nothing. I didn't bring any, that's all."

"Vanilla pudding." Wheat joined in.

"Toll House cookies right out of the oven," Jenny said.

"Thanks a lot. You guys are a great resource."

"Bananas," Wheat tried again.

"Yuck," Jenny said.

"My mother used to make this dessert with vanilla pudding and bananas," Wheat reminisced. "It had vanilla wafers in it, too."

"Focus," I chimed.

In the end, we agreed on a Milky Way. I slipped it in my daypack with a bottle of water, and Luke did a fancy number on his official windbreaker: by pulling tabs and flaps, he made the cloth badge on front and STATE AGENT on the back disappear. Magico Presto, he was wearing an ordinary black windbreaker over his gun.

We took off, down around the lake and up the old hunting track. We moved at a decent clip, but it took us a good twenty minutes to reach the place on the trail where I'd bushwhacked over to the "hand." My marker was a dead fir suspended between two live ones. The bark was long gone, the silvered trunk twisted, the branches broken to stubs. It looked uncannily like an enormous vertebral column tossed aside by some meat-eating giant.

I stopped to let my heartbeat slow. Luke and I didn't speak. Then I nodded at him and he nodded back, and I clumped on through the woods, making as much noise as I could to mask his movements behind me. I snapped off dead branches, whacked them against passing tree trunks, tossed them into the brush, and hummed "Stand by Your Man." (Bizarrely, it seemed to be the only tune that popped up from my memory's jukebox.) When I paused to listen for Luke's step, I was reassured to hear nothing but the wind.

I walked out of the woods into the clearing. I felt as if I were in a dream, stepping out onto an empty stage. Still humming, I casually strolled over to the rock where I'd left the cake. The container was still there. In the exact position in which I'd left it. The Tammy Wynette inside me dried up. I felt a tug of disappointment: she wasn't here, after all. She'd collected her snow and gone. Her cave was somewhere else. I scooped up the plastic box. It felt empty. I shook it. No soft bump against plastic. No tiny rattling of dry crumbs. I pried open the lid. The inside of the box was so clean, it might have been run through the dishwasher. For a second, I felt a spasm of doubt: *I did leave a piece of chocolate cake in here, didn't I?* Then: *She took it!*

I stared at the empty box. My mouth felt dry. I slipped off my pack and sat down on the rock facing the wall of boulders. I took my time and, moving from left to right, "read" between the rocks. None of the spaces looked any bigger than a rabbit hole. The only movement along the wall was the irregular twitching of dry stalks in the breeze. I unzipped my pack. It sounded very loud. Could she hear it? Was she watching, as I had fancied?

I took out my water bottle, unscrewed the top, and took a long drink. Then I reread the wall. Nothing. Nor could I discern any change in the paths scooped out of the snow on the slope above the boulders. They looked exactly as I had left them earlier in the afternoon. Except for the "thumb" with its new, narrower extension, all four fingers were the same width. I sat there on the rock and stared at them. If she had made each finger successively, the first ones should have been fatter than the later ones. The first scrapings would have had more exposure to sunlight, would have melted sooner.

I heard a rustle behind me. Heart thumping, I turned slowly. Luke was standing quietly at the edge of the woods. His face was expressionless, but I could feel him steaming. I turned my back to him and faced the rock ribbons in the snow. The girl must have made all four fingers at the same time. Had she made four giant snowballs, rolled them into her cave, then chipped away chunks as needed? How had she melted them? She wouldn't have risked a fire. Had she packed in a stove along with her handmade bow and store-bought arrows? Had she packed in food—and her toothbrush—as well? Evidently, not enough food to last. But why had she stayed around?

I fished the Milky Way out of my pack, put it in the plastic box, sealed the lid. Then, on an impulse, I reopened the box, took out the candy bar, unwrapped it, and chomped off a large happy bite. The idea was to reassure her, to "prove" the candy harmless, like those slaves who used to test imperial food for poison. But the taste test ran away with me. I chewed slowly and sensuously. I ran my tongue around my teeth, half-closing my eyes like a X-rated actress. Shamelessly, I sucked the taste of chocolate off my lips, my fingers. An Academy Award performance. (Did the girl actually witness it?) Mustering up my self-discipline, I re-wrapped the bar and left it for her in the box.

LUKE WAS waiting for me on the trail, his mouth tight and angry, his eyes blazing under the bill of his cap. He gave me an abrupt nod, and I followed the back of his windbreaker down the trail. When we were safely out of range, he stopped and turned. "What exactly do you think you were doing?" His voice was carefully modulated, but steely.

"Putting on a show for her."

He let go of his control. "You agreed to go in and come right out!" he burst out. "You went in and sat there like it was some kind of picnic! You were completely exposed!"

I took a long breath. "I'm sorry."

"You think I could have stopped her from killing you? Do you?" The force of his anger seemed to bulk him up. He took a step toward me.

I held my ground. "Luke, the box looked like she'd licked it clean. She's there. She's there somewhere." I felt a rush of exhilaration.

"No way you're going back up there."

"Listen, it worked out." I did a small prance of victory. "*Yes.*"

"You're crazy."

I flashed my best grin. "Huh. Never heard that before."

"I won't be responsible for you, Lee."

Suddenly I was angry, too. Childishly, perhaps. I wanted applause, not a scolding. I swept past him and headed on down the trail.

I GOT BACK to my kitchen feeling meaner than an old-time trail cook and by all accounts, the men called "Cookie" were a surly, temperamental breed known to ruin the coffee out of spite or hoard the best side of the bacon for themselves and feed moldy scraps to hungry hands. When Wheat and Jenny asked, "Hey, how'd it go?" I rudely told them to ask their boss. They retreated, leaving me feeling guilty, exhausted and wired all at once. I uncorked my flask, and, in keeping with chuckwagon tradition, chugged a finger and poured another. Drunk seemed like a good idea. However, after punching around my chapati dough, after whacking off tender little balls of it and slapping them around, oblivion didn't seem quite so urgent. I slowed down on the whiskey and allowed myself to listen to Luke droning away on his radio.

Although he usually took the handset out of earshot and paced up and down the meadow as he talked, this time he parked himself just beyond my kitchen. No doubt, I was meant to overhear. "Our girl's up there," he told Webb. He made no mention of the way I'd played my part. Their discussion was all logistics, strategies. Gradually I gathered that Plan A was on. Tomorrow the troops would arrive. Webb and a "perimeter" team made up of deputies, wildlife rangers, and tribal police would hike in. "I don't care if it takes you till noon to get up here," Luke barked at Webb. "I won't have choppers up here!"

Tomorrow I would try to coax the girl out of hiding—"If she's still up for it," Luke said with a sideways glance at me. It dawned on me that we were playing for real. Suddenly I felt like an utter fraud. What did I know about crisis negotiation? About psychopaths? My mother would have a better shot at bringing in "Artemis" than I would. As much as I hated to admit it, even my ex-husband would have been more likely to succeed. (Like my mother, Clint was a certified shrink. In fact, he had been one of my mother's students—which is how we met. Last I heard, he was working as bereavement counselor somewhere in Colorado.)

By the time Luke got off the radio, I was feeling panicky. "One condition," Luke warned.

"What?"

"You follow the script this time."

"Okay," I agreed contritely.

"Webb and I will walk you through it tomorrow. You'll do fine." Now that he'd let me in, suddenly I was qualified.

"Right."

"You're worried?"

"Don't you have a consultant—some kind of expert on conflict resolution?"

He grinned cockily. "You're talking to him."

Was he serious? He met my gaze, measured my doubt. His grin subsided. "Let me see what we can do." He got back on the radio.

As I worked on supper, I kept seeing the arrow embedded in Roland's eye. I concentrated on the chapatis. Using the stubby dowel I carry as a back-country rolling pin, I rolled out the dough balls into tortillalike rounds. Jenny and I cooked them on a frying pan over our campfire. They behaved exactly as they were supposed to. They puffed up into giant blisters (always amazing, given the lack of yeast in them), then deflated as soon as we took them off the heat. If I had been cooking my last meal, I couldn't have wished for better. Perhaps my sense of doom helped. Or the fact that I'd mellowed out on bourbon. Whatever, the sweet fragrance of cinnamon and cumin wafted out of my Bombay curry and mingled with the scents of wood smoke and wheat bread. We ate with our fingers, tearing the chapatis into wedges and using them to scoop the curry into our mouths. As we hunched over our bowls in the firelight, I felt a kind of atavistic communion with all the women through the ages who had cooked for hunters. I thought of Eddie's mother cooking for hunters who had themselves become victims. She had lived to tell the tale. Eddie's father had not.

Jenny and Wheat cleaned up while I talked on Luke's cellular phone to a therapist/negotiator in Helena. It was not a satisfying conversation. The woman's voice at the other end of the line was warm and sympathetic. If she hadn't kept murmuring "beautiful," I might have gotten weepy and negotiated all my neuroses into her ear. As it was, "Alice" (she did not provide her last name, nor any credentials) wasn't much use. She talked vaguely about "establishing trust" and "nonjudgmental listening," but she was more interested in caressing my self-esteem than passing on any useful tips. I hung up, annoyed.

To my surprise, I heard myself tell Luke, "I want to call my mother."

He looked surprised himself. "Sure." He glanced at his watch. "I've got a couple more calls to make. Can you wait? It's now, what—about ten in Washington? Is that too late?"

"Nope."

He looked slightly worried, like a thoroughbred owner on the eve of a race. "You all right?"

"I'm not calling to say my last good-bye. My mother's a psychologist. I thought it might be a good idea to touch base with someone a bit sharper than Alice in Wonderland."

"You didn't like her?"

"You know her?"

"No. Webb suggested her."

"You think he goes to her?"

"Webb?" He let out an incredulous bark of laughter.

"What's so funny?"

"Webb in therapy." He chuckled at the thought.

"You go to family counseling."

Instant chill. "That's different."

I raised an eyebrow. "Maybe you should try Alice, cry a little feel good about yourself."

He peered at me as if I were mad.

"God, you cops are tough. Really turns me on."

"I thought you didn't like the woman," Luke said, exasperated.

"I didn't." I giggled. "I don't recommend her."

He took a breath. "How about some coffee?"

"You think I'm drunk?"

"I'd like a cup of coffee."

I kissed the air in his direction. "Good idea."

IT WAS after midnight in Washington when I got my mother on Luke's phone. I sat cross-legged in the meadow, swathed in poly pro fleece and guarded by llamas. A waning moon had risen over the eastern ridges and silhouetted the animal's proud head against a smoke-colored sky pricked with pale stars. Our satellite connection was astonishingly clear. My mother might have been sitting beside me in the moonlight. I ran through the situation for her as concisely as I could. She interrupted a few times, asking for clarification on one point or another. To my relief, her voice was businesslike, crisp. I recognized her emergency voice—the one she used with suicidal patients.

"So you're going to go up there with them tomorrow," she stated. I listened for a note of protest, for a suppressed maternal wail, but she was gently professional.

I took a deep breath. "Yes," I said. And suddenly I knew for certain that I would go. I told her about my chat with Alice, made overlong with complaint.

"What did you want from her?" my mother inquired.

"I don't know! A clue, something to watch out for, something to say, a plan—a *map*. I want to know where there be dragons."

"A map?" She seemed to find the idea humorous.

"I'm afraid I'll say something wrong and blow the whole thing," I insisted.

"There are no reliable maps for the wilderness of the soul," my mother said matter-of-factly. "But there are landmarks."

"Such as?"

"Your goals. You need to keep what you want to accomplish in focus. You may not be able to reach your goal," she added gravely, "but if you keep it in sight, you won't get lost."

"I don't even know what my goal is," I complained. "I don't know why I'm doing this."

She waited, allowing me space to explore, but I closed up. She was, after all, my *mother*. Over by our camp, Luke and Wheat and Jenny stood around the fire, dark figures in conversation, their hands and faces catching orange light as they kicked a log, stepped to avoid a spume of sparks.

"You will have to find for yourself where the dragons are," my mother informed me. "You have the tools. Use them. Listening is a tool. And so is breathing. It is important to *breathe*, Lee. Breathe and listen and keep your inner eye on your goal."

"Yeah."

"Breathe. Breathe and listen," my mother soothed.

I breathed in and out, exaggerating for her benefit. The llamas heads turned. I saw Luke crossing the meadow toward us, his step purposeful. "I have to go now. Thanks, Mom. I mean it."

She hesitated. "Do you remember our conversation about the Calydonian Boar?"

I suppressed a groan. "Yes?" I said.

"It is interesting that you have snow there. In one of his twelve labors, Hercules climbed Mount Erymanthus to capture a wild boar—"

"Mom," I interrupted, "I'm sorry, but they need the phone now." I stood up. We said good-bye and disconnected.

I handed Luke the phone. "My mom's got boars on the brain."

"Bores?"

"Wild pigs. The kind people used to hunt. If I remember correctly, boar's head was a delicacy in Merrie Olde England."

Later, as we rustled into our sleeping bags, a memory from childhood sailed up into the darkness of the tent. I couldn't have been more than three or four at the time—I was old enough for a "big bed," but one with side rails. What I remembered was the vision of my mother standing in the doorway of my room in a black cocktail dress with a black velvet top and a full, Mamie Eisenhower-type taffeta skirt. I thought I had never seen anyone so beautiful. I remember diving into the shimmering black skirt and the watery swishing sound it made—a harder, crisper sound than the nylon of our sleeping bags. I remember pulling the dark folds of her skirt over my head and, for a brave moment, costuming myself in her beauty before I burrowed for the safety of her legs.

I wriggled inside my bag, waiting for warmth. Night began to settle around us. "Tomorrow?" I said to Luke. "What's the plan?"

"I'll walk you through it in the morning." He yawned. "Get some sleep."

A minute later I said, "Luke? What's our goal?"

"What do you mean?"

"My mother said I should focus on our goal."

"That's easy. Bring her in."

Duh.

Then he added severely, "*Your* number-one goal is to stay

alive.'' Outside, an owl hooted. Luke cleared his throat. ''I care what happens to you, Lee,'' he said.

Clearly, it cost him something to say it. But I couldn't let it be. ''Would your tongue turn black if you said the L-word?''

Silence.

''The problem is,'' I went on recklessly, ''I think I'm in love with you.''

Neither of us moved. Then he rolled over and pulled me toward him and held me, as if I were a sick child, until I fell asleep.

SEVENTEEN

WHEAT AND JENNY left before sunup. They didn't wait for breakfast—or even for my coffee to perk. I made them sandwiches to eat on the way and, in a parting burst of generosity, tossed in Rose's million-calorie macadamia-nut killers. We shook hands all around and they walked off across the wet meadow, Jenny in the lead, Wheat with his birding binoculars dangling from his neck.

Luke and I drank a cup of coffee, then led the llamas down to the lake for a drink and back up to an ungrazed section of meadow. As if someone were turning up a rheostat, the dusky light over the meadow turned rosy. The western ridges glowed purple and the predawn breezes died. The llamas stood at attention, facing east expectantly. Together, we watched a liquid rim of sun squeeze itself up against the dark line of mountain. After a moment's hesitation, the sun burst over the horizon into a colorless sky. The llamas lost interest. Luke was intrigued. "It's as if they *cared* about the sun coming up," he said.

"According to Pete, the Incas regarded them as servants of the sun god."

Luke turned from the llamas to me, pulling me into a hug. "Alone at last," he said, his eyes mischievous. The time and place were right, and the length of him was taut and urgent, but I felt about as sexy as a wet rag. "What's the matter?"

"I don't know. I'm twitched."

Expertly, his hand massaged the back of my neck.

I closed my eyes, tried to get into it, then pulled away. "We need to talk."

"About what?"

"About what I'm going to do when I get up there. I need to know."

It was my own fault. I'd summoned up the professional in him, and like the genie in the brass lamp, there was no turning back. The playful, sexy, companionable Luke vanished. Suddenly he shifted into a sort of canned solicitude. I suppose "canned" is too harsh—I know his concern was genuine—but his voice exuded a kid-glove kindness that made me feel like a stranger. Suddenly I knew exactly how he talked to witnesses and crime victims. "It's not too late to change your mind," he soothed. "Webb and I can handle it together."

"Let's cut to the action, okay?"

"Okay," he humored me. He paused, organizing his thoughts, then started the lesson. "The way this works is by trade-off. Step-by-step trade-offs. She does something for you. You do something for her. At first, she may be just a voice. You need to establish eye contact with her, to get her out in the open so you can read each other's faces. She needs to see that you're sincere, that you care about her. Like George Burns said, 'The greatest thing you can have is sincerity; if you can fake it, you've got it made.' "

"Cute."

"What I'm saying, Lee, is you need to get her to like you. You think you can do that?"

"No sweat."

"I mean it. If you need to, lie. Tell her how she reminds you of your little sister. But watch your body language. People tend to pull back, look away when they lie. Lean forward, maintain eye contact when you're talking to her."

"Sort of like you're talking to me now."

He shot me a look of exasperation and went on. "The name of the game here is power. You need to hold onto as many chips as you can. So we aren't going to sit her down and feed her a nice meal and then say, 'Now come along with us.' It doesn't work that way. You give her everything at once, you've got no leverage. So first you give her something salty—usually we give them a ham-and-cheese sandwich and potato chips. Then they get thirsty, and you've got another bargaining chip. You can negotiate over the Coke. When she asks for something, you make her wait. You tell her you're only a grunt, that you have to get permission. Then you leave, you walk over to me nice and slow, we talk it over, you go back to her."

"Where are you?"

"I'm visible the whole time. As she moves closer to you, I

move closer, too. We work as a team. You make the contact, find common ground, keep the communication rolling. I stay in the background, the authority figure."

"The old good-guy/bad-guy drill?"

He smiled. "You're showing your age. That went out when I was still in cop school." Then he was serious again, his voice calm and soothing. "What we want is to create a safe space for her. She needs to believe we're both there to help her. Tell her we care about her future. You can say that it's the first day of the rest of her life."

"You actually *say* that?"

"It works. If you're not comfortable with it, you can tell her it's an opportunity to do something good for herself." He stopped. "What's the matter?"

"Prison is an opportunity to do something good for herself? She's going to buy that?"

"If she likes you, you can sell her on it." He read the scruples in my eyes. "Lee, you don't know where she's coming from. For some of these—" He stopped, censoring his word choice. "For some of these people, prison is a step up in the world, believe me. The main thing is to set up a peaceful climate."

To that end, he gave me three Don'ts. I was not to use the word *murder*. "You want to downplay what she did," Luke instructed. "Keep your language bland. Talk about 'the incident,' or 'the problem between you and Roland.'"

"Got it. Avoid plain English," I said sarcastically.

Luke took a breath. He knew I was scared. "You are trying to defuse the situation. To disarm the suspect," he explained. "Language helps. If I ask a suspect to write a 'confession,' he's going to say no way. If I ask a suspect to write a 'letter of apology,' he'll think about it."

There were two other Don'ts. Don't touch her. Don't ask her why she killed Roland. Touch, Luke maintained, was tricky—the girl's associations with touch might be bad. It was safer not to "reach out" physically. As for not asking why, he explained, "People kill for stupid reasons. 'She put the toilet paper in backward.' 'He spilled my beer.' And when the reasons aren't stupid, they can be shameful. Maybe Redhawk abused her. You don't want to embarrass her. We don't need to know why she shot him. We can get that later. Now, we just want her to give herself up."

"To do something good for herself," I said darkly. The words felt poisonous in my mouth.

Luke opened his eyes wide. They were guileless. "Believe it," he urged earnestly.

THE PERIMETER TEAM reached us at nine-thirty. To keep them out of the girl's sight line, Luke confined them to the dip in the lower end of the meadow where we had picketed the llamas. There, a tongue of trees screened a shallow bowl of grass that made a natural pasture. The team was all men. They ranged from hefty to skinny, from pink to brown, but all looked fit enough to jog up the mountain several more times before lunch. Webb was with them, sweating in a black windbreaker that matched Luke's. The two of them went into conference. The others dropped their packs and weapons in the grass and stood in clusters, thumbs hooked in their belts, boots apart, chins high. One group marched over to inspect the llamas and, as I watched, their macho postures eased. Perhaps it is difficult to maintain a heroic strut around creatures with ears as silly as a medieval Fool's cap. In any case, around the llamas, the men clowned like Boy Scouts with badges in pumping iron.

Among the khaki and denim, a purple-and-black striped shirt stood out. It was large enough to have been cut from a Lenten awning. Then I realized Pete was wearing it. He had hiked in with the backup team. I called and waved. He turned, saw me, and waved back. With his smooth brown face and his hair pulled back into the stubbiest of ponytails, he resembled a smiling Buddha. A few minutes later, he walked over and enfolded me in a large bear hug. I hugged him back hard. The simple mass of him was comforting. I was more nervous than I wanted to admit about the job ahead and, perversely, Luke's studied calm only made it worse.

"New shirt?" I asked Pete.

"Dolores gave it to me for my birthday."

"When's your birthday?"

"August."

"Leo."

Pete dismissed his horoscope with a shrug. "So how's it going? Stove holding up okay?"

"No problem. Carbon had a sore on the side of his mouth after the hike up, but it seems okay now. I put some Neosporin on it. You might want to check his halter. How was your hunt?"

"Good." He nodded his large head gravely. "Good," he repeated. While Luke and Webb poured over topo maps with the perimeter team, Pete and I caught each other up. Councilwoman Bernadette Walker had dropped by his house while Dolores was at school and had tried (unsuccessfully, according to Pete) to pump Rose about me.

"Rose likes you," he said. He sounded mildly surprised.

Gwen Mears had called again, demanding a refund. "Don't you dare!" I protested. But his dark eyes were bland—which made me suspect he was considering it, if he hadn't already agreed. "Pete?" I challenged.

He let out a heavy sigh and changed the topic. "Eddie McNab died yesterday afternoon. His daughter found him in his recliner. Didn't look like it was any kind of struggle."

"Oh shit, Pete." A wave of sadness washed over me and left a sandy prickling of regret: I realized I'd been counting on seeing Eddie again. I wasn't sure what I had wanted to tell him—if anything—but I'd been counting on it. The news of his death distanced Roland's and Charlie Herron's: like an abandoned jigsaw puzzle, the various pieces of their murders no longer compelled me.

Pete's eyes were pained. "You'll miss him," I offered.

"Yeah."

"Shit," I said again.

"Funeral's going to be Monday, they think. I didn't know whether to tell you." His hand encompassed the waiting men, the mission ahead of us.

"I'm glad you did." And I was. Pete's matter-of-fact report from the world below made me feel more normal. Somewhere down there, I had a life waiting for me, new students to teach, new poems to write, new mansions to sit. I had funny, loving friends and, despite our quarrels, a family that was thicker than water. A family ruled by a dowager soothsayer.

"What do you know about wild boars?" I asked Pete.

He brightened. "Actually, Paul and I saw one on TV the other day. Ug-ly!" He laughed. "But they're supposed to have a keen sense of smell. This one, the West German police had trained to search for drugs and explosives. Supposedly, she'd found things buried as deep as three feet, sniffed them out, and kept at it with her tusks till she dug them up."

"My mom's been warning me about wild boars."

Pete had heard me before on the subject of my mother's Delphic pronouncements and had always maintained the safest position when it comes to psychic phenomena and other people's mothers: on the fence. This time was no different. He scratched the back of his neck and said, "Boars, huh? Had a client once who'd been boar hunting. Back before I bought the business—back before *you* bought the business." He cocked an eyebrow at me.

"Back before Cyrus Strand bought the business," I contradicted him. "It was Cyrus's money, if you recall. Go on."

"We took this guy out for elk over on the Sun Preserve. Year before, he'd gone boar hunting with a pack of dogs. He said you can't ambush hunt a boar because they don't follow regular trails."

"Where was this? Not out here?"

"Someplace in Tennessee, I think. He said they lost a couple of dogs—boar charged and gored them to death before he could kill it. Said it took him six rounds to bring the critter down. Turned out its hide was two inches thick."

"Neat," I said gloomily.

He looked at me speculatively. "There's two kinds of animals in this world. Runners and killers. The runners, like deer and elk—and llamas—have their eyes set closer to the sides of their heads, so they can look all around them. The eyes of the killers—the bears and wolves and boars—are set more in front, so they can see their prey better during pursuit. But there's only one killer who sees its prey with perfect binocular vision. That's us." He paused, then added with a shrug, "Keep your eyes open."

I nodded gloomily.

"Use your binocular vision," he repeated, "and I'll lend you a llama to watch your perimeter."

"What do you mean?"

"Llamas have excellent eyesight. Dolores and I have seen them spot deer on a hillside over half a mile away. The llamas won't make a sound, but they all look intently in the same direction. If we follow their gaze with binoculars, after a while we can pick out the deer. I'm thinking you oughta take Fluffy up there with you. I'm betting he'll find her before you do—and without making any kind of fuss over it."

The suggestion flabbergasted me. "Fluffy, the royal llama?"

He smiled his slow smile. "The Incas used to save white llamas for sacrifice."

"You want to me *sacrifice* Fluffy?"

"I'm not planning on any kind of sacrifice. If you lose him, you owe me four hundred bucks. I was just thinking he might help you out. Not just his eyesight. Llama have a calming effect. We've seen deer jump our fences to bed down among them—the deer seem to take comfort in their presence. Works the same way on people. I know a stressed-out dentist who jumps into the pasture with his llamas every day after he gets home from his office. He swears it's as good as two vodka martinis."

I looked over at the llamas, their heads rising disdainfully above the heads of curious humans. I liked the idea. "Run it by Luke—he's the man with the money. But why Fluffy? Why not Jake or Oreo?"

"Jake's my kitchen llama," Pete said firmly. "You want Oreo?"

"It doesn't matter. I was just wondering."

A sparkle danced up from the depth of his black eyes. "The girls really go for Fluffy. If I was in the market, all I'd have to do is shampoo him up, blow him dry and parade around with him a bit, and I'd be beating women off us both."

Pete went off to confer with Luke about Fluffy while I started packing my seduction lunch. Then Luke came over with a bulletproof vest. "So," I said cheerfully. "Are we counting Fluffy in?"

"A llama kneeling there, quietly chewing cud Pete thinks it might help defuse things." He looked at me with concern. "If you're comfortable with it."

"I'm 'comfortable.'"

"How you doing?" he probed in his social-service tone.

"Stop it!" I bridled.

"Stop what?"

"Talking to me like an undertaker."

For a moment he looked wounded. Then his bland mask recomposed itself. He held out the vest in his hand. "Try this on."

The vest was stiff and heavy and made for a woman a size smaller than me. "I think you underestimated me."

"Never," Luke countered. He smiled his old smile. I felt as if the sun had just come out. He tugged on the nylon straps. "You want it snug."

"How am I supposed to *move* in this thing?"

"I'm not asking you to shake it for her."

I rapped my knuckles on my chest and let out a gorilla-style hoot. "What's in here, anyway? Kevlar?"

"Yeah, but arrows go through Kevlar like butter. Same with knives and ice picks. This one's got a ceramic insert."

"My jacket's not going to zip up over it," I fussed.

"Lee," he said firmly. "It's not too late to change your mind."

"I'm not going to change my mind. Jesus! Can we get on with it?"

EIGHTEEN

BY NOON, Luke's partner, Webb, had the perimeter in place—an invisible radio-linked chain that looped through the woods below the snowfield and back behind the ridge above it. Fluffy was not happy about leaving his pals; as I tugged him away, he set up a shrill hum, twisting his head back over his shoulder. Reinforced by Pete's drill-sergeant bark, we trotted him across the meadow and down the track to the lake. Once away from Pete, however, he balked. His legs folded up underneath him as if wiped away by an invisible eraser and down he plopped, blocking the narrow trail like a giant woolly duster. We pushed and yanked, clapped and shouted, trying to startle him back up to his feet, but it only made things worse. He let out short bleats that sounded like the toy horn on a bike. His head tilted back, and I could see his cud sliding up his long neck. "Uh-oh," I said. We backed off. Luke jogged back up to camp to get Pete. Fluffy's toots subsided into a nervous hum. We eyed each other warily. "I know how you feel, bud. Believe me," I assured him.

Pete inspected Fluffy's halter, cinch, and rear crupper, and finding no evidence of sores, decided it was an attitude problem. He slid his hand between the llama's rear legs, and Fluffy sprang to his feet. "Now move it," Pete instructed us. "Keep the momentum going." Off we marched, Fluffy obediently in tow, Pete riding shotgun.

"That maneuver of yours back there?" I asked. "Looked something like sexual harassment."

"Naw. That was a jump start."

"Would you like to share the magic?"

"A little pressure on his penis sheath. He's real sensitive in that area."

"Who would have thought."

Pete's dark eyes glinted with humor. "Works every time."

I glanced back at Luke. He was talking intently into his handset. Pete walked with us as far as the lake, keeping an eye on Fluffy, but there were no more problems. The llama's natural curiosity got the better of his separation anxiety. His high hum softened into sporadic sighs of resignation. "Lookin' good," Pete said, including me as well as Fluffy in his approval. He had loaned me his birthday shirt to wear over my arrow-proof vest. "See you later, then." He touched his headband in a two-fingered salute and as he turned back, I felt my own spasm of separation anxiety.

We hiked on up the trail on the far side of the lake. With Fluffy on the end of a red nylon lead and Pete's purple-striped shirt flapping around me like a party tent, I could have passed for a clown in a circus parade. All I needed was a pair of giant shoes. By the time we reached the clearing, however, I wasn't feeling very festive. The sides of my armpits felt rubbed raw from the vest, my undershirt was soaked with sweat, and my head was spinning with fragments of advice. *Breathe,* said my mother's voice. *Use your eyes,* said Pete's. *Don't say murder,* instructed Luke's.

According to plan, I was unarmed. Luke declared that he didn't see any need to "get Western about it" and that suited me as well. Luke himself was packing his official nine-millimeter and a canister of pepper spray. He agreed to stay at the edge of woods, out of sight until I made contact.

I led Fluffy out into the clearing and staked him beside a scraggly clump of wild currant bushes below the "sign of the hand." Then I took off his panniers, fished out a backpacker's stove, and set it up on a level bare patch. We had decided to leave Pete's heavy-duty two-burner Coleman in camp, and at Luke's request, Pete had brought up a spidery little Whisperlite in his pack. I hooked it up to a bottle of white gas, set up its foil windscreens, and laid three strips of bacon in an aluminum frying pan not big enough to hold more.

I pumped up the stove, got a clean blue flame going, and put on the bacon. It was cool and sunny. In my pan, the bacon puckered and became transparent, sending its aroma up toward the snowfield. After sampling the currant bush and stray tufts of bunchgrass, Fluffy settled down in the "kush" position. The bacon browned. I forked it out of the hot fat onto a paper-towel-lined pie plate, then covered it with a blue-and-white dish towel. Under the thick fringe of his eyelashes, Fluffy's round black eyes watched me attentively. His ears twitched, then lowered like airplane wings on either side of his narrow face. What was he hearing?

I added new strips to the pan. The fragrant fat crackled and spat. I thought of all the cold school mornings of my childhood when I'd awakened to the smell of bacon cooking downstairs. Bacon was salty, bacon was familiar, and back before cholesterol was invented, bacon was safe. Hardworking fathers brought it home; early-rising mothers cooked it in warm kitchens. Now I was cooking it to bring in a killer. If she didn't show up, Luke and I would have bacon sandwiches for a late lunch. Saliva flooded my mouth. Bacon sandwiches on white bread. Along with the stove, Pete had packed in a loaf of air bread. Last night's leftover chapati's were not going to cut it, Luke assured me.

I scanned the rocks below the snowfield for movement, took the second batch out of the pan, broke off a piece, and popped it into my mouth. I was on my knees, draping a third batch into the fat, when I noticed Fluffy staring fixedly at a spot above us in the jumbled wall of boulders. How long had he been silently "pointing"? Squinting against the glare of snow, I followed the direction of his stare, and saw nothing—only grey rock, stumps twisted like driftwood, and the autumnal yellow leaves of a willowlike shrub stirring in the breeze. Fluffy remained absolutely still, intent on the rocks above us. My stomach clenched. Breathe, I reminded myself.

I caught a small metallic flash some hundred feet above us. *Shit,* I thought, *she's got a gun.* A cold stab of fear hit my chest. My adrenaline kicked in—a hot, blinding rush. Then I saw her. She was standing on a flat shelflike rock at the snowline. Behind her, the exposed strips of rock reached up like a giant claw. She was smaller than I remembered, almost frail, but still in the camo fatigues familiar from the video. The knees were coated with mud. Over a bulky dark sweater, she wore a tattered grey shirt that was almost indistinguishable from the rocks around her.

She moved slightly. Again I caught a small pop of light. I could see no sign of a gun, however. She had both hands on a makeshift staff—a hefty stick of dead pine, weathered silver and spiked with broken branches—like a shillelagh. She shifted her weight, leaning on the stick. Another twitch of light, this one lazier. Then I saw the dark green garbage bag hanging at her back; as she moved, light from the snow behind her slipped off its slick surface. She was wearing it like a superhero's cape.

Despite the dazzling snowy light and the drama of the dark clawlike pattern behind her, she didn't fit the picture of Wonder Woman—or Artemis, for that matter. She looked like one of the homeless on the sidewalks of Washington, D.C.—those androgynous smelly lumps of humanity who stew in layers of wool in the summer and freeze in the same layers in winter. Instinctively, I looked away, as if she might ask me for "spare change." *Establish eye contact*, Luke had said. But back on the streets of D.C., the rule was to avoid eye contact. It could only spoil your day.

I hunkered over my stove. *Where was her bow?* I turned over a strip of bacon and glanced up. She was having no qualms about staring at me. Using her spiky staff, she took a step forward for a better look. No bowstring crossed her chest, no bow tip poked up over her shoulder. And no red sneakers: wherever they had come from, they weren't hers. She was wearing brown leather hiking boots caked with dried mud. The left boot gaped open.

I met her eyes for a second, gave her a pleasant, noncommittal nod, and returned to my pan. I lifted the bacon out of the bubbling fat, deposited it under the blue-and-white towel, and started yet another batch. Fluffy breathed softly behind me. The meaty steam wafted upward like an offering before an altar.

"Hey," she called. "What are you doing?" Her voice was harsh, urgent. Gone was the spacey, almost dreamy intonation I remembered from our first encounter by the lake. Had I imagined that, along with the red sneakers?

"Cooking lunch," I called back.

Her face remained blank. "What's that?" she demanded. She indicated Fluffy with a jerk of her stick.

"That's a llama. His name is Fluffy."

She stared at Fluffy. "Will he carry me?"

"If you're under sixty pounds," I told her, shrinking the limit *If you need to, lie.* She was slight and starved, her cheeks sunken She didn't look as if she weighed more than ninety. Fluffy might have carried her in a pinch—at least, for a short distance "They're pack animals," I said. With my fork, I pressed white bumps of bacon down into the fat.

"Hey," she called again.

"My name's Lee."

"Yeah, well, whatever. You got a cigarette?"

A cigarette. Screw the bacon, why hadn't we thought of cigarettes? I felt a blast of panic. I wanted a cigarette. Badly "Sorry," I called back with sincere regret. A ding went off in my brain: *Bargaining chip,* it prompted. "We can get you a pack later on."

"We?"

"I came up here with my boss. We wanted to see if we could help you out. We've been worried about you." I turned to the woods behind me. "Hey, Luke," I called.

He stepped out into the clearing, hands raised casually.

"Stay right there!" the girl yelled. "Don't come any closer!"

He stopped, raised his arms a notch, splayed his fingers into flat surrender. He waited a moment, then half-turned on his heel and retreated back against a lodgepole pine. After another endless moment, he slowly lowered his arms and folded them over his chest in a casual I'm-here-for-the-duration position.

"You!" She indicated Luke with her chin. Her voice was shrill. "What do you want? What are you doing here? Answer me!"

Luke gave me an over-to-you nod.

I repeated, "We thought you might need some help."

"What are you? Cops?"

"I'm a cook."

She frowned and stared at Luke. "*He's* a cop."

"What's your name?" I asked.

She turned her head half a degree and sniffed the air. "You're burning that bacon," she accused angrily.

I looked down. She was right. I turned down the flame. "It's okay," I told her. "We've got plenty more. You want a piece?"

She didn't answer.

"Tell you what. You tell me your name, and I'll bring one up to you."

Silence.

I shrugged. Then I reached under my blue-and-white towel, pulled out a piece of bacon, and ate it. I took out another one, but before I got it to my mouth, she called out, "Raven. My name's Raven."

"Okay, Raven. I'm coming up. My boss is going to mind the stove. Okay?" I held up the piece of bacon, a fragile flag of truce. I approached the boulders. Luke, hands raised, walked slowly toward the stove. The girl didn't move. I climbed up toward a rock that was close enough for easy conversation, but beyond the reach of her spiked club.

"Raven. Listen to me. I'm going to put your piece of bacon on top of that big rock below you. But you need to put your stick down. I'll do it after you put down your stick."

Her eyes moved back and forth from the bacon in my hand to Luke below. "Okay?" I asked, meeting her eyes. The morning she'd killed Roland, there had been black stripes smeared across her face; they were still faintly visible, smudges of grey across nose and cheeks, but the circles under her eyes were darker. She lowered her club.

I left the bacon on the rock, a red-brown ruffle on dark stone. It looked as transient as a leaf. With quick grace, she scrambled down, swooped it up, and ate it. I looked at her right boot: it wasn't untied. The black laces were drawn tight, making flat X's, but on one side of the tongue, the laces crossed a wedge of bare skin: even without a sock, the boot wouldn't close. Her ankle was badly swollen.

Below me, a puff of wind ruffled the fur on Fluffy's throat. Luke was poking through the panniers. He took out a plastic container, dumped out my supply of candy bars, then poured hot bacon grease into it. I felt a surge of annoyance. What was wrong with the man's eyes? I'd packed our grease jar in the same pannier as our candy box. It even had G-R-E-A-S-E written on it in blue Magic Marker. I took a breath and looked over at the girl. She was sucking bacon grease off her fingers, but her eyes were on Luke. Now he was putting the candy bars back into the pannier.

"Raven. That's a pretty name," I tried. *Neat line, Squires.*

She'd heard it before. "My mother got it out of a book," she replied automatically.

I flashed on a paperback bodice ripper, the cover in pink and blue, a raven-haired heroine, eyes closed in ecstasy, embraced by a man in a full-sleeved poet's shirt. "Raven what?"

"Davisson. With two s's."

"Davisson," I repeated.

"It was my mother's name. That's what I go by."

"Your mother's maiden name?"

She scowled. "It was her name."

"You use it on your driver's license?"

Her face darkened. "What do I need a fucking driver's license for? You think I drove out here in a fucking Cadillac?"

Fucking good going. Now ask her for her Social Security number. "Raven," I said, "You're going to be okay. I'm trying to help you get out of here. Can you tell me where you live?"

"What's that got to do with the price of beans?"

"Nothing. I was just curious." The wind shifted momentarily, pulling away the meaty aroma from below and I caught a whiff from her lair, an acrid animal scent of leaf mold and stale urine. "I bet you could use a sandwich," I said.

She studied me, decided to test the waters with a toe. "One time, I used to live in Michigan. Up near Cheboygan." She met my eyes and I saw something familiar. It looked like despair.

Unexpectedly, I felt a shift, a spark of contact arching between us. We were strangers, but in the space of a few seconds, we had become intimate strangers. "You need something more to eat," I decided. "I'm going to go down and make you a sandwich. Then we can talk some more."

BACK DOWN on the ground, I piled five pieces of crisp bacon on a slice of white bread and laid the top on lightly. A featherweight sandwich. Hurriedly I wrapped it in a paper towel. "Keep cooking," I told Luke. "It's working. Something's wrong with her right ankle. It's all swollen."

"Probably the reason she's still here. Tell her we can help her out, give her something for pain. Tell her we'll get a doctor to look at it for her. Anything else?" he probed.

"She's from Cheboygan, Michigan. Her last name is Davisson. She said it was her mother's name." I hesitated.

"Yes?"

"I don't know. I got the feeling maybe her mother is dead. At least, something's going on there. It seemed like a sore point."

"Don't press on it, then. See if you can get her to give up her bow before you let her have the sandwich. You're doing great." He turned on his old grin, full wattage.

I felt the rough edges of my heart soften. "Don't lick your chops yet," I warned.

"Speaking of chops, this bacon's killing me!"

I smiled. "You know how to delay gratification."

"Get back up there!"

I climbed back to my perch. Although I was only a hundred or so feet above the clearing, it was like climbing into another dimension, a place where inchoate rules flickered and shifted with the light, where honest nouns and verbs were more dangerous than indulgent half-lies. Beneath the stiff tangles of her hair, the girl's eyes watched me like a wary animal's. They were pale, set in a face that tapered down to a narrow chin. Her jaw had a skewed look, as if she had needed orthodontic work as a child and not gotten it. She looked about twenty-five, but there was something disconcertingly childlike about her manner. "This is your sandwich, Raven," I said, showing her the towel-wrapped packet. "But before I give it to you, my boss wants you to answer a couple of questions."

"Yeah?"

"Where's your bow?"

"It broke."

"It broke?"

"That's what I said—it broke," she said dully.

"Did you make it?"

"No." I felt her struggling with it. I waited.

"It was old. I leaned on it, and it broke." Her voice was defensive.

"Was this after you hurt your ankle?"

"Yeah, the first time."

Stay on track. "I need to see your bow."

"I told you, it's broke. Kaput. Get it?"

What now? Subtly communicate the fact that I'm scared she'll whack a steel broadhead into my eyeball? Tell her: *Baby-doll, seeing is believing?* What I said was, "We're here to help you, Raven. We don't want anyone else to get hurt." I heard myself and felt a twinge of repugnance at my tone: I sounded like my ex-husband—like my mother, as a matter of fact. "Show me the bow," I said in my own voice. I did a little here's-your-carrot wave with the sandwich.

She turned and dropped down onto all fours. Her garbage-bag cape fluttered behind her as she crawled into the shadows. I felt a quick pang. She might have been playing an animal, a sheep, a leopard in a school play. A moment later, she was back. The bow was, in fact, broken in half. She held up one piece of the stave in her hand. The rest of it dangled at the end of the bow-string. She swung it out over the rocks, as if she were fishing with a drop line, and jiggled it in my direction. "Happy?" she taunted.

I moved up, deposited the sandwich on the rock, and withdrew. She hopped down, snatched it up, and retreated. Given her puffed-up ankle, she was surprisingly agile. Still standing, she shoved half the sandwich into her mouth and chomped down. Shattered fragments of bacon popped out. She wolfed down the sandwich as if it might be snatched away, then checked the folds of her sweater for bonus bits.

Her absorption in the search made her face look less pinched. But under the grey smudge across her nose and cheekbones, her skin was sallow, her cheeks sunken. It brought back the way Rachel, my daughter, had looked before she died. The brush of shadow under her small, waxy cheekbones. The wisps of dull hair against the clean hospital sheet. Pediatric pink, the sheet had been stamped with cheery little nosegays of unidentifiable flowers.

Raven's face had the same starved look as Rachel's—understandable enough, given the circumstances. More unsettling was the fact that Raven's eyes had the same look as my daughter's a knowingness that made you want to look away. There was the sense that, even if I didn't want to talk about it, both dying child and killer woman knew exactly what the score was.

Raven squatted down on her right leg, left leg extended, and retrieved a crumbled piece of bacon. Nothing wrong with her knees. Or her quads. She might be starving, but she was still strong.

"You up for another?"

Raven considered me. "Yeah. Sure, I'll eat another one for you."

"Right. Do me a favor."

She smiled slightly, as if caught in the act, and amended in a mocking singsong, "Yes please, Mom, I'd like another one."

I said nothing.

"You want me to say 'pretty please'?"

"What happened to your ankle?"

"I tripped." She let out a blast of contempt. "Talk about stupid? You guys could of had me right afterwards. I was, like, *crawling* up here. I thought I'd fucking *broken* it." She looked at her boot. "Maybe I did."

"Hurt now?" I asked.

She thought about it. "Yeah. Some. I packed it up in snow, stayed put. Swelling went down. I could put some weight on it. Thought maybe it was going to be okay. Thought maybe I'd just sprained it." She smirked. "I made it over to your camp." The smirk widened into a death's-head leer.

You are nothing like Rachel, I stormed inwardly. *Nothing!*

"Did you notice?"

"What?"

"I stole two of your cool ones."

She was asking for admiration. I felt like throwing up. "No," I lied. "We didn't notice."

She caught the frost in my voice. "That was when it started acting up on me again," she whined. "I think maybe it's broken."

I forced up a dose of sympathy. "You need an X ray. We can get you to a doctor. Get you something for the pain."

"I broke my mother's bow." She met my eyes and again, I

glimpsed despair. "I leaned on it and it broke. I showed it to you."

"Yes."

"It wasn't any good anyways," she argued, as much to herself as to me. "It was old. Like, it had a permanent set."

Whatever that was. "Your mother made it?"

"She made it out of juniper wood. Yew would of been better. I don't know why she didn't use yew. They've got yew up in Michigan. I looked it up." She found another speck of bacon on her sweater, plucked it off and swallowed it. Then she looked at me. "An old wood bow like that? It don't hold energy. It don't take the energy from you, not like a new one. That's why I had to get in so close."

I nodded sympathetically, then eased us off collision course: "Where'd you learn to shoot?"

"My foster dad. He was in this kinda like a club. Hey," she protested, "you said you were going to get me another sandwich."

"Okay. You need something to drink?"

"I wouldn't mind a Coke."

"Sorry. I didn't bring any soda. O.J.?" I offered. "Actually, it's Tang."

"That's okay. I got water." She glanced up behind her at the scrapings. "I guess that's how you found me, huh?"

I nodded. "You can see it from our camp. How'd you melt the snow? You have a stove?"

"I had garbage bags," she bragged. "Ever heard of solar power?"

"Neat," I approved. If nothing else, the girl had survival skills. "How did you find your—what is it, a cave up there?"

"More like a hole under the rocks. One side's been dug out. It's pretty tight. You can't really sit up inside, but it goes in a ways. Once you're in, you can stretch out okay." She shrugged. "I found it by luck. I'd figured on going out the other way afterward. You know, up over the top, pick up the trail down to Turquoise Lake, and out onto Eighty-three?"

"Mm," I said.

"But then I hurt my ankle and I was getting kinda thirsty so I decided to hang out over here for a bit. I was climbing up here to get some snow and out pops this coyote. Man. He looks at me, I look at him, then off he trots, tail between his legs! Reckon I scared him off." She grinned her death's-head grin. "So I took his hole. He never did come back." She broke off. "What's he doing?" she demanded sharply. "Who's he talking to?"

I turned. Luke's eyes were fixed on us, but he was talking into his handset.

I took a breath. "There's a bunch of people up here with him. They hiked in this morning. We're surrounded." If I sounded like a B-grade movie, she didn't object. Nor did she express any surprise. Her face was grave, as if the expected had come to pass.

Now or never, I thought. I made my pitch: "Not many people could manage to survive the way you have, Raven. Most people wouldn't have made it through the first night. You're smart, you're strong, you're young. You've got a lot going for you." In her eyes, I saw doubt wrestling with the desire to believe. Suddenly I felt sorry for her. "We aren't here to judge what happened," I told her. "What happened in the past doesn't matter right now. What matters is your future. It's time for you to start thinking about getting yourself out of this mess. We can help you. Think about it. Will you think about it?"

After a moment, she nodded solemnly. "Good girl," I praised her. "Now I'm going to go and get that sandwich for you."

NINETEEN

I SPENT THE NEXT three hours climbing up and down between Raven and Luke. The idea was to keep the pressure up without having her lid fly off. Like a master of the rack, I was supposed to turn the screws with a light hand and let pain do the heavy work. Problem was, there were no dials or gauges—or, as my mother had put it, no map for the wilderness of the soul. Up on the snowy side of a mountain, Raven Davisson with two s's swung back and forth from fatalistic calm to agitated anxiety. And I banged back and forth between compassion and disgust.

Something said or unsaid would set her off. She would start gnawing her knuckles. Her eyes would well up with tears of despair, her bony shoulders would twitch under her garbage bag cape, and she would careen into anger. I couldn't sort out various names she blamed and her narratives kept looping around into a tedious snarl of self-pity. I made rote listening noises and stared at the deepening blue of the afternoon sky. But during one rant, she veered onto Roland. "He got what was coming to him," she fumed. "He killed my mother."

I sat up, electrified, and stared at her. "Roland killed your mother?"

My surprise made her regroup. She looked around as if she'd misplaced something, then settled on sarcasm. "No, Santa Claus killed my mother."

"Did you know him? I thought you didn't know him."

"But I knew his name," she retorted with a smug smile. "Roland Redhawk. My grandma used to sing it when she got shit-faced. 'Roland Redhawk killed your beautiful mother,' " she mimicked in a drunken wail. "You couldn't get her to shut up. Over and over, like some rock-a-bye-baby song: 'Roland Redhawk killed your beautiful mother.' Yeah, I knew his name, all right." She paused. "Then I saw it when I was living in Madison. They have this store there that's sorta like a museum, only small like a store, and I was walking by the window and saw all this Indian shit. Bowls and bracelets hanging on a dead branch and a bunch of beaded bags laid out on white sand, like they'd washed up on a clean beach. One of them had this cool-looking bear on it, and I kept looking at it. Then I noticed this little sign that said, 'On loan from the collection of Roland Redhawk.' So I went in and asked the woman there about it and she told me he lived in St. Ignatius, Montana."

Then, for no discernible reason, her mood would switch and she would become curious, ask me where I lived, where was that. She had never heard of Washington, D.C., although she recognized President's Clinton's name. She wanted to know if I had a car, did I take the bus, how did I get out here then? When I told her I flew, she brightened. "I've never been in an airplane," she said. She ate two more sandwiches and two candy bars and washed them down with melted snow sucked through a straw in the lid of a convenience-store mug—a quart-sized orange-and-blue number from Town Pump. My own stomach growled but I was too strung out to eat. Luke made coffee and the aroma wafted up to us. On my trips down, I drank it, spooning in the sugar, but Luke refused Raven's request for a cup. "Let's hold onto that one for a while," he directed.

We talked about getting her to a doctor. She didn't know what an X ray was. *Where has she been?* I wondered. I explained about X rays. "Colored pictures?" she wondered. "No, black-and-white," I said.

She was more interested in getting a lawyer than a doctor. (She'd seen O.J. and his lawyers on TV.) She also wanted to know how we were going to get her back down.

On horseback, Luke decided. "I'm not going to call in a chopper. This isn't a medical emergency. She's put up with that ankle this far, she can ride out. We'll put her on a plug, get her something for the pain."

"How about a downer for hors d'oeuvres? It's already a bumpy ride, and we haven't even gotten her on the pony."

"Something like Valium? I'll check with the medics."

"I was, ah, trying for a smile here, Luke."

He looked at me. "You okay?"

"No. Tell the EMTs to send me up a Saint Bernard. The kind with the little barrel around its neck."

"What was that you were saying earlier? Something about delayed gratification?"

RAVEN HAD NEVER ridden a horse. She was at once dubious and pleased by the idea. I promised her that I'd ride down with her and suggested to Luke that he use Pete's horses—or least horses that were used to llamas. We didn't need a string of horses freaking out at the sight of Fluffy. Luke agreed, but it took a lot of back-and-forth on the radio and even more waiting. Dolores had to get home from school, load her old mare and Pete's big gelding in their van, pick up her brother and two more horses, then ride up from the trailhead.

Meanwhile, we decided to try two Tylenol capsules. "Hey, Raven," I said. She was sitting back against the rocks, eyes closed. She opened them. "You allergic to any drugs?"

She frowned. "No."

"Look, here's something for your ankle." I put the offering on our halfway rock. "It'll help the pain."

Curious, she climbed down, but when she saw the pills, she started to shake. "No!" she shouted angrily. She scooped them up and hurled them at me. Below us, two deputies with rifles stepped out of the woods. Luke waved them back. "You can't make me!" she yelled. Her eyes were afraid. "You can't make me!"

When she calmed down, I climbed back down to Luke.

"Jesus," I said. "What was that about?"

His face was tense. "Whatever it was, you brought it down okay. That was good work, Lee."

But his praise gave me no boost. I felt shaky and, oddly enough, guilty—as if, in some nightmarish way, I had turned the pills to poison.

AS THE afternoon wore on, Luke worked himself halfway up the wall of boulders while Webb and an another man came out of the woods to establish a position next to Fluffy. Raven and I settled onto our respective perches. We were both tired, and if we didn't trust each other, at least the mood had become companionable. Gradually, the brilliant silvery light off the snow softened to a gold-washed vermeil. The dark spaces between the rocks widened, as if leaking shadows from the Underworld. Below us, radios crackled—static from a busier sphere.

I relayed messages back and forth: "Dolores is at the trailhead, the horses are on their way."

"Tell him I want a cigarette. You said I could have a cigarette."

"Let her wait. Tell her no one up here smokes."

"Tell him bullshit. And don't let him get me no menthols either. I don't care for menthols."

FOR A MARLBORO and a cup of hot coffee, Raven traded an owl-fletched arrow. There was no way to tell if it was the one she had yanked out of Roland's heart: to the naked eye, it was clean of blood. In my hand, the high-tech carbon shaft felt smooth and cool as pencil lead.

Luke called for an evidence bag. Above us, Raven lit up. The tang of tobacco cut the cooling air. I inhaled deeply, catching nothing but old memories. On we haggled. She insisted she had no more arrows. "She hasn't given it all up, yet," Luke said grimly.

"How do you know?"

"I know. She's holding onto an ace, and I don't think more Malboros are going to cut it loose for us. Ask her if she's got a gun."

I climbed back up to her. "Raven. My boss wants to know if you have a gun."

She let out a sarcastic little snort. "Where am I gonna get the money for a gun?"

"Do you have a gun?"

"I told you. I don't have no gun. They never let me have a gun. I never even got to try one," she said wistfully.

They? I didn't ask. If she was lying, she was world-class. We waited some more. A mantle of shadow stretched across the clearing. Finally we heard horses in the forest. A pair of tribal Fish and Wildlife men rode into the clearing, each leading a saddled horse. From our separate perches, Raven and I watched them dismount and turn the horses over to Webb and the deputy.

"Which one's mine?" she wondered.

"I don't know."

Luke climbed up beside me and briefed Raven. "You're going to put your hands up on your head," he told her. "Lee and I will come up and check you for weapons. Then we'll help you get down and onto a horse. If you do what we tell you, you won't get hurt."

"But which one's mine?" she repeated anxiously.

"Let's get down there. Then we'll see. Okay? You ready? You ready for us to come up there?"

"Wait!" she burst out. "I can't leave yet."

Luke's face was impassive. "Why not?"

"I need something."

It took another five minutes to get it out of her. What she wanted was her pack. She said she had hidden it in the woods on the east side of Lost Pipe Lake. She had intended to pick it up "afterward," but after she hurt her ankle, she had not been able to take the weight of it. She had taken out her mug, her remaining food (two cans of SpaghettiOs), her Virginia Slims, and a box of garbage bags. Now she wanted the rest of her things. She worried about animals getting at them.

Luke showed no irritation. "What do you need out of it, Raven?"

She ignored him. "I want my pack," she said to me.

I let out a tired sigh and looked at Luke.

He thought about it. Finally he decided, "Okay. We'll get it for you."

She gave us directions. Half an hour later, Webb carried a battered navy blue day pack up to Luke. "Raven," Luke said. "Is this it?"

"Yeah."

"Is there something special you want out of it?"

"It's mine."

He shook his head regretfully. "I'm afraid it's also evidence at a crime scene. I can't let you have it. But I promise we'll take good care of it for you." He started to climb down with the pack.

"Wait!" she cried out in alarm. "It's mine!"

"You have some personal items here?" His voice was sympathetic. "Something of a personal nature, I might be able to let you have. But I need you to help us out here, Raven. I need you to give us something in return."

She scowled. "I don't have nothing."

"I think you do. You're a smart girl. I think you still have a weapon."

"I already told *her.* I don't have but nothing."

"Like I said, Raven, you're an intelligent young lady. You know that sooner or later, you're going to have to give it up. Why don't you make it easier for yourself? Let us have it now."

He hunkered down on the rock and unzipped the pack. I caught a pungent whiff of old socks and wood smoke. He pulled out a greasy sleeping bag, dirty underwear, a pale blue orlon sweater, Tampax, deodorant, a Goofy toothbrush, a roll of duct tape, and finally, wrapped in a pair of black jeans, a small varnished cedar box that said "Pigeon River, Michigan" in black script on the lid.

Luke opened it up. Inside, on tomato red velvet, lay a sad tangle of costume jewelry: a pin set with plastic "aquamarines," gilt chains, a class ring, an enameled daisy, a silver ID bracelet, a man's stainless-steel wristwatch with a yellowed face. Luke held up a knotted string of small graduated pearls. Maybe they were cultured.

"Those are mine!" Raven shouted. "They were my mother's!"

Fluffy's head lifted. The horses shifted nervously. I felt triumph trilling through Luke, but his voice remained serene. "Give up your weapon and I'll let you have them."

She jerked her head to the side, as if hearing something suspicious, then stumped a step back, a step forward. She had given up her stick, but moving around without it seemed to cause her little pain. Finally she reached under her shirt and pulled out a hunting knife. It looked capable of filleting an elephant. She lay it down on the rock at her feet, straightened up, and looked at Luke. Without taking her eyes off him, she found a handhold in the boulder beside him, balanced herself on her good leg, and nudged the knife over the edge of the rock with the toe of her left boot. It fell ten feet, clanged off a rock, and slid into a crack. "All gone," she chimed.

Luke and I looked at each other. Then Luke nodded to Webb who climbed up, retrieved the knife and without making a display of it, unholstered his Smith & Wesson. Luke gave me the pearls. I held them up. "I'm going to bring your necklace up to you, Rachel—I mean, Raven!" I let out a sharp, nervous laugh. Raven looked startled.

"It's okay," Luke soothed us both. "Raven, put your hands up on your head."

Nonchalantly, she laced her fingers together, put her hands on her head, and waited for us to climb up to her. Her ledge was wider than it looked from below, a kind of rock-studded landing that backed into the snowline. One end had recently been used as a toilet; the snow was trampled and stained. How had I not noticed? Yesterday I had climbed within ten feet of it. The entrance to her hole was easier to miss; it was hidden by a scrubby mountain alder. Above the den, where she had gathered snow, the melted paths glistened in the dying light like a wet claw.

"I want my necklace," Raven pouted. Her laced hands pushed the mat of her hair forward, like a loose wig.

"Hang on," Luke said cheerfully. "You can have it as soon as we get these on you." As he walked around behind her, he reached behind him under his windbreaker and pulled out a pair of cuffs. Her eyes, following him, widened at the sight of them. It was as if her pupils were imploding into a black hole. She let out a small whimper. I stepped toward her, reaching out to reassure her but not sure exactly how, a touch, a hug at least let her have her necklace—but in the next instant, Luke snapped a cuff around her right wrist.

She exploded. Her arms flew up and out into the air as if blasted away by a bomb, and Luke fell back under the impact. Flailing, she cawed hoarse cries of distress. The loose cuff whipped through the air as she frantically tried to shake it off. It caught the side of my head and I reeled backward. "Raven!" I cried in shock. She looked up and recognized me. "You!" she bellowed. Furious, she attacked, lashing out at me with the cuff.

I fended her off with my arms, saw Luke diving for her legs. She went down with a howl, falling against me, clawing blindly at me as if she wanted to tear me into pieces. I twisted away, tripped off the ledge, and did a face plant onto a boulder ten feet below.

The next thing I remember was hearing Raven's screams on the ledge above: "Don't, don't, don't! Oh, please don't, I'll be good. I promise I'll be a good girl, please don't!"

What were they doing to her? I heard Luke's voice over my head: "Get an EMT up here. Now." I felt confused. I was lying on my side, somebody's jacket folded up under my head. "Don't move, Lee," he said kindly. "You're going to be okay."

I tried to push myself up and felt a stab of pain between my right wrist and elbow. I rolled onto my knees and tried to speak. Luke was leaning over me, his arms easing me into a sitting position. I gagged and spat and saw a dark clots of blood hit the rock beside me. I hoped I wasn't spitting out bits of my tongue. Raven kept on screaming, a grating, steely noise that bounced off the rocks and keep on going right through my skin.

"Let's get some snow on that," Luke said to someone. "You've got a cut under your lower lip," he said to me. "Looks like your teeth went right through."

I made a noise.

"Take it easy."

"Can you move your toes?" asked a new voice.

Luke held something wet and icy against my chin. It stung like yellow jackets. Someone's hand carefully moved sticky strands of hair out of my eyes. I felt a wave of nausea, pushed away the cold pack from my mouth, and spat more blood. Then I focused on my right hand. It was still in a fist and bleeding. Raven's flying cuff had gashed the tops of my fingers. I opened my fingers and saw her pearls. Smeared with blood from my fingers, they lay in the palm of my hand like a pile of just-extracted baby teeth.

TWENTY

I REFUSED to let Luke call in a medevac—even after he said he'd pay for it. No doubt I looked alarming: I was not only drooling blood; my nose had spurted like a Villa d'Este fountain, and I had multiple lacerations from the flying steel handcuff. My right forearm hurt, but I could feel nothing out of place under the skin and I decided it was only bruised. Moreover, despite my face-first landing, my neck was unbroken, my jaw still moved and when I tested my teeth with my finger, none had that sickening wiggle that spells January in the Caribbean for your dentist. (Given the fact that my pearly beiges were not covered by my major medical, a cervical fracture would have been cheaper than fake choppers.)

I had to ask for a boost onto Pete's big bay, but I rode out with Raven, as promised. A form of self-punishment: Raven wouldn't have noticed if I'd sprouted wings and carried her out like a stork. She shrank into a rigid autistic silence. Luke was solicitous toward her—obviously, he was compensating for not having warned her about the cuffs. Apologetically, he explained that she would have to wear a belly chain on the way down. She showed no reaction. A pair of nervous deputies wrapped it around her waist and clipped her cuffed wrists to it, but the only noise was the clinking of loose chain. When they raised her up onto Dolores's mare, they might just as well have been loading a brace of two-by-eights onto a packsaddle. ("How's she look over on your side, Tommy?")

Needless to say, it was no pony ride down the mountain, but I don't remember a lot of pain. What I remember is how kind everyone was, how gentle the faceless male voices were in the dark. I got the shakes on the way down—I remember the same deep mortal chill on the delivery table after Rachel's birth—and I almost chattered out of the saddle. The deputies halted our procession, peeled off their jackets, wrapped me in blankets. Their rough makeshift cloak fell over the back of my horse and down to my stirrups, so that I rode through the night forest like a medieval queen in disguise.

Two ambulances were waiting at the trailhead, spinning red light against the pines. One for me, one for Raven. I would have preferred to ride in one of the black-and-whites, but when it came to getting off my horse, my legs gave out and I ended up on a gurney. Dolores, who had hiked down with the Fish and Wildlife men at the head of our procession, rode with me to the hospital. She said Pete and her brother would bring the llamas down the next morning. Luke, still in his "I-care" mode, rode with Raven.

In the ER at Polson, nurses drew curtains around me, pulled off my boots, hooked me up to an IV. I lay under bright lights, and various medical and law-enforcement people looked in to console me with the same joke: "Boy, you sure took it on the chin." As if that were a virtue.

"What time is it?" I asked Dolores. My words slopped out like seawater from a loose bucket. "Ten of ten," she said. It felt like 2:00 a.m. I asked her to call my mother for me. "Tell her I'm fine. Tell her I'll call tomorrow."

Rose showed up with coffee in foam cups and a Big Mac for Dolores. "How you doing?" Rose asked. She peered at my lip, and shook her head. "You aren't going to feel like any serious kissing real soon." She gave me a lewd wink. The meaty smell of fast-food grease wafted through the cubicle. My stomach turned. "You look a bit green," Rose informed me. "You want a pail?"

I waited and dozed and listened to conversations on the other side of the curtains. Raven was in the next bed: I could hear her chains clinking when she moved, but she answered questions in a droned mumble I couldn't make out. Then they wheeled her off to X ray, and a man complaining of stomach pain moved in. More correctly, his wife complained. She described the peculiarities and preferences of his intestinal tract with perverse satisfaction and in stultifying detail. ("He can't take cucumbers, not even the burpless kind, nor green peppers either, and onions, they act up on him same way, but you can't tell him anything about it....")

I lay behind my curtains and heard pages coming over the PA, canned laughter from a TV, and Luke and a male voice in the hallway talking about Raven's X rays.

"You're saying she's broken that same ankle before?" Luke asked.

"See this? I'd say it never was set."

"How long ago?"

"Good long while. A childhood injury. Right leg's an inch shorter than her left."

"We looking at abuse?"

"Or neglect."

"It's not broken now?"

"A bad sprain."

TO MY ANNOYANCE, my X rays showed a simple fracture of the ulna. It had cracked under the impact either of my fall or Raven's handcuff. A doctor in green encased my forearm in an excessively large white cast. He was young and polite. Another doctor in a heathery shetland sweater came in to sew up my lip. This one looked about my age and was less polite. There was grey in his trim brown beard, his features had a chiseled intellectual cast, and his voice was dry. He pulled on rubber gloves, turned yet another spotlight on my face. Rose went out for a cigarette with Dolores. "Wait a sec," I said to the doctor. "You a plastic surgeon?"

"No." He prodded at my lip.

"You done this before?"

"A couple times." He squirted something cold into the open flap under my lip. He mopped and squirted with authority, pulled tugged, pinched, and started sewing. Webb came in, a welcome distraction. He said that Luke had taken Raven over to the county jail and would see me later. He peered over the doctor's shoulder and grimaced in distaste. "She gonna have a scar there, Doc?" he wondered.

"A night crawler," said the doctor.

"Ha, ha," I growled without moving my mouth.

"By the way," Webb said to me. "Did Luke tell you about Charlie Herron?"

"Uh-uh."

"A fax came into the office while we were up on the mountain.

Turns out, back in the seventies, Herron used to work for the FBI. He ran the St. Paul office."

"Uh?"

"Our friend Roland Redhawk was one of his snitches."

"Huh."

"Hang in there," he told me and he left. I watched the doctor's long, sweatered arm pulling long, almost-invisible threads through my lip, and considered the late Roland Redhawk. Roland had attended the tribal tourism conference and heard Herron present his "low-impact" ski resort-casino scheme. Roland must have recognized Charlie Herron right from the beginning. Herron, however, didn't recognize his former underling. Roland looked vaguely familiar to him, as he had remarked—more than once—on the way up to Lost Pipe Lake. "I never forget a face," he said the evening he was killed. But taken out of context, memory can fail. The produce manager of the supermarket is unrecognizable standing in line at the movies. Did Herron finally make the connection? On the night he died, did Roland's former identity break the surface of his Scotch-soaked brain? Suppose it had. Suppose Herron had said suddenly: "Hey, I know you. You worked for me back in Minneapolis." Was this motive enough for murder: a twenty-five-year-old boss-underling relationship? Had Roland killed Charlie Herron to protect his self-cherished persona as an AIM warrior? And what was Roland's connection to Raven's mother? Had he actually killed her, as Raven believed? My mind felt lazy. Images of the afternoon drifted through my head: Raven swinging her broken bow; Raven greedily eating bacon sandwiches; Raven exhaling cigarette smoke into the cooling air.

The doctor pulled off his gloves, wrote me a prescription, and gave it to me. "This is good shit. If you don't need it all, you can sell it on the street and make your copay." His delivery was deadpan.

"You're too kind," I told him.

I LEFT THE HOSPITAL with Dolores and Rose without seeing Luke. The town had closed up for the night and there was no easy way to get the prescription filled. Annoyed, I tore it up. The local wore off in the small hours and I got up to check my chin in the mirror: under the sutures on the outside, there was only the finest red line. Inside, however, it felt like a barbed-wire implant. I ate two aspirin and went back to Pete's and Dolores's big bed. Dolores had insisted; she took the sofa bed downstairs, saying she had to get up early for school.

The next day was Friday. Rose made me a chocolate milk shake for breakfast. I called my mother collect and drooled out a damage report.

"Oh, Lee!" she exclaimed several times in distress. Gradually, worry yielded to relief. I imagined her in her office, leaning back, inch by inch, in her ergonomic tweed chair: her worst fears had not been realized. I had survived. To tell the truth, I was relieved myself.

"So," I said giddily. "How's the weather back there?"

"Perfect fall days. Cool and sunny. We have not had the air-conditioning on all week and again this morning, the sun is pouring in through my window. I can see how badly it needs to be washed!"

"It's raining here." I was talking on the upstairs extension, sitting on the side of Pete's and Dolores's bed. Opposite me, a small window under the eaves looked down on a hay field. A dirty mist hung over the wet stubble.

"What happened to the girl?" my mother inquired.

"Your wild boar? They took her away in chains." I told her about Raven, chronicled her manipulations, her odd gaps of knowledge, her free-form bursts of panic. I was hoping for a diagnosis. I wanted my mother to say, "Ah, yes," give it a name, hold out a cure. "They think she might have been abused as a child," I offered.

My mother was not impressed. Child abuse was a routine fact of her professional existence. She was more interested in the state of my psyche than Raven's. This should have consoled me, but her dismissal of Raven only made me cranky.

"And how are you—otherwise?" she probed tactfully.

"Oh, just great," I snapped.

She waited. A gust of rain scratched the tin roof. I cast around for something to toss her, an innocuous bone. I was certainly not going to cry on her shoulder about the imminent end of my fling with the only lover I'd had in the last five years. Nor did I feel like "venting" my frustration at the fact that he was a kind, upbeat, decent man who was trying to make a go of his marriage. I pushed aside a sour cloud of guilt and, suddenly, in the closet of my memory, found a pair of faded red sneakers, tied with brown laces and splotched with blood. "I think I'm losing my mind," I said.

"Really?" There was a maternal smile in her voice.

I told her about the sneakers.

She perked up, a hound on the scent. "A false memory. How interesting."

"What, that your daughter's going insane?"

She made a small noise of impatience. I could see her hand flicking away my worry, my grandmother's diamond catching the sunlight from her window. "Do you remember the red sneakers you had?"

"Me?"

"I think you were eight or nine."

"Mom, I never had red sneakers. You always bought us navy blue ones. So they wouldn't show the dirt, you said. I remember wanting white ones and being jealous when Johnny got them because he was starting tennis. You never bought me red sneakers."

"You wanted red," my mother insisted. "I thought they were déclassé. But in the end, you won. 'Perseverance furthers,'" she quoted wryly. A favorite bon mot from the *I Ching.*

"*I* had red sneakers?"

"I think there is a picture. Your 'declaration of independence.' I can check in the album for you," she offered.

"That's okay. I believe you. I just don't get it."

"It is not so difficult. The goddess is an aspect of your Self. Artemis appeared to you 'in your shoes,' as it were."

I was too stunned to argue. I could not remember wearing red sneakers. I could not see them on my eight-or nine-year-old feet. And what about the blood? Had I actually seen Roland's blood on Raven's boots? Or was I remembering my own blood? "Did I ever cut myself when I was wearing these alleged sneakers?"

"Oh, Lee, you cut yourself all the time!" she scolded. "You were always racing around, falling off your bike, running after your brother and his friends. You were always scraping yourself up!" She laughed. "Nothing is changed!" she declared ruefully. Something beeped. "Excuse me. There is another call. It may be a patient. Don't go away!"

I waited. She was right. Nothing had changed. I was still getting bumped for her patients, still sipping the sweet poison of self-pity.

"Lee?"

"I'm still holding. It's your nickel."

"Where were we?"

"Sneakers," I said glumly.

"But there was something else—oh, yes, I wanted to tell you about Hercules' boar. It really is amazing how things pop up when you need them! The night before your—encounter?"

"Yes?"

"You called me on your detective friend's phone?"

"And?"

"And while we were talking, I remembered the labors of Hercules. Of course the association is obvious, but I'd completely forgotten that one of them involved a monstrous boar. You remember we were talking about Artemis's boar? Well, I am sorry I did not tell you about this one. Perhaps it would have helped."

"A hint from Hercules?"

"Lee," she objected mildly. "Do you know how Hercules captured the boar of Erymanthus?"

"No, Mom."

"He forced it out of its lair, high up on the mountain. Then he pulled it into deep snow, and when the animal was exhausted, he carried it on his shoulders down to the king!" Her voice was bright with triumph.

"Well," I said slowly, "I'd call that a miss. Your crystal ball needs a polish. For one thing, it happened on rock, not in the snow. That's how I got hurt, landing on a big rock."

"I understand how you were injured. I am not pretending to be prescient," she stated indignantly. "I was worried about you. This story came to me as we were talking that night. If you had allowed me to tell it to you, you might have considered the snow. That is all. Now I must return my patient's call."

Of course, she was right. Dr. Marcella Romann-Squires, Soothsayer, was my own handy projection. Beneath it there was a woman I scarcely knew, a woman who, despite her considerable skills and experience, still harbored the maternal insecurity of every other mother on earth. "Wait. I'm sorry," I apologized. "What happened to the wild boar?"

She was not entirely mollified. "I imagine they ate it," she said.

TWENTY-ONE

LUKE DIDN'T CALL until Saturday. Rose and Dolores were busy cooking for Eddie McNab's wake—a three-night tribal affair. I was of no use in the kitchen, thanks to my heroic cast, so I passed the morning with Paul, visiting Fluffy, Oreo, Jake, Ringo, and the other llamas. Paul and I were "helping" Pete in the tack room in the barn, when Dolores brought me out the walk-around phone. It was Luke. I drifted out the tack room into the vaulting dark of the barn's central aisle.

Luke sounded jaunty and genuinely apologetic for not having called sooner. On Thursday night, he said, he had taken Raven from the ER to the county jail. There he had "Mirandized" her and invited her to tell "her side" of the story. By dawn, he had six hours of interview on tape. Since then he'd been working full tilt trying to wrap things up. He was due back in Helena on Monday morning.

"So how's she doing?"

"Okay I guess. I haven't seen her since the interrogation."

"Can I hear the tape?"

My request disconcerted him. "I can't do that, Lee. It's evidence in an criminal investigation."

"Did she have a lawyer present?"

"Nope. She didn't want to wait."

"Up on the mountain, she said she wanted one."

"What she wanted is an ear. It's what they all want. If I do my job right, I'm their best friend."

The darkness smelled of hay and earth and engine oil. "It doesn't bother you?"

"What?"

"Conning people like that."

"No way," he declared cheerfully. "All you have to do is think of the victim."

"Roland?"

He said nothing. I looked up at the stretch of missing roof at the far end of the barn. The exposed rafters made a dark rib cage against the bright blue sky. *Quit raining on the man's parade, Squires.* "I'd really like to see you, Luke," I said.

"I was going to ask you if you wanted to have dinner with me."

"And now you're not?"

He laughed, his high spirits restored. "What I mean is, can you eat?"

"Definitely not steak. Macaroni, maybe. But I can drink."

"I know that."

I laughed. "You'll have to pick me up. I've got this insane cast on my right arm, and Pete's machines are all stick shift."

"Around six?"

"Six?"

"Too early?"

"On the contrary. 'Tis twenty year till then!'" I quoted. I waltzed into a shaft of sunlight. Paul stared at me from the doorway of the tack room. Overhead, a swallow swooped through open rafters.

There was a smile in Luke's voice. "How 'bout I aim for five-thirty? No guarantee, though."

So what else is new? "I'll be right here, pawing the earth."

It was closer to six-thirty than five-thirty when he drove up, but never mind that. The cast made getting ready tricky. Dolores had to help me into my bra and, so I didn't have to slit the right sleeve of one of my own shirts, Pete lent me another one of his, this time a cream-colored flannel shirt, worn soft as a baby's hand-me-down cottons. (His blood-soaked striped number was still soaking in a bucket on the porch.) I sat in the kitchen, and little Paul watched with interest as Rose brushed and braided my hair for me. "It's so pretty. You should wear it loose," she protested.

"I don't like it in my face."

"Your poor face," she sympathized.

With my left hand, I gingerly tested my nose. I looked like the bride of Mike Tyson. My lip bulged like a sutured sausage, my mashed nose gleamed rawly with ointment, a Band-Aid covered the cut on my forehead and a half-moon of deepest purple hung under one eye. Dolores's efforts with a concealer stick only made it more repulsive. "What you need is a veil," she decided.

When Luke saw me, he winced. "It's a test," I told him. "If you can bring yourself to kiss me, I turn into a princess."

He peered at my face and scratched his neck. "The question is, where?" In a show of gallantry, he raised my left hand to his lips.

I pulled back my hand. "That doesn't count."

"You can't afford to be too picky."

THE RESTAURANT was a upscale café located on the lake north of Polson. Luke had heard "you could get something besides steak" there. The varnished log walls displayed sepia blowups of old photographs: steamboats ferrying across the lake and early model pickups in newly planted cherry orchards. The ambiance, however, was more California than Flathead Lake. It was the sort of place where "wait-persons" pushed "cabs" and "chards." Our wait-person was young, tanned, and stony. She marched us to a corner table, slapped our menus down onto the dark green tablecloth, and promptly abandoned us. "What's the matter with her?" Luke wondered.

I brushed away three white petals from a chrysanthemum in a bud vase. "She probably thinks you beat me up."

"I'm a cop," he objected.

"She doesn't know that. Besides, cops never beat their wives? Tell me another one."

We picked up our menus. The fare was not *listed*, it was anthologized in ludicrous paragraphs any one of which would have earned my comp students a big fat F. Take the salmon (and I am not making this up):

> Salmon steak with local dried cherries poached in homemade court bouillon flavored with fresh sorrel, pink peppercorns, and purple basil, served with mango salsa and crème fraîche over black beans on a bed of organically grown wild greens.

How about fish sans fruit? Was the mango salsa "on the side" or mixed in with the crème fraîche? What exactly was the provenance of the "wild greens." Did we get free Tums for dessert? Our wait-person was not available to answer these or any other pressing questions. She bounced from table to table, assiduously avoiding eye contact with us. I wanted a drink. Luke looked antsy. "Flash your badge, if you think it would help," I suggested.

Finally Luke pushed back his chair and stood up. "What do you want?" he asked.

"Double black Jack on the rocks. And a straw."

He strolled over to the bar: the tall, lanky stranger ambling into the saloon. No unshaven yuppie barfly laughed when he ordered red-eye instead of chardonnay. A few minutes later, he came back with my bourbon and a frosted mug of beer. A few minutes after that, our wait-person sullenly took our order.

"What'd you do?" I asked.

"I told them we were celebrating the arrest of your husband."

"You didn't."

He grinned. "I told them if they were too busy to serve us, we would leave."

"How manly. I love it. Thanks." I raised my glass to him, sucked on the little red straw, tasted an icy thread of sour mash. "Now. Tell me about Raven Davisson."

"Not a lot to tell." He took a swallow of beer and considered me. "You look pretty bad," he said ruefully. "Does it hurt?"

"We aren't going to do a real wild good-bye thing, I can tell you that."

He gave a shy little shrug that tore at my heart. I changed the subject. "What about Raven?"

"Most of it you already know. It was just a question of filling in the gaps in what she told you up on the mountain. You did a great job, there, Lee."

"Thank you. So what'd she say?"

He frowned. "What do you want to know?"

"I don't know. You were the one who talked to her for six

hours. What about the mother? Did Roland really kill her?''

He sighed. ''We're still working on that one. Raven was only a year old when the mother died. The mother was part Objibwa. Martha Mary Davisson. Marty Davisson. She attended parochial school up in Michigan, got a full scholarship to Boston College, and dropped out after a year to work for AIM. She was at Wounded Knee for the duration, then went home to Michigan to have Raven. No father listed on the birth certificate. The next year, 1974, she was down on the Pine Ridge reservation. She was picked up one night, dead of winter, lying beside the road. She was wearing no coat, was seriously beaten up, bleeding and reeking of alcohol. The local cops dumped her in jail, but instead of sobering up, she died. No autopsy, no investigation.''

''You think she was murdered?''

''Hard to say. During those years, there were a number of unsolved Indian murders at Pine Ridge. The AIM people were at war with the FBI, and the tribal council was a corrupt bunch of goons. A lot of casualties were swept under the rug.''

''Was Raven there? Was she along with her mother at Pine Ridge?''

''Don't know that. I know that her grandmother in Michigan raised her. Then the grandmother died and she was put in foster care.''

''How old was she then?''

''Nine. I talked to both the foster mom and social services this morning. Sounds like the foster parents made a living off the payments they got for the kids they took in. They had a regular turnover, six kids at a time. She took care of them, he pumped gas part-time and the rest of the time collected disability and played with a survivalist group.''

''He taught her how to shoot, she said. With a bow and arrow. He wouldn't let her try a gun.''

Luke nodded. ''According to the foster mom, Raven didn't get to eat unless she grew it or killed it herself. She thought he was a little hard on her at times but she didn't like to interfere."

"Jesus."

"She said Raven was more than a handful of trouble, but she was good with the little kids. That's why they put up with her for so long."

"How long was that?"

"Till she was thirteen. She ran away. 'Never appreciated alls we did for her,'" Luke imitated in a whine.

Our wait-person brought my soup (shrimp bisque) and Luke's beef filet. "We'd like some bread," he said. "And another round, please."

Her mouth tightened. "Anything else?"

"How about a light for our candle?"

"Yessir." She turned away.

"And how about no tip for you, sweetie-pie?" I muttered darkly, hoping she'd heard.

Luke scraped chic goo off his steak. It looked respectable enough underneath. I spooned bisque into my mouth and felt a warm drool on my chin. I dabbed with my napkin and tried again.

"How's the soup?" he asked.

"Good. What hasn't leaked out tastes like shrimp. They used real cream."

He nodded approvingly and started in on his steak. The waitress came back with our second round and lit our candle. It made a warm circle of flickering light on the dark green cloth, softened Luke's lean, slightly lopsided features. He was wearing his soft charcoal jacket and a crisp white shirt with thin blue Wall Street stripes on it. I remembered the sweet contours of the body underneath the shirt and felt an acute pang of lust followed by a surge of annoyance at the condition of my own body. Well, we'd just have to work around it.

We listened to the couple sitting behind me talking too loudly about coffee. It sounded like a first date. The woman said, "I've only had half a cup, and my heart's flittering." The man said, "You should be able to float a horseshoe in it that's how I like it. Caffeine doesn't bother me. Here, take my pulse. You're a nurse."

"Sub-tle," Luke muttered.

I giggled. "What does Romeo look like?"

"About fifty. Stocky, five eight, one-ninety. She's younger, maybe one-forty."

"Is she taking his pulse?"

He shook his head in mock sorrow. "You win some, you lose some."

"Tell me more about the foster mom."

"Mrs. Porter? She said Raven came back to visit in July. She said she was real surprised."

"I'll bet."

"Raven stayed a couple days. When she left she took Mrs. Porter's jewelry with her and a juniper bow Mr. Porter spent a year making." Luke looked around for the waitress. "She didn't bring our rolls."

I felt stunned. "You mean Raven's mother didn't make the bow?"

"Mrs. Porter claimed her husband made it. The pearls, she said, were a graduation gift from her own mother. She's still steamed about it. Itemized the jewelry on the phone for me. Gold chains, pearls from her mother. Plus his class ring. They reported it to the authorities up there as a theft."

Behind us, the nurse was educating her date: "The heart's a muscle. It's got these little fibers in it called heartstrings. I've seen them under a microscope."

I took an icy swallow of bourbon. "What about the broken ankle? Did you ask about that?"

"Said she didn't know anything about no broken ankle. She got pretty defensive. Said the girl was a pathological liar. Told me she's taken in over a hundred children over the years and there's never been any complaint, that she loves every one of them just like they were her own, and that she and her husband were good Christians who sacrificed everything to give them a home."

I put my spoon down. Suddenly the soup didn't seem worth the trouble.

"It could have happened when she was living with the grandmother," Luke pointed out.

"...the blood goes in and out through valves..." The nurse's voice was flirtatious. I sucked at my whiskey.

Luke went on. "We checked the elementary-school records. Raven was referred for psychological testing twice. On one test, she showed up as mildly retarded. The other said she was gifted and talented. They put her in special ed. Chronic absenteeism, chronic discipline problems. After the Porters took her, she had home schooling. It was part of their survivalist thing." He forked in a mouthful of steak.

"We managed to run down the social worker. One of the sheriff's men interviewed her by phone on Friday. Raven was one of her first cases. She didn't remember anything about a broken ankle. But she did remember paying a home visit to the Porters'; the child's wrists were all swollen and chafed. She suspected rope burns."

"And she didn't do anything about it?"

"I didn't talk to her. I assume she tried to do something."

Suddenly I felt exhausted. My head was spinning. "You think that's what Mrs. Porter meant when she told you her husband was 'too hard' on Raven? That he'd tied her up?"

Luke winced. "It would explain why she lost it when I cuffed her."

"You think he—"

He put his fork down. "It happens." His voice had an angry edge.

"I can't stand this."

"...then your nerves send electrical impulses to your heartstrings," chirped the nurse behind me.

I wanted to turn around and tell her to shut up. Instead I asked Luke, "What about Raven's real mother—Marty? She was at Wounded Knee the same time as Roland?"

"Apparently."

"So Roland could have been Raven's father?"

"It's possible."

"Are you going to find out?"

He let out a weary sigh. "We can barely keep up with the

caseload, Lee. It's not often I have the luxury of chasing down as much information as we've got." He looked at me, his eyes full of concern. "Don't let this thing eat you up."

"No," I agreed.

"Thata girl," he approved.

"I just don't like it. I feel as if I *betrayed* her."

"You aren't going to like me to say this, Lee, but whatever you did up there on the mountain, it was just a drop in the bucket."

"You think I'm being grandiose?"

"No."

I tried to smile, felt the pull on my fat lip. "Liar. You're a hard man, Luke Donner.

"Seriously. What would you have done differently?" he asked.

"I don't know. My mother says if we'd gotten her up into the snow to make the arrest, I'd have had a softer landing."

"And if I hadn't rushed it at the end, if I'd taken the time, showed her the cuffs, talked her through it, you might not have had a landing at all. I don't feel real good about that, Lee. Every time I look at you, I want to kick myself."

"Yeah, well, I forgive you." I raised my cast in a priestly gesture of absolution.

Luke raised his beer mug. He took a long swallow, then carefully studied the inch that was left. "We make a good team," he said. Something about the elaborately casually way he said it made my heart stop. He met my eyes.

"Yeah," I said—half statement, half question.

He leaned forward over his plate. Candlelight flickered on his face. His expression was open, earnest, as if he were a birthday boy about to make a wish. "Maybe you should stick around."

I felt a sharp little kick of hope. "What do you mean?"

"You told me you weren't teaching this semester. Why don't you come back to Helena with me?"

"And do what?"

He raised a comical eyebrow. "Let me take care of you."

"Ah." I moved the saltshaker sideways an inch, like a pawn

on a chessboard. "You play doctor, and what about Barb? She going to be the nurse?"

He grinned sheepishly. Then he took a large breath and announced, "We're divorced."

I almost knocked over my water. "You're divorced?" It came out too loudly. Heads turned, then turned away. I leaned forward, lowered my voice. "You're divorced?"

"Hm."

I stared at him. "Since when? If I may ask."

He looked embarrassed. "It was final last November."

Thud. Something inside me collapsed. Folded up and went flat line. "Almost a year ago? Why didn't you tell me?"

"There's no good reason, Lee."

"You lied to me."

"I'm sorry," he said sincerely.

"Now I'm supposed to jump up and down with joy?"

His jaw tightened.

Behind me, the woman prattled on. "I believe a heart can literally rupture," she declared. "They've documented cases where people have died of a broken heart."

Romeo declared, "They told me mine's as strong as a twenty-year-old's."

Luke made a wry face at the man's boast. His eyes were sympathetic, guileless. He grinned his charming grin.

"You mean to tell me," I said slowly, my voice as cold as black ice, "that when I flew out here last Christmas and we did that noble good-bye thing at the airport, you were already divorced? You dumped me for—what? Ex-sex?"

Luke studied the rim of his plate.

I took a breath. "I have to say, my own ex has never been a temptation, but I've heard people swear by it. Or was there someone else in the picture? Was Christmas a test?" I let out a bitter bark of a laugh. "I guess I came in second."

"Lee."

Our waitress appeared. "Is everything all right?" she scowled.

"Fine," Luke said impatiently.

She looked at me. "We're fine, thank you," I confirmed.

"You need anything else?" she pressed.

"No, we're fine." My voice sounded curiously pleasant.

She removed our plates. Luke leaned across the table, his face worried. "Lee, honest to God, I'm sorry. I'm sorry about that. I was scared. Last Christmas? The morning of the day you left? Barb called. And I jumped. Same old story. She was only jerking me around. Now it's over."

"But you never bothered to let me know."

"I wish to God I had. I don't know why I didn't!" he burst out in anguish.

I said nothing. We all run on different timetables. I should have known better than to expect Luke's to match my own. But I couldn't help feeling betrayed.

He put his hand to his heart, patted it proudly. "I swear to you, Lee. In here, it's over with Barb."

I felt nothing. Nothing at all.

"I care about you. We make a good team," he said for the second time.

"What if we hadn't bumped into each other?"

He looked genuinely puzzled. "But we did."

I shook my head. "I'm not sure this can ever work."

WE SKIPPED COFFEE. Luke paid the check with a credit card. I didn't ask how much or if he'd tipped. On the drive back to St. Ignatius, it started to rain. He turned on the wipers. I asked, "What do you think will happen to her?"

"To Raven?"

"Yes."

"I've done my job, Lee. What happens next is not my department." It sounded like a rebuke.

I don't remember getting out his car. I don't remember saying good-bye. I do remember trying to protect my cast from the rain on the way into the house.

I FELT SHIPWRECKED. Like an inept actor stumbling ashore in a production of *The Tempest,* I staggered into the Bonsecours' kitchen. It was warm and bright and crowded with women. The sharp fragrance of coffee cut through the heavier smells of damp hair and cigarette smoke and somebody's lily of the valley. Pete was the only man in the room, a large masculine anchor with a slow smile. The women's voices splashed over his head. They all had just come back from Eddie's wake. I kept blinking at them. I recognized some of the faces from Roland's funeral. "Where's Dolores?" I asked.

"She's putting Paul down," Rose said. She pushed forward a squarely built woman about my own age. Her brown hair curled onto the shoulders of a fuchsia pink jacket. "This is Ellen White Cloud," Rose said. "She's a medicine woman."

Rose turned back to Ellen White Cloud. "This is who I was telling you about."

"Lee Squires," I said. "Nice to meet you." I tried my cocktail-party smile. It was out of order.

Rose said to me, "Ellen was a friend of Eddie's." There was a nudge of significance in her voice. Then it clicked. Ellen White Cloud must be the healer who had encouraged Eddie to go up to Lost Pipe Lake. "Oh," I said.

To Ellen, Rose said, "Tell her what you told me about that girl who killed Roland."

The voices around us quieted down. Ellen White Cloud regarded me with mild eyes. "I knew her mother," she said. "Marty Davisson. I met her at Wounded Knee, then again at a rally in Pierre. By that time, Raven was born. Marty had the baby with her in Pierre. She was still nursing. This was just a month before she was killed at Pine Ridge." She stopped, as if to mull over old memories, then went on.

"Marty was smart. She'd been to college in Boston, but she wasn't only book smart. She knew her way around. And she was *totally* committed to the cause. She knew Roland Redhawk was a Fibby plant. She'd watched him operate at Wounded Knee, she'd watched him snuggle in with the leadership, and she recognized him as the enemy. She told everyone and anyone who would listen. She was confrontational, passionate, articulate. Her AIM brothers wrote her off as hysterical."

"You think she was murdered?"

"Of course she was murdered. For one thing, no one who knew her had ever seen her take a drink. Marty used to say that her mother—Raven's grandmother—drank enough for the two of them. The night Marty was killed, she was staying with friends and got a phone call. She never said who it was from, but the friends she was staying with said she was excited, like really *up*. Only thing she said was that Roland was finished. She went out to meet someone that night and never came back. For over a year, we tried to get an investigation going, but nothing ever came of it. At Pierre, she told me she'd been getting threatening phone calls, that Roland had spread the word around that *she* was the rat. The leadership shut her out, but she kept on making noise, ruffling their feathers." Ellen White Cloud allowed herself a small feminist smile.

"You think Roland killed her?"

"One way or another. I heard he was in Duluth at the time."

No doubt Herron, Roland's spymaster, knew the story. Was that why Roland, more than half-drunk, shot him through the heart? Out of fear that Herron would loose Marty Davisson's ghost in the Mission Valley? Perhaps Herron, in his own drunken stupor, had suddenly connected Roland's face to his past, and tried to squeeze Roland into his corner to facilitate his ski scheme. Kevin had overheard his dad talking about wanting "a favor." Perhaps Herron, for the second time in his life, had tried to use Roland Redhawk. There was no way to know for sure. They were both dead. But I felt as if another piece of the puzzle had suddenly snapped into place. I felt a small blast of excitement. I wanted to tell Luke. Then I remembered.

I focused on Ellen White Cloud. "Was Roland Marty's lover at Wounded Knee?"

There was another lull in the conversation. Everyone in the room was listening. The healer's face was impassive. "Does it matter?"

I flushed. "No. I just thought it might explain—I mean—" I stopped awkwardly.

Ellen White Cloud smiled. "You mean, Hell hath no fury like a woman scorned?" She looked around at the listening faces. As much to them as to me, she said, "From what I heard, none of the women at Wounded Knee would go near Roland. They thought he was a creep. As for Marty, she was in love with AIM. Roland was the enemy. She hated him, pure and simple. It's almost as if she passed that hatred on to Raven in her milk."

Her audience murmured approvingly. "Thanks for the coffee," she said to Pete. "I've got to get back."

He nodded. "Dolores must have fallen asleep with Paul," he said. "Thanks for coming by."

"See you tomorrow," Ellen White Cloud told the others. "Nice to meet you," she said to me. She scanned my face with professional interest. "If you want to walk out with me to the car, I've got some ointment there that might help."

I followed her out into the night. It had stopped raining. She opened the trunk of an old Chevy Nova and rummaged through a basket made in Taiwan. "Here," she said, handing me a familiar-looking plastic jar.

"Cold cream?"

"Recycled container. It's aloe. I get it wholesale from a health-food store in Missoula."

"Thanks. How much do I owe you?"

"Nothing."

I thanked her again. In the trunk light, her face was thoughtful.

"Something else," she said. "You were asking about the girl's father."

"Yes."

"There's no need for this to go further," she warned.

"No," I agreed.

She took a breath. "Marty and I were both at Wounded Knee. Like Roland, Marty was in and out, running supplies. So we never got close until later, when we met at that rally in Pierre. We talked for three days nonstop. And that was one of the things she told me, who the baby's father was. I told you she was in love with AIM. Well, at Wounded Knee, Buster Littlepond was its incarnation. I understand you met him.''

I blinked. ''Buster Littlepond? But he's such a pig!'' The words were out of my mouth before I could stop them.

She wasn't offended. ''Back then, he was par for the course,'' she stated without irony.

Frames from the reel of my meeting with Buster whirred through my head. ''He claimed he knew all along that Roland was a spy.''

''I don't think they'd have shut Marty out if they'd known. Maybe they suspected she was right. But they couldn't accept the word of a woman.'' She paused, then added wistfully, ''Marty was something else. If she had lived, you'd have heard about her.''

The back door opened. Voices bubbled into the night. ''I thought I might give Buster a call. His specialty is damaged kids. He might want to get a defense fund going for the girl. Make a federal case out it—as it were.''

BUSINESSES ON the reservation closed for Eddie McNab's funeral. It was held in St. Ignatius Mission which, despite its vast size, was crowded. I sat squeezed in with Pete and Dolores, Paul and Rose, in a center pew. Again, the watery blue light gave me an underwater feeling. We were sitting inside the vast, overturned hull of a sunken ark. Above our heads, along the keel line of the ceiling, the painted medallions of saints floated like rows of air bubbles escaping a wreck. I listened to the piercing wails of the Salish choir and tried not to think of Luke. I don't know exactly what set me off. Maybe it was the way Paul's small dark, fuzzy head was nestled against Pete's shoulder. Maybe it was the way Pete, in an unguarded moment, looked at Dolores. I started to weep. Dolores passed me a folded pink tissue, but that only made it worse. A loud squeak escaped me. I could feel Pete's and Dolores's embarrassment. I lurched over Rose's legs, out into the aisle, ducked my head and scurried toward the door at the back of the church as if I were running a gauntlet. I felt heads turning. No one else was making a display. Eddie's mourners had to wonder why I was crying so hard for someone I scarcely knew.